The
Complete
Bostock and Harris

THE
COMPLETE
BOSTOCK
AND HARRIS

Leon Garfield

THE NEW YORK REVIEW CHILDREN'S COLLECTION

NEW YORK

THIS IS A NEW YORK REVIEW BOOK
PUBLISHED BY THE NEW YORK REVIEW OF BOOKS
435 Hudson Street, New York, NY 10014
www.nyrb.com

Library of Congress Cataloging-in-Publication Data
Garfield, Leon.
 [Novels. Selections.]
 The complete Bostock and Harris / Leon Garfield.
    pages cm
 Summary: Two stories published separately in the 1970s, in the first of which
the boys experiment to see if a wolf will adopt Harris's infant sister, Adelaide.
In the second Harris offers Bostock the affections of his sister in exchange for
the brass telescope of Bostock's father and starts a string of misunderstandings
about who is courting whom.
 ISBN 978-1-59017-783-9 (hardback)
 [1. Best friends—Fiction. 2. Friendship—Fiction. 3. Brothers and sisters—Fiction. 4. Courtship—Fiction. 5. Great Britain—History—1789-1820—Fiction.
6. Humorous stories.] I. Garfield, Leon. Strange case of Adelaide Harris. II.
Garfield, Leon. Bostock and Harris. III. Title.
 PZ7.G17943Cn 2014
 [Fic]—dc23

                              2014013612

ISBN 978-1-59017-783-9
Also available as an electronic book; ISBN 978-1-59017-803-4

Cover design by Louise Fili, Ltd.
Cover illustration and chapter-head illustrations by Nathan Gelgud

Printed in the United States of America on acid-free paper.
10 9 8 7 6 5 4 3 2 1

Contents

For Patrick Hardy

The Strange Affair of Adelaide Harris

Chapter One

A MUSTY, dusty, leathery smell of boys, books and ink. Words drone and a family of flies stagger through the heavy air as if in pursuit of them. But they turn out to be of Ancient History so the flies blunder moodily against the parlor window beyond which the June sun ripens tempting dinners at roadsides and down by the strong-smelling beach; day after day after day.

"Among the customs of ancient Sparta," says Mr. Brett at the twelve enormous, crumpled boys before him, and then goes on to tell of mothers bidding their sons come back with their shields or cold and dead upon them. He gazes at his twelve and reflects that Spartan mothers knew what they were about. He looks particularly hard at Bostock and Harris whom he hates and fears; day after day after day...

Thin, depressed, humane man—though with a touch of youth still remaining—Mr. Brett was employed to teach Classical Education at Dr. Bunnion's Academy in Brighton. There was something of a mystery about Mr. Brett; he was a well-spoken, gentlemanly sort of person, quite out of the usual run of schoolmasters. It was generally supposed that he'd fled from a well-to-do family in the north after committing some horrible crime and had found sanctuary in Dr. Bunnion's obscure school. This notion lent him a certain melancholy distinction in the eyes of the pupils and helped to explain why he never left the school for more than a few hours—even remaining through the holidays—and always tended to start and grow pale whenever there was a knock on the door.

From time to time, with the object of trapping Mr. Brett into betraying his crime, some ingenious pupil would ask seemingly innocent questions about parricides, fratricides and what were Mr. Brett's thoughts on poisonings (of which matters Ancient History was interestingly full), and then sit back and closely observe him for signs of guilty dismay.

Oddly enough, such questions did seem to disturb Mr. Brett in quite a striking way, and when some sly and brutish boy at the back, or the terrible Harris in the front, inquired how finely glass needed to be powdered before it might be used to commit murder, he would always falter and look alarmed...Then there'd fall an absolute silence on the class; the pupils would stare at Mr. Brett and Mr. Brett would stare at the pupils, and each would be struggling with his private thoughts of the other; and only God Almighty knew which was nearer the truth.

But now the day was almost done. Ten of the boys appeared to be asleep and Mr. Brett dropped his voice for he did not want to awaken them. Only Bostock and Harris still seemed to be interested in him. Side by side they sat in the front row and watched him attentively. Bostock was the larger of the two, but Harris was the deadlier. Though Bostock had caused more destruction and would, most likely, end on the gallows, Mr. Brett believed Harris to be his evil genius. Or would have believed it did not "genius" suggest a high intelligence—

which Harris did not have. But there would be no more of them; so far as Mr. Brett was concerned, they were the end of their line. Harris had only a quantity of sisters and Bostock was a single child, so Mr. Brett thought that even his parents were appalled by what they'd done and would do no more.

Ten minutes of the lesson remained and Mr. Brett struggled on with the customs of ancient Sparta. A fat boy at the back was actually asleep with his mouth open. Mr. Brett had a childish desire to throw an ink pellet into it, but did nothing of the kind. The fat boy was a boarder at ninety pounds per annum and so worth three day pupils. Not for worlds would Mr. Brett have risked Dr. Bunnion's anger and, therefore, his situation. He was desperately anxious to remain. *Desperately*...

"Beg pardon, sir," said Harris, cupping an ear and leaning forward earnestly. "Can't quite hear you. Could I have that last item again?"

There was an unwholesome light in Harris's eyes. Uneasily Mr. Brett wondered what could have been the cause of it. He hoped it was a fever as he did not care to think of its being an idea.

"Little children," repeated Mr. Brett, as softly and tenderly as he could, "quite tiny infants exposed on the mountain side by their parents..."

Harris nodded shrewdly, and Mr. Brett caught himself wondering why the custom was ever abandoned. He would like to have lived in ancient Sparta—or, better, he would have liked Bostock and Harris to have lived there.

As these thoughts drifted into his mind, the bell rang and thunder from aloft proclaimed that Dr. Bunnion's Religious Instruction had finished for the day. Then all the little academy rocked and shook as Major Alexander's twelve rose from Arithmetic in the back parlor and all the six and thirty sons of merchants and gentlefolk tumbled fiercely out into the five o'clock sun. Even the fat boarder had gone—not to join his friends, for he had none—but to the kitchen, and Mr. Brett was left alone with his strange secret...

The unearthly light was still in Harris's eyes. Bostock noticed it and held his tongue. There was no point in interrupting his friend's thoughts; he would be told of them when Harris was ripe.

They lived in neighboring streets, about a mile and a half from the school, so there was time enough. As they walked, the sun streamed down and gave them immense shadows which fell like black phantoms among the half-built houses that littered their way—as if haunting them prematurely with the ghosts of tragedies to come. Their pace was slow; their manner winding, but sedate. There was no hurry. After some minutes of silence, Bostock stole a glance at his friend but it was plain that Harris's thoughts were still in the furnace, and at white heat. So Bostock scowled and punched an imaginary enemy. He was angry; he was often angry. It was part of his nature. Fits of anger came over him like waves of the sea till he longed to hiss and seethe and hurl stones like the sea itself. His father was a retired sea captain and he put it all down to that. Harris had once explained it to him—this notion of in-herited passion—and Bostock had nodded fiercely, feeling at one with the elements. Harris's father, on the other hand, was a learned physician, so Harris was able to explain his own advanced manner of thinking in the same way.

They suited each other very well, did Bostock and Harris. Each had what the other lacked—and was always ready to part with it: Harris with his powerful mind and Bostock with his powerful limbs. In a way they represented the ancient idea of soul and body, but in a very pure state. Harris was as weak as a kitten and Bostock was as thick as a post. They were the greatest of friends and had the utmost respect for each other.

"I think he admires me, you know," said Harris abruptly.

"Who does?" asked Bostock, curious but not surprised.

"Mr. Brett."

"Oh," said Bostock, and waited. Whenever Harris opened his thoughts, the strange light in his eyes seemed to go out—like candles snuffed in an emptied room. But the light was still on, so Bostock knew there was more to come.

"Haven't you noticed how he looks at me and drops his voice like we was the only two in the room?"

The friends halted and Bostock stared down towards the wide, glittering sea where distant fishing vessels seemed like faint perforations on a blaze of silver. They had reached the corner of his street. Far away the clock of St. Nicholas's began to chime six and the setting sun, striking on the walls of the square flint houses, rosied the cobbles as if to show that even stone, when scrutinized by the eye of heaven, might have cause to blush.

Harris laid an inky finger on Bostock's torn, blue sleeve. Bostock stared and withdrew his eyes from the bright sea. "Old friend," murmured Harris, his large face seeming vague and luminous in Bostock's sun-dazzled eyes, "what do you say to this?"

Then he told Bostock what he had in mind. As he murmured on, now rapidly, now slowly, a wisp of cloud passed across the sun; the flushed houses changed their complexions and an unearthly gray pallor fell across the little golden street. There was a brief chill in the air—and Bostock shivered.

"Well?" said Harris softly.

Bostock gazed at him in terrified admiration. Harris wanted to expose an infant.

Among his numerous sisters, there was one of seven weeks

old who was peculiarly suitable, and he was quite willing for Bostock to carry her up and expose her on the Downs. "It's a warm evening," he concluded with unusual humanity, "so I don't suppose she'll come to much harm. And anyway, my pa says it's wonderful what they can stand."

He stopped; the light had gone out in his eyes so Bostock knew he had finished. Bostock frowned. He knew Harris was not mad. There were good reasons behind Harris's scheme— very good reasons indeed. Only Bostock had not quite taken them in. A real tidal wave of anger at his own stupidity swept over him. He kicked a stone violently and watched it bounding down the street. Having no sisters of his own, he didn't presume to judge of Harris's generosity with his. The only living creature that Bostock had to share his meager thoughts and confidences with was a great brute of a ginger cat called Jupiter. Not for worlds would he have exposed Jupiter; but then he supposed cats were different. So Bostock, who would have trusted Harris with his life, helplessly nodded and hoped to understand everything in time.

Adelaide was the infant's name and Harris swore she was fed at six and then put down till she howled about four hours later. She wouldn't be missed.

Bostock felt himself being gently tugged towards the neighboring street where the Harris family lived a shade more elegantly than did the Bostocks. Already he could hear the faint shouts of the Harris girls and wondered, with a little pang, which was Mary's—for she had a thin, wild beauty that Bostock greatly admired.

"Quiet, Bosty—quiet as a mouse!"

Tiny Adelaide, fed and happy and dreaming her muslin dreams, snoozed in her crib while her giant sisters squabbled in the garden and the rest of the household obligingly forgot her. Of a sudden, she dreamed she was lifted into the air in a big fluffy cloud. She bubbled and chuckled and tightened her creased-up eyes against any interruption. She flew... she flew...

Bostock had got her partly under his coat. Leaving their loud boots in the street, the friends had entered the house, crept upstairs and abstracted the child. The fine weather had drawn everyone out of doors and only a kitchen maid had glimpsed them as they'd vanished through the front door. But she'd taken no particular notice. Master Harris and Master Bostock always came and went like ghosts—and were just about as welcome.

Once outside, the friends paused only to put on their boots before turning northward and hastening towards the Downs. This first, easy success of the scheme filled them with a trembling anticipation—though Bostock, heavily burdened, still did not know for what.

Already evening was coming on and the little town, lazy in the warm, buzzed only with the ever-busy flies. Silently the friends passed along the quiet, narrow streets; but always on the shady side. Ahead of them rose the great shoulders of the Downs where dark shadows were sweeping, like giants' hands lifting in abhorrence at the deep, inquiring brother and his patiently following friend. For, though Bostock was immensely strong, Adelaide was portly and her weight hampered his stride and kept him to the rear.

Tiny Adelaide dreamed she was in the branches of a tree and the wind was bouncing her up and down. She smiled into the musty darkness of Bostock's coat and her fat fingers found a waistcoat button...

"Harris!" Bostock's voice was sharp with alarm. "I—I think she's leaking or something. I'm all wet, Harris."

Harris hurried back and examined his sister. "I think she's peed, Bosty." For a moment the friends stared down at Adelaide in her cocoon of shawling—as if for the first time divining her to be vaguely as themselves, subject to the same pains, pleasures and natural laws. Then they observed the rapidly deepening sky and hastened on till the road dwindled away and became no more than a finger scratch of broken chalk through the stubby green.

On and on went Harris, across the uneven ground and skirting the chalky hollows that glared up abruptly, like the bleached sockets of half-buried giants' skulls. It was plain to the panting Bostock that Harris had one particular spot in mind. At last they reached it, and Bostock knew it well: a place of mystery, trysts and blackberries. It was a steep declivity, carpeted with close turf and bordered on three sides by thick, mysterious walls of bramble. This dense darkness was always full of strange rustlings and sudden cracklings as unseen denizens went about their sharp affairs.

"There," breathed Harris, pointing to the turf. "Lay her there."

Bostock hesitated, and Harris looked surprised. Then, and only then, did he understand that Bostock was totally ignorant of his purpose. At once a great warmth filled him as he realized the scope of his friend's trust. That Bostock should have come so far, and on so strange an errand just because he, Harris, had asked him, spoke volumes for the power of friendship. Harris blinked. Even though Bostock must have thought he was mad, he'd followed him without a word.

"Old friend," he whispered moistly. "You an' me's going to behold wonders."

Rapidly and eagerly he explained everything. Did Bostock recall the tale of the two Roman infants that were suckled by the she-wolf? Bostock frowned and nodded. Few things ever got into his mind, but when they did there was no getting them out again. They stayed there like the alien fixtures of another man's house—a source of passing wonder and bewilderment. He did not have the creative imagination that seizes on matters, apparently of little use and far apart, and instantly divines the link between them.

But Harris had. When Mr. Brett had mentioned the she-wolf, Harris's mind had leaped to the vixens that roamed the Downs; and when Mr. Brett had told of Spartan infants being exposed, Harris had thought at once of Adelaide. Then, putting all together in a sudden blaze, he'd hit on the inspired notion of seeing how native wildlife accepted a human baby in its midst. He had every hope, he whispered excitedly, of a vixen with full dugs coming to suckle Adelaide!

Bostock stared at Harris in awe. "Well?" said Harris; but Bostock was unable to speak, so Harris, mistaking his silence for doubt, said defensively, "Anyway, she's my sister and if she perishes it'll be me what'll have to bear her loss. Go on, Bosty—lay her down, old friend..."

Fat little Adelaide smiled and dreamed...dreamed she was being laid among buttercups and daisies on a cradling green...

Bostock and Harris crouched down to the windward in a patch of long grass through which only disconnected parts of them could be seen; and there, with bright, sharp eyes and pounding hearts, they awaited the arrival of the vixen with full dugs.

Harris never doubted for a moment that something of the

kind would turn up and they'd witness an extraordinary phe-
nomenon in nature; and Bostock never doubted Harris.

This is the most exciting moment of my whole life, thought
Bostock; with difficulty. Harris is a real genius and he's my
best friend. I'm so excited I could jump and shout and kick
the grass. Something's going to happen. I don't know how to
keep still. Who can I tell about it? I must...no, I mustn't. I
wish I could think. Oh, I'm so horribly excited and Harris
looks so calm. I wish I could stop thinking—someone might
hear me...

Harris's thoughts, though no less turbulent, were of a more
advanced nature and concerned the youngest person ever to
read a learned paper before the Royal Society. Faintly, in his
inner ear, he heard the bravos peal out like a storm of church
bells on Judgment Sunday, and he bowed his head to hide his
happy tears...

Suddenly the two friends grew still in mind and body. A
sound had petrified them. A faint but unmistakable panting
and snuffling and crackling of bramble. Then there was a
crunching of dry twigs. Harris's face, briefly blossoming in
the long grass, was ashy with expectation.

Little Adelaide, deep in her blind sleep, chuckled and dreamed
she was about to be fed again...

It was coming, it was coming! The vixen—the vixen with full
dugs!

Chapter Two

YOUNG, pretty and in yellow muslin, Tizzy Alexander, daughter of the fiery Major who taught Arithmetic, was in a condition of terrified excitement. Her heart was thumping half out of her bodice and she kept clutching at her scarf to hide it. She must have been mad to have put herself in Ralph Bunnion's way but wild curiosity had at last overpowered her. Ralph Bunnion—cricketer, horseman and hero of the school. What was he like—this terrible, handsome, heartless breaker of hearts? Tall, fashionable and, so far as could be judged from the ends of them, clean-limbed.

The use of this last expression had given her a brief feeling of maturity but it had gone when she'd stolen glance after glance at Dr. Bunnion's dashing and notorious son. It was said he'd once fought a duel—and everyone knew he drank prodigious quantities of claret at the Old Ship Inn with three young men almost as famous as himself.

Oh, Tizzy, why ain't you back in the school, safe with your ma and pa? She shook her head. In her heart of hearts she knew she'd always have regretted it. She knew that, if she missed this chance, she'd have dreamed and wondered all her life long what it would have been like to have been swept off her feet by a Ralph Bunnion. Only once in a lifetime did such an adventure befall a young girl.

With a start she felt his hand on her arm and she realized they'd walked all the way from the school to the beginning of the Downs. All her instincts bade her fly back home; but she could not. The sun was dropping down and warning shadows were pooling in the rough, tufted ground like treacherous black pits. Tizzy—Tizzy! When will it begin? Oh, Tizzy, what a little fool you are! Thus her fears and hopes raced hand in hand.

He was talking to her, had been for some time, but she'd been too engrossed in her own confused sensations to know what he'd been saying. All she'd noticed was that, as he laughed, his teeth flashed like bayonets.

Lord! He was handsome! He wore a mouse-colored coat with smart tails and a waistcoat embroidered with a design of love-lies-bleeding.

"D'you know," he said, laughing gently, "the last time I walked this way was with poor Maggie Hemp?"

"Oh dear," said Tizzy. "I saw her only yesterday in Bartholomew's. I didn't know aught was amiss—"

"Then—then she's not—not drowned?"

"Oh no—"

"Thank God!" breathed Ralph fervently. "I say thank God for that!"

"I never knew," began Tizzy, when Ralph shook his head as if the subject was painful to him. But in a little while he overcame his distress and admitted to Tizzy that Maggie Hemp had threatened to throw herself off Black Rock and into the pounding sea.

"Why?" asked Tizzy. Ralph glanced at her a shade coldly.

"Who knows the secrets of a woman's heart?" he wondered aloud; and then went on to explain that Lizzy Cooper had come between them. He believed it possible that Maggie's affections were more deeply engaged than he'd supposed, and it distressed him very much. He wished such things wouldn't keep happening to him for he was, by nature, retiring and shy. "As I was saying to Dolly Packer, only last night at the Assembly Rooms, she shouldn't set her heart on me..."

"And poor—poor Miss Cooper?" whispered Tizzy, in deeper waters than ever she'd supposed. Ralph sighed, shrugged his broad shoulders and tightened his grip on her arm. Tizzy moaned inwardly and saw herself poised on some cruel eminence with the wind blowing her pretty ringlets, crying, "Ralph!" as she leaped to a popular oblivion.

"You women!" said the hapless Ralph, laughing ruefully. "We men don't stand a chance!"

Imperceptibly their pace had quickened. Ahead lay a dangerously romantic-looking hedge of brambles that crowned a scooped-out bed of turf. Such mysterious trysting places had often figured in Tizzy's dreams—such lovers' couches of green with leafy curtains to shut out the eyes of the world.

Her heart fluttered and she looked, half yearningly, back along the way they'd come. With a pang she saw the humdrum little town far below. It looked for all the world as though it had slipped down the green hillsides and come to rest at the edge of the wide swallowing sea for the greater convenience of Ralph Bunnion's unhappy loves.

"You snare us and trap us with your charms," said Ralph, laughing bitterly now. Tizzy waited, nervously hopeful of discovering which of her charms was proving the deadliest. But it was not to be. Instead she learned to her dismay that Ralph was as clay in women's hands. Somehow or another they always seemed to be attracted to him. He didn't know why, but wondered if there might be some sort of shining about him.

He paused and eyed her with an air of weary expectancy. Tizzy blushed and looked hurriedly down at her black shoes popping in and out of her daffodil gown and carrying her onward to her fate. Ralph laughed, frowning this time, and admitted that his mysterious attractiveness was really quite unwelcome. There were times, even, when he dreaded it and envied his friends who might go anywhere without so much as a single admiring look.

Could she, Tizzy, understand how wretched it was that every time he stood up to dance at the Old Ship Assembly Rooms everyone fell back to watch? Yes, he *was* a fine dancer; but then so were many others. Yes, he *was* a brilliant cricketer; but so were several others. Yes, he *was* a remarkable horseman; but there were others almost as good. So what was it?

He felt so—so foolish about it all. More often than not he longed to be at home with a good book; but it was never to be. What *was* it about him, he demanded of Tizzy. Was he— here he laughed incredulously—was he really so outrageously handsome?

"No—no!" breathed Tizzy, confused and grateful to have been brought into the conversation.

Ralph glared at her. He'd underplayed his hand and been too modest. It was a weakness of his. He kicked a lump of chalk, laughed fiercely and said, "Dolly Packer once said I was like a Greek statue..."

Tizzy looked up. The dark and secret hedge of bramble was almost upon them. She thought of the soft green bed it screened but, to her surprise, she felt nothing of the terrified expectancy with which she'd set out. Perhaps she was being swept off her feet without knowing it? She sighed. Was life always such a disappointment? Was she never to learn that her eyes were like mysterious twilit pools and her lips a pair of kissing cherries? Was she never to share those high, sweet passions with which the lovers of old led each other up the mountains of bliss?

"Dolly said my profile was extraordinarily Greek..." He presented this aspect of himself for Tizzy's admiration. Unluckily Tizzy was still brooding on life's disappointments, and her expression was touched with something very like boredom. Fatally offended, the handsome Ralph felt one of his rages coming on. As through a veil of red, he saw Tizzy just ahead of him. She was picking her way round the bramble hedge to the very edge of the soft, grassy couch. Angry, lustful thoughts inflamed him. He would teach her what it meant to be out with Ralph Bunnion. There was a terrible look in his eyes, and with a savage laugh he launched himself at Tizzy, meaning to seize her and bear her to the amorous ground.

At the selfsame moment Tizzy saw, of all amazing things, a tiny human baby, lying all alone, asleep in the grass. She cried out, "Lord save us! A baby!" and rushed to gather it up.

Thus it happened that, with nothing in the way to halt him, Ralph Bunnion, still laughing savagely, flew a goodish way across the declivity before coming down and striking the ground with his face. He gave a sharp, loud cry of pain, but Tizzy urgently begged him to be quiet as the baby was sleeping.

Tiny Adelaide dreamed of deliciously frightening storms and thunder; then she chuckled as she fancied herself to be borne up and floating in a sea of milk... gently, gently towards some crisp, entrancing shore...

"The shame of it," murmured Tizzy Alexander, walking

with the greatest care and tenderness as she bore her precious burden. "To leave such a sweet thing to die! Lord, what's the world coming to? What can have come over the mother to part with her darling soft morsel?"

Ralph Bunnion did not answer. He was not interested. He followed after Tizzy with a handkerchief pressed to his face. He had suffered severe scratches and bruises and his nose would not stop bleeding. He feared it might have been put out of shape. He had heard of such things. He was consumed with hatred for Tizzy and the infant in her arms.

"What should we do with it, Mr. Bunnion? We can't just let it go on the parish. Perhaps it could go to the Foundlings? But wouldn't that be a shame? It's such a darling. And—and finding it so. I get a queer shivering that we were *meant* to come on it as we did...as if it's something special like Moses in the bulrushes or—or Perseus in his ark. Maybe it's going to grow up into a saint or a hero or something. Oh, Mr. Bunnion! D'you think we could keep it? It wouldn't be no trouble. We could give it every love and care and Pa could teach it Arithmetic..."

Thus Tizzy prattled on, her motherly feelings shining in her flushed and sweet young face. All the benefits of love, affection and learning could be lavished on the mysterious infant. Nothing would be denied it...

A little way behind her stalked Ralph Bunnion, his face—and particularly his nose—blazing with pain. Dimly he thought of revenging himself on Tizzy, but was too upset to determine on how. Vague images of dark figures overwhelming her filled his dazed brain. He shifted the handkerchief and discovered that the blood still flowed. He hoped he'd not lost too much; and above all he hoped he'd not stained his father's best cravat which he happened to be wearing. More and more passionate grew his hatred of Tizzy Alexander...

A little way behind him, taking skillful advantage of every bush and sheltering hollow, crept Bostock and Harris, awed beyond measure by the fate that had overtaken Adelaide. Though Bostock had been deeply moved by Miss Alexander's tenderness and the wonderful prospect she'd held out for the infant, he knew it wouldn't be right to let Adelaide go. He peered towards Harris whose face was of a terrible whiteness. So Bostock held his peace till he should be told what to do. Harris would think of something. Harris was nobody's fool . . .

Thus thought Bostock as he followed Harris who followed the famous Ralph Bunnion who followed Tizzy Alexander and Adelaide in strange procession towards Dr. Bunnion's Academy . . .

Chapter Three

MR. BRETT, despised even by the cook for never flaring up like the lively Major Alexander and bearing every humiliation as if his very life depended on staying at Dr. Bunnion's, sat at dinner next to the fat boarder whose name was Sorley. Though there were two other boarders at ninety pounds per annum each, Sorley came first in the headmaster's estimation. He was the son of a baronet at Cuckfield and Dr. Bunnion had hopes concerning a sister of Sorley's and his own son, the ever-popular Ralph. But he was a sensible man and kept these hopes to himself, and only assisted them by throwing in Sorley's way any little advantage or courtesy that might be reported back to Cuckfield. Naturally he looked to his staff to do the same. In his heart of hearts he considered his ambitions not unreasonable; Sorley, in common with the rest of the school, looked up to the handsome Ralph as to a prince... and surely must have talked of him at home.

"Here, boy," said Major Alexander, leaning across the table and thoughtfully helping Sorley to more mutton pie. "We must look after you, eh?"

Mr. Brett, who was sitting next to Sorley and so might have performed the same action more easily, bit his lip. As usual, his thoughts had been elsewhere so Major Alexander benefited by a smile from Dr. Bunnion while he received a look of contempt from the doctor's stately wife. Mr. Brett lowered his eyes and wondered if life was worth living.

It was then that there came an agitated knocking on the door. It was a rapid and urgent sound; the door seemed to tremble and before Dr. Bunnion could speak, it burst open.

At the same moment two faces of supernatural terror appeared at the window, then vanished like spectral dreams, blown by the wind. No one in the room had seen them nor felt the stare of their wild eyes. They had made no sound nor even misted the glass with their breath. They had not dared to breathe.

But in that instant Bostock and Harris had seen Harris's infant sister in Miss Alexander's arms being presented at Dr. Bunnion's dining table like an extra course. Ralph Bunnion was not with her; she and Adelaide stood alone before the astonished company. Harris thought madly of tapping on the window and coming out with: "Please can we have our baby back?" but natural dread of the unlucky affair being told to his father killed the idea stone dead. If there was any hope at all—for him, for Bostock and for little Adelaide—it rested in the god of boys and infants, to whom Harris unscientifically prayed.

"And what, miss, were you doing on the Downs with Mr. Bunnion?" Major Alexander, being an ex-officer of Engineers, had a fiery and explosive sense of honor which he was inclined to lay like mines under friends and enemies alike. Generally no great harm was done owing to the Major's natural deviousness. He tunneled too far and explosives were apt to go off at too great a distance from the events that had provoked them; thus his fury often seemed more the result of brooding on some unworthy trifle than the instant anger of an honorable man.

But this time he'd exploded his mine with military speed and success. Instantly Adelaide was forgotten and Tizzy's tender pleadings on the baby's behalf were blown to smithereens.

"Well, miss?"

The Major was standing. He was a short, square, formidable man with flashing eyes. Tizzy went very red and Mrs. Alexander, a German lady, shrugged her shoulders and muttered something in her native tongue.

"I—I—" stammered Tizzy, guiltily recalling the dreams with which she'd set out. "That is, Pa, we was walking—"

"Indeed, miss?" said Major Alexander in a low, shaking voice. "Alone—with Mr. Bunnion? I rather fancy you are lying to me. I rather fancy he has—compromised you, miss. As I see it, this is a matter of honor."

The word honor was delivered like a sword thrust, and Ralph's father felt a warning stab at his heart.

"My dear Major," began Dr. Bunnion, hurriedly attempting to calm his touchy Arithmetic master, "even allowing for your—um—impulsive—er—nature, there's really no need... a trifle, really—"

"A trifle?" The Major clenched his fists. "My daughter's honor a trifle?"

"My dear sir—I didn't mean that. You misunderstand me. I would never dream of implying such a thing." The headmaster spoke with almost trembling sincerity. He was a man who valued discretion above all and the conversation was becoming painful to him. "Miss Alexander herself has said they were just walking. She brings no charge—no charge at all. And I assure you, sir, my boy Ralph is the soul of gentility. To my knowledge he has never harmed a fly. I beg of you, sir, most earnestly, to—to control yourself, if you'll forgive the expression. Of course I respect your feelings, but I am certain, quite, quite certain that you are mistaken...indeed, damned nonsense!"

This last remark had been quite unintentional, but the headmaster was deeply agitated. He kept glancing at Sorley as if wondering how much of the scene would be reported to Cuckfield.

"Fetch my son," said Mrs. Bunnion coldly, "and put an end to this at once. Whatever that girl" (here she glanced contemptuously at the scarlet Tizzy) "may say, my son will tell the truth. Rest assured of that, Major Alexander. Mr. Bunnion will tell you your odious suspicions are as absurd as they are insulting."

Dr. Bunnion, while wishing his wife had not spoken out so plainly, none the less agreed that Ralph ought to defend himself and put an end to the wretched scene. So he was sent for...

Unluckily, Ralph—after congratulating himself on having reached his room without being seen—had not yet restored his dapper appearance. Such was the unexpectedness of the summons that he'd scarcely time to remove his damaged coat and his father's cravat before presenting himself to the company in his fatal waistcoat with its design of love-lies-bleeding, and with a similar design, executed in blood, on his brow and nose.

Mr. Brett's lips twisted in a bitter smile.

"I see my child defended herself," said Major Alexander harshly. There could be no reasonable doubt that the young man's injuries had been inflicted by the desperate and outraged nails of the Major's daughter. "I rather fancy I am entitled to—satisfaction."

At once there was a terrible silence in the room. The scene which had, at the very worst, been disagreeable and awkward, took on an edge of steel. Dr. Bunnion stared aghast at his son and the smoldering Major and seemed to see phantom bullet holes in their breasts—and all his dreams and ambitions sinking in a sea of scandalous blood.

"My God," he whispered. "You—you cannot mean a—a duel?"

Now Major Alexander had not meant a duel. Nothing had been further from his thoughts. He had meant to say "compensation" but thought it sounded too mercenary and so had said "satisfaction" instead. He was as shocked as anybody by the turn affairs had taken; he frowned uneasily at the athletic Ralph who did not look the sort of opponent to be trifled with. There was an unpleasantly fearless look about him that the Major could not help disliking; and in a moment his worst fears were realized. Ralph, conscious of the adoring eyes of the three boarders fixed upon him, drew himself up and said coolly, "I am at your service, sir."

"For God's sake!" cried Dr. Bunnion. "Can we not talk this over?"

"Yes!" said Major Alexander eagerly.

"Pa! Mr. Bunnion!" moaned Tizzy in terror—when the infant in her arms, disregarded till that moment, woke up and began to scream and scream.

Tiny Adelaide had opened her eyes. Huge strange faces filled her sky and whirled like furious suns as far as she could see. She struggled to put up her fat little hands to push them away...

"Get rid of that baby!" shouted Dr. Bunnion. "Get it out of here!" The wailing of Adelaide, filling the little Academy with its despair, had set up a multitude of echoes in the head-master's head till he could no longer think. Tizzy pleaded and begged for the infant to go to the Foundlings—as it no longer seemed probable that she'd be allowed to keep it—but Dr. Bunnion, who had a mania for discretion, was all for quiet-ness; so, still shouting above the infantine uproar, he insisted it be taken and left in the church porch for the vicar to deal with. Tizzy protested that it was inhuman and that they were all beasts and brutes who thought only of themselves and that it was shameful to turn away one so young and helpless.

"Hold your tongue, miss!" snarled the Major. "It's you who are inhuman to think of a damned baby when your pa is pre-pared to sacrifice his life to clear your honor!"

"I'll take it," offered Ralph. "I'll ride like the wind, sir..."

"You're savages, savages!" wept Tizzy, clinging to the baby which seemed to her the only real and warm thing in the whole demented room. They were a very sweet and touching sight—the girl and the crying baby—but it was only Mr. Brett who pitied them as they were parted, and Adelaide was given up to the eager, handsome Ralph.

Like brooding spirits Bostock and Harris moved from under the window and followed the wailing that had come out into the air.

"We'll get her back from the church," breathed Harris, and thanked the god of boys and infants for so aptly answering his prayers.

Pressed against the wall they waited for Ralph Bunnion to emerge from the little yard, high on the school horse. There was something wild and noble about the headmaster's son as he leaned forward against the evening sky with one hand on the reins and the other about the crying child. There was something of an ancient story and a deathless ride as he clattered away in a cloud of frightened sobs.

Bostock and Harris followed after, at first cautiously, then faster and faster till their boots seemed winged. On and on they sped, leaving behind them the little Academy which was now trembling in the grip of its own, quite separate calamity.

Presently the sound of the infant's wailing stopped as the motion of the horse rocked it back into sleep; then the sound of the horse itself died away and all that could be heard was the groaning breath and stumbling footfalls of the two pursuers as they mounted the hill towards St. Nicholas's.

"There he goes!" panted Harris as he looked up and saw the dark shape of the great horseman bending low over his burden; but it was only for a moment—the strange pair vanished almost instantly into the stony bulk of the aged, sometime haunted church.

"Hurry—hurry!" urged Harris. He was horribly afraid they'd be too late and Adelaide would be snatched inside before they could recover her. At last they reached the shadow of the church. There was no sign of horse or rider. Ralph Bunnion, master horseman, had been true to his word; he had come and gone like the invisible wind.

White of face and silent of step, the friends crept through the churchyard. Suddenly a movement disturbed them. They melted amid the monuments and with fearful eyes observed a solitary mourner—a gypsyish widow—rustle tragically away. Once or twice she stopped to look back, then she vanished like a ghost.

"Look, Bosty!" whispered Harris, pointing to the dark porch. "She's still there!"

Bostock looked; a quiet bundle lay upon the step. "Thank the Lord!" he breathed, and sped like an arrow to gather it up and follow his friend down the hill.

With hearts almost bursting but with spirits high, they ran and ran till they reached the fateful corner of the street where the adventure had begun. As they did so, the clock of St. Nicholas's chimed a quarter to ten. Fifteen minutes remained for the friends to return Adelaide to her crib and call it a day.

"Best give her to me, now, Bosty," said Harris when they were but yards from his home. Thankfully Bostock handed over the still quiet bundle to its lawful flesh and blood.

"You know, Bosty," murmured Harris with unusual tenderness and affection, "I'm glad we got her back. I mean, after all, she is my sister..."

He unwound a corner of the shawl to see how his sister did. He trembled; he moaned; he shook so violently that the infant almost fell and Bostock put out a hand to save it.

The tiny face, sleeping in its wrappings, was of a crumpled brownish color, with scanty hair as black as sin. Even in the fragile light of the broken moon, there was no doubt. It was not Adelaide. They had got the wrong baby.

Far, far away, tiny Adelaide opened her eyes and gurgled with joy. Mistily she saw a golden bird hovering over her head. She reached up to pluck a feather from its wings... pretty bird...

She lay under the lectern, not in St. Nicholas's but in the church at Preston beyond, where Ralph Bunnion had left her. The master horseman, up on the school horse—which he was not allowed to ride as often as he would have liked—had been unable to resist the temptation of galloping further afield than to St. Nicholas's and back. So he had gone on to Preston...

"Are you sure, Harris?" whispered Bostock, dimly sensing the enormous disaster and struggling to deny it. For answer

Harris glared at his friend with terrible eyes set in a face be-side which the pallid moon was rosy. Of course he was sure. What was to be done? Piteously Bostock gazed at Harris for instructions. Such was his admiration and the size of his heart that he would have done anything for his friend. He would have plucked the cock from the church steeple; he would have brought him an alderman's ring or the mayor's chain if only Harris would speak and command.

But what could Harris do or say? Even had he ten Bostocks at his command, there was too little time. Minutes alone re-mained to fill the empty cot in the Harris nursery and dispose of the beetle-browed babe in his trembling arms.

Then panic inspired him. "Bosty," he whispered. "We'll have to put it in Adelaide's place."

Bostock stared at him in veneration; then a doubt soiled its edges. "But—but won't they notice?"

Harris shrugged his shoulders. Having decided on his course, a feeling of deathly calm had overcome him. "What else can we do, Bosty? Answer me that. What else *is* there?"

The two friends gazed at each other over the head of the sleeping baby; the one resolved, the other still hesitant. Then Bostock knew, in his heart of hearts, that Harris's was the only way. "You're a genius, Harris."

Palely, Harris nodded and, returning the infant to Bostock, beckoned him on. As they neared the unsuspecting house, once more they removed their boots and flitted on with phantom stealth. A moment later, the small street was de-serted and the riding moon stared down on the empty boots which lay like mysterious vessels on the shore of adventure...

Chapter Four

MR. BRETT lay in his bed in the awkward attic where even the moon came in contemptuously. It laid a silver finger across the humble blanket as if wondering whether it was a man or a mouse that lay so quietly beneath. Wake up, wake up, James Brett, it seemed to say, or be buried forever in this dull spot!

But Mr. Brett did not seem to heed the moon's warning; instead he brooded on the evening's alarm. Though he was a peace-loving man, opposed to all violence save in the Ancient World where heroes battered each other's immortal brains out till a turn of the page resurrected them, the prospect of a duel between Major Alexander and Ralph Bunnion excited him enormously. Like the worried father, he, too, dreamed of phantom bullet holes in proud breasts, but, unlike the father, he cared not in which. Both the adversaries had cast their shadows across his secret life, and he detested them equally.

Mr. Brett's secret led him down strange paths and gave him bloody thoughts. But they were only thoughts, for his secret itself was of the softest kind. He was in love! Helplessly, frantically, wildly and, above all, hopelessly, he was in love with

Tizzy Alexander. The very sound of her footfall made him tremble and the sight of her face obstructed his heart. He no longer knew whether he'd come to this state little by little or whether, in the winking of an unguarded eye, he'd fallen into the midst of the sea of desire in which he now floundered.

But however it had begun, it was now an exquisite torment and a marvelous misery. He dared not breathe a word of his passion; he was violently terrified she would laugh at him and so extinguish the forlorn hope he still nursed. So he quaked and turned pale to every knock on the door and endured all the miseries of life in Dr. Bunnion's school. He became a walking knot of complicated emotions that daily tightened about his heart and caused him to snarl and snap at the one being he loved to distraction.

He sighed and gave a tortured smile. Whether or not the duel and the possible deaths of the Major and the headmaster's lecherous son would improve his situation was doubtful; but he didn't see that it could do any harm.

Suddenly there came a knock on the door. The smile left his face and a look of uncertainty and dread replaced it. He sat up. "Who's there?"

The door opened and Tizzy Alexander in her shift with a netted black shawl about her shoulders came in. Amazed and intoxicated he stared at her, and, before he could utter a word, she raised her finger to her lips and gently closed the door. "You must help me," she whispered.

"For pity's sake," he breathed, "go back to your room! What—what would your mother say?" His heart thundered as passion and propriety fought a battle in his breast beside which the fury of Hector and Achilles was as but a tiff between children.

"Ma sent me," said Tizzy, with a worried smile that was intended to reassure Mr. Brett, but did not.

"In heaven's name, why?" Such was Mr. Brett's terror and excitement that his voice took on an edge he deeply regretted.

"She said you was the only one in the house with any sense," said Tizzy nervously. "She said you was the only one who could stop them fighting..." Then Tizzy, quite overcome by the horrible circumstance, sat down on the edge of the bed and began to cry. "They'll kill each other," she wept, "and I'll be to blame for it."

"Isn't that what young women dream of?" muttered Mr. Brett bitterly. "To have men fight to the death on their account?"

Once again he regretted his words. That Tizzy had come to him filled his heart with joy; but that she'd come only to beg his help in preventing the very thing he half hoped would happen was a deep humiliation. None the less the sight of her weeping in the moonlight moved him almost unbearably and it was as much as he could do to stop himself folding her in his aching arms. The coldness of his words had been more to cool his own ardor than to reproach Tizzy. But she, who knew nothing of this, raised her eyes and looked at him in utter misery.

"I thought...I thought you would understand."

"Oh, but I do understand!" said Mr. Brett rapidly, and went on to lash himself still more with his own cruel tongue. "I understand very well, Miss Alexander! I understand you're frightened out of your wits for what your silly, flirting little heart has brought about! I understand that you don't know where to turn for escape! I understand that you're willing to do anything—even to come to the wretched, despised Mr. Brett in the attic to implore him to save your lover from the wrath of your father—"

"He's never my lover!" sobbed Tizzy furiously. "I hate him! I hate you! I hate everybody!" She stood up and wore the moonbeam from the window like a sash. "I wish I was dead! I—I'll drown myself like—like—"

"Ophelia?" offered Mr. Brett savagely.

"No," said Tizzy with sudden dignity. "Like Maggie Hemp."

With that she swept from the room leaving the moonbeam empty and Mr. Brett in an agitated torment of misery, wondering why he was always his own worst enemy. You fool, you fool! he groaned to himself, you've killed your only hope! Why did you do it? Why do you always do it?

Then, as the storm subsided, the answer came to him cold and clear. It was because he despised himself more than anyone else he knew. Not even in his dreams of ancient grandeur could he ever aspire to anything. The armor of Achilles would have crushed him and the very sight of Hector's nodding plume would have sent him shrieking from the field. He was a pygmy, a dwarf beside whom even that lout Ralph Bunnion stood up for a man.

Tizzy and Mr. Brett were not the only ones denied the ease of sleep. Dr. Bunnion was restless, too. He had dozed off but his dreams had been of so alarming a nature and a sharp creaking of floorboards or joists had so fitted in with the dread of a leveled pistol that he'd woken with a faint cry and had not dared close his eyes since.

The thought of the duel fell like the hand of death across his imaginings. Although in private the fiery Major had offered to withdraw his challenge, his conditions had been as hateful to Dr. Bunnion as the prospect of the fight itself. To wipe out the stain on his family honor, the Major had had the impudence to propose a marriage between the handsome Ralph and his own child, the penniless, wretched Tizzy. He had said it and stood back with almost a smile. It was plain he'd not budge an inch.

Dr. Bunnion scowled into the darkness of his bed and contemplated informing a magistrate of the duel and so having the Major jailed for two years. This at least would save Ralph, and if news of the affair could be prevented from reaching Cuckfield, there would still be hope for the baronet's daughter. But, on the other hand, it would deprive the school of its Arithmetic master and of Mrs. Alexander who taught German.

He sighed and gently eased his huge body out of the bed where Mrs. Bunnion slept like a stately ship, rising and falling at anchor. He paced the room, then, shaking his head, quietly opened the door and went out in search of a solution to his problems.

He passed along the passage until it joined another where his candle illuminated both ways as if to give him a choice of direction. He paused, frowned, then seemed to make up his mind. Quietly he moved down one passage while his shadow seemed to go down another.

There were a great many such passages in the upper part of the Academy, linking, dividing and turning sharply away. Sometimes there were stairs between—not flights but single steps that seemed like spies from lost battalions, lying in wait and wondering where the rest had gone. All this was in consequence of Dr. Bunnion's desire to expand his premises. He had knocked through and thrown out in so many directions that the house itself had come to resemble a pupil, endlessly outgrowing its suit of bricks. Had there been such a word, Dr. Bunnion would have called himself an educationalist; he got his living from education and was dedicated to expanding that living by expanding his capacity to educate.

Such then was the hapless complication of corridors that the prowling headmaster did not meet with Tizzy who, having left Mr. Brett, was drifting round strange corners like a melancholy ghost. Her agitated tears still flowed and, having more pride than sense, she would not return to her room from which her mother could have heard her sobs of distress.

"Come in!" breathed Mr. Brett. There had come a second knock on his door. His heart had leaped; she had forgiven him! Now for certain he would tell her of his love. His voice trembled with hope...

The door opened and Major Alexander slipped in with the air of looking for somewhere to lay a mine.

An unreasonable anger seized Mr. Brett, and it was so apparent that the Major felt obliged to apologize for having disturbed him. Mr. Brett neither accepted nor rejected the apology, but seemed to leave it in the air like an invisible third party between them.

"Brett, my dear fellow," murmured the Major, shifting restlessly round the little room. "I've come to beg a favor." He had reached the window and frowned out on to the night world; then, with sharp, sidelong glances at the foot of the bed, went on: "I know you and I haven't always seen eye to eye but I've always understood our differences were honorable." Here he looked inquisitively at the top of Mr. Brett's head. "We've differed on principle alone—but I've always felt our natures, underneath it all, to be sincerely friendly."

Mr. Brett, who had felt no such thing, mumbled feebly into his blanket and the Major nodded. "Truth of the matter is, Brett, I need your help. This—this shocking affair...if it comes to anything (and we all pray it won't), well, the upshot is, I'd like you to act as me second."

"What?"

"Second, my dear fellow. Arrange all the details: weapons et cetera...time and place...surgeon..."

Mr. Brett sat bolt upright. Weapons? Surgeon? He knew nothing about such matters. He knew nothing about dueling.

"You ain't engaged for the—um—other side?" asked the Major, whose first instinct was to assume everyone was as devious as himself. "If so I'd rather you came out with it openly, Brett. You know me—man of honor—can't abide subterfuge—all in the open—no excuses—"

Mr. Brett stared at him and wondered that such a father could have produced such a daughter. Then the unworthy thought struck him that such a father had not produced such a daughter and that Mrs. Alexander had been swept off her feet by some unlawful broom...He smiled, and the Major, mistaking his expression, darted up to him, shook him warmly by the hand and exclaimed, "Thank you, Brett. From the bottom of my heart. Knew I could count on you. Pays to open one's heart...always..."

With a last affectionate squeeze of Mr. Brett's helpless hand and a last reference to his heart's bottom, he vanished from the room, leaving behind a faint smell of brandy and sweat as if in token of having briefly opened that secret place in his breast. Once outside, the Major paused for a moment, cocked his head towards the door, then departed, wearing that curious smile that nature has drawn on the jaws of snakes and crocodiles.

He moved swiftly and silently, and even as the pale skirt of his nightgown whisked round a corner a flickering light and accompanying shadow approached from the opposite direction.

◆

"For God's sake, what now?" groaned Mr. Brett, and his third visitor came in.

Dr. Bunnion, gowned and candled, seemed to fill the tiny room like some immense spirit on a dreadful errand to guilty beds. This severity of aspect was, however, the work of nature and could not be helped. Within was a very discreet and hopeful gentleman, even timid at times.

"Jack," he murmured. "I may call you Jack, I take it?"

Mr. Brett nodded. His name was James, but it did not seem to signify.

"This unhappy affair, you know. Of course, one cannot blame Alexander. These military men and their honor... where would we be without them? I blame the girl, I'm afraid. But still, what's done is done and we must all face the consequences and look to the future..."

He drifted on in this way for some minutes while his candle tilted and shed its wax on Mr. Brett's folded breeches. Angrily Mr. Brett watched and, each time the headmaster paused for breath, attempted to draw attention to the circumstance.

"So, Jack, you understand why I'd rather it was you than any of Ralph's wild friends. So long as there's a chance of reconciliation, it's important to have someone of good sense acting as his second." The headmaster smiled painfully. "Thank you for bearing with me, Jack. And above all, thank you for standing by me—standing by the school, I should say—in this time of trial. But then I knew I could count on you, Jack..." He shifted his candle so that a final little cataract of wax fell on the folded breeches before wishing Mr. Brett a heartfelt good night. A moment later he popped his large head back into the room and murmured, "All this is only if the worst comes to the worst. But I've every confidence that in the clear light of day everything will be cleared up. Let us pray for it, Jack, eh?"

Once more he departed, this time finally, and left Mr. Brett in the impossible situation of having agreed to act as second to both parties because he'd been too cowardly to utter a word in objection.

Indeed, the only soul he'd spoken to with any passion had been the unlucky Tizzy who still wandered, gently sobbing, along the maze of passages and up and down the lurking stairs.

Mercifully the intricate architecture of the Academy's upper part continued to hide her grief from the other wanderers in the night, each of whom pursued his separate winding way like a nightgowned thought in the coils of some dark, gigantic brain.

Suddenly she stopped. Somewhere a door had opened and shut. A breathless silence seemed to fall on all the house. The creakings and gruntings of boards were stilled; then, slowly, but dreadfully sure, came the sound of stealthy steps...

Ralph Bunnion, half frightened, half excited by the prospect of the duel, had not gone out that night. Instead, he'd remained in his room, brooding on blood, weapons and cold death upon some gray dawn. Still in his fatal waistcoat, he'd saluted his reflection in the mirror and raised imaginary pistols and swords.

He had almost decided on pistols—one of his friends owned a very fine pair—but still he hesitated. He was not a coward but, if by ill-luck he should fall, a sword thrust was likely to prove less injurious than a pistol shot—which might well be fatal.

He opened a bottle of claret to oil his thoughts. He was very used to claret. At the Old Ship Inn a bottle did no more for him than impart an ease and lightness to his gait. So he drank quite freely and without any sense of care or constraint. The fact that he'd had no supper to lay the claret's foundation,

so to speak, had quite slipped his mind; by the time he'd finished half the bottle the ease and lightness that should have
tempered his limbs had reached his unsuspecting head.

Matters of life and death slipped effortlessly away and various extraordinary notions, robed in crimson fumes, filled
his brain. Lust, anger and the memory of his downland fall
inflamed him. In his mind's bleary eye he saw again the
tempting, insolent back of Tizzy Alexander whirling away
from his outstretched grasp. He clenched his fists and brought
them down fiercely on his writing table. Then he drank some
more claret to clear his head.

He stood up and stared at himself again in the mirror. For
a moment he was shocked at the sight of his injuries; his chis-
eled features contorted in fury and humiliation. In vain he
called up images of his many conquests—saw them fall like
painted leaves before the wind of his passion. But always
Tizzy interposed with her look of weary disappointment; and
again he lived through his frightful fall.

He drank the last of the claret to wash her memory away.
But the dangerous fumes within only boiled the more fiercely
and his lust and hatred knew no bounds. He snarled and
moved vaguely towards the door. If only he could find it, he
would move along the corridors like a ghost—like a wolf...
He would take her in her arrogant bed...he would stifle her
screams and—

At last he found the door which had unaccountably eluded
him. He opened it. Like a wolf towards his wild design, he
began to move. Slow, slow...but dreadfully sure, his stealthy
feet moved on...

Chapter Five

THE MOON, the same inquisitive moon that had laid its silver finger on the troubled bed of Mr. Brett, gazed down on the other distracted household in the town—the home of Dr. Harris—as if coldly noting the connection.

Between the two houses lay the silvered windows and phantom streets from which thieves, murderers and lovers alike all shrank into the concealment of the shadows. But their thoughts and schemes ever ventured abroad, crossing, linking, tangling, till the whole world seemed covered with a web of obscure motives in which even angels might be caught.

The old nurse who had looked after all the Harrises had been the first to scream. She'd gone to wake little Adelaide for her ten o'clock feed.

"Come, little one," she'd crooned. "Come to—"

A beetle-browed infant with hair as black as sin opened its eyes and glared at her. She screamed; she shrieked; she ran distracted out of the room pursued by alien cries from the usurped crib.

Then terror, confusion and frantic grief seized the house

till the very cobbles of its walls seemed turned to bulging eyes, all stony with amazement. Every window blazed with light as the Harrises rushed from room to room as if hoping to come upon Adelaide in some unexpected part of the house. Then they went out into the garden and called and rummaged among the bushes; then Dr. Harris ran up and down the street.

Not that anyone had any clear idea of what should be done, but everyone felt they should be doing something—even though, in their heart of hearts, they knew it to be in vain. Several times Dr. Harris went back into the nursery and stared, bewildered, at the crumpled, shrieking infant that lay in his daughter's place. The loss of Adelaide by itself would have been a terrible thing but this substitution—this *change*— was weird and uncanny. It was beyond all normal experience and reasonable explanation. Wretchedly Dr. Harris shook his head. He was a good, learned, persevering sort of man; a man of sense, not given to idle fancy.

"For pity's sake, *do* something!" wept his wife. "Look again before it's too late!"

"Too late for what?"

"I don't know—I don't know!"

So once again Dr. Harris joined in the despairing search; and, of all that troubled household, the most eager, the most urgent and the most anxious to look and look again was the only son, young Harris himself. It was he who was ever in the forefront, full of hopes, ideas and sudden sights that, alas, came to nought. It was he who thought he saw Adelaide at the bottom of the garden; it was he who thought he saw her in the attic.

Deep and subtle consideration had suggested this course to Harris as being the most brilliant way to avoid suspicion. His absence from the scene, or even his lagging behind, would surely have seemed unusual and so might have led to the horror of discovery. So he threw himself into the search with extraordinary vigor and invention. But all the while, under this dazzling counterfeit, his brain was steadily at work.

At last it became tragically plain to the family that Adelaide was not going to be found; and, in spite of the younger Harris's urgent entreaties that they should look just once more, they gathered wearily in the front parlor to decide on what next should be done.

"Bostock," said Dr. Harris gravely. "I'll have to call Bostock."

At this, the son of the house started in horrible alarm, till he understood that his father had meant Bostock the sea captain—his friend's parent—who was a Justice of the Peace. So Captain Bostock was fetched from his bed and informed of the unnatural disaster that had struck at the home of Dr. Harris.

He listened, yawning and frowning the while and fixing his piercing blue eyes upon one member of the family after another as they broke in with uncontrollable agitation. This gaze of his which, in its day, had subdued mutinous sailors and almost the sea itself, had the effect of calming the parlor. Everyone dropped their eyes; but not the younger Harris whose mounting dread of discovery would have given him strength to outstare St. Peter himself. He sat and glared, with terrible fixity, at Captain Bostock, being entirely convinced that one turn of his head would reveal its guilty contents. Then, little by little, as the sea captain talked, his dread diminished and his brain resumed its underground activity.

Though Captain Bostock was, as he himself freely admitted, a sturdy, straightforward and even blunt fellow, many years on the Bench had taught him a great deal. He was, he owned with a sigh, no stranger to the webs of deceit in which men raveled themselves. In his time he had come upon many affairs as curious as the disappearance of Adelaide. He did not say this with any idea of belittling the Harris family's grief, but merely to establish an authority over it.

None the less Mrs. Harris looked plainly resentful at what she took to be Captain Bostock's insinuation that they were all making a great fuss over nothing. The sea captain, anxious to correct the false impression, hastily admitted that there were certain aspects of the Adelaide affair that distinguished it from the commonplace.

In his opinion—for what it was worth—it was not so much the disappearance of Adelaide that was extraordinary, but the *appearance* of the unknown infant in her place. He took it for granted, he said, in view of his long friendship with Dr. Harris, that the family were not mistaken and the infant was not their own. Here Mrs. Harris could not be restrained from telling the sea captain that his long friendship with Dr. Harris might go to the Devil; a mother knew what was her own child and what was not, and that the newcomer was a male infant which, somehow or another, seemed to her the worst thing of all. Then she began to sob and Captain Bostock said, "Madam, madam," several times in an effort to atone for his unlucky remark. At last Mrs. Harris was brought to a temporary calm and Captain Bostock admitted cautiously that the situation was one that called for an inquiry of *peculiar* delicacy...

The younger Harris's heart leaped and thundered. The very word "inquiry" tolled like the bell of doom inside his breast. Nor was what followed any less alarming. He sat, cold and deathly, as the consequences of his and Bostock's experiment in Natural History grew and grew till it was like a monster whose tentacles reached into every corner of the living world.

Naturally, Captain Bostock would institute inquiries (that terrible word again!)—and here he tapped the side of his weathered nose down which ran a neat, straight scar—but he would advise Dr. Harris to take certain steps himself.

At the Old Ship Inn there happened to be staying a certain Mr. Raven—Mr. Selwyn Raven. Had Dr. Harris heard of him? Well, well, perhaps not. Unless one had cause, one did not hear of such as Mr. Raven. Such persons are rather more discreet than most. The nature of their trade is against advertisement. None the less, in his, Captain Bostock's opinion, for what it was worth, the Harrises could do no better than consult Mr. Raven whose reputation, among those who had cause to know it, stood very high indeed for pursuing inquiries of *peculiar* delicacy. There could be little doubt that Mr. Raven, once in possession of the facts, would quickly arrive at the truth.

At the word "truth," the younger Harris's blood all but congealed. He felt like some rare and lovely creature caught in a forest of implacable hunters seeking to destroy him. He twisted, he turned, he darted this way and that in the secret places of his mind to escape. But outwardly, by reason of his almost superhuman strength of character, he appeared quite still, and with an air of utter calm. There was a small, remote part of Harris that was able to observe this, and even to admire it.

At last Captain Bostock rose to go and Harris, still brilliantly counterfeiting an inward peace, courteously offered to attend him. He had reached a conclusion and determined on a course of action.

For a moment Captain Bostock fixed him with his piercing eyes which seemed to go right inside Harris's head, but apparently he saw nothing there for he patted the lad's arm and suffered him to lead the way to the neighboring street.

Harris waited for the sea captain to shut his front door, then, with easy stealth, he floated round to the back of the house and summoned his friend by means of a stone at his window. Bostock appeared, disappeared, then appeared again and came looping down through an ancient apple tree that grew against the house, pausing only to embrace Jupiter, his brutish ginger cat who waited on a bough for some necessary bird.

The friends shook hands; then Harris told Bostock about the consternation in the Harris household and the mention of the man who was staying at the Old Ship—the inquiry agent, Mr. Selwyn Raven. Bostock looked at Harris in terror. He could see Harris was alarmed; and to him Harris's alarm was as the cracking of a temple or the shaking of a star in the sky.

"But I've thought of something, old friend," whispered Harris reassuringly; in a curious way, Bostock's simplicity seemed to reassure both of them. Bostock's great faith gave Harris confidence, and the more confidence Harris displayed, the greater grew Bostock's faith. There was really no limit to it all. "I think I know where she is."

"Who?"

"Adelaide. I've put two and two together, Bosty—and there's only one answer."

"What's that, Harris?" breathed Bostock, who was not strong on Arithmetic.

"She's back in the school."

"How do you know?"

"Human nature, Bosty."

Bostock frowned; he did not like to question Harris, particularly about human nature.

"Mark my words, Bosty, at this very minute my sister's asleep at the school, snug in Miss Alexander's bed."

"Then—then Ralph took her all the way back again?"

Harris tapped the side of his nose. "Human nature, old friend. He fancied Miss Alexander; Miss Alexander fancied Adelaide. Two and two, Bosty."

"Human nature," nodded Bostock, but with a note of uncertainty in his voice. Then Harris smiled and Bostock was reassured.

"Let's go, Bosty."

"Where, Harris?"

"To the school. We've got to get her back, you know. It wouldn't be natural to leave her."

"Right now, Harris?"

"Right now, old friend. Safest and best. They'll all be asleep at the school. After all, what can have happened to keep them awake?"

The moon stood in the sky above the two distracted households like a scimitar: it illumined a thread between them like a silver worm winding through a world of black. Along this thread, which here and there vanished under interrupting shadows, moved the double shape of Bostock and Harris and, a little way behind, a smaller, quicker shape that stopped and started, then went arrow straight.

The brutish Jupiter had left the birdless apple tree to follow his master into the night.

"Go back!" pleaded Bostock at intervals, and Jupiter would pause and stare at him meaningfully; then, when the friends went on, he would follow after with the quick, stiff-legged walk of an elderly but still powerful cat, no longer able to hunt for himself but eager for others to oblige.

Though the two friends were as familiar with the way to Dr. Bunnion's as with each other's pockets, it now became mysterious and uncanny. The solemnity of the night and the desperate nature of their journey lent an unearthly aspect to the well-worn streets. The houses—now the tombs of sleep— seemed curiously insubstantial, as if their very walls had only been bodied forth by the dreams within and a touch would dissolve them into wide vistas...

But Bostock and Harris were real. No dream could have

bodied them forth, and no touch could have dissolved them. They crept among the shadowy plots of half-built houses where ambitious builders were extending the scope of the town. Stealthily they removed a ladder and carried it with them until they reached the school.

All was in darkness. The Academy was wrapped round and round in a deep silence. Harris pointed upwards. Miss Alexander's room lay under the roof at the side of the house. The mystery of the Academy's upper architecture was as an open book to a mind like Harris's.

Harris smiled. The window was open to the warm night. He nodded. Nature herself was on the side of the two friends. Cautiously the ladder was raised and settled against the wall. Harris signed to Bostock to mount while he steadied the ladder's foot.

Bostock shook hands with Harris and began to mount. As he did so, a rapid shape passed Harris. Jupiter, with hungry green eyes, had gone up after his master. Harris saw them enter the window almost together, with Jupiter scrambling over Bostock's shoulder.

Harris waited. For a moment there was silence. Then there was a loud and dreadful cry followed by the sound of something heavy falling. Then Jupiter reappeared and descended the ladder at a great speed with Bostock after him. Bostock looked very white. Harris paused till Bostock was down, then the two friends fled for their lives. They did not stop running until they were back in Bostock's garden. There they leaned against the apple tree while, in the branches above them, Jupiter cleaned the blood from his claws.

A terrible thing had happened. Inflamed by vengeance, lust and wine, Ralph Bunnion had accomplished his monstrous errand. Unseen by the other wanderers in the night, he had somehow unraveled the maze of passages, stairs and corners and found out Tizzy Alexander's room. A wolfish smile had disfigured his handsome features. Quietly he'd opened the door. Then had struck disaster. The bed was empty; but the room was not. A shape of strange, inhuman aspect was at the window. Outlined against the sky it seemed, to Ralph's crimsoned mind, to be part man and part beast; from its human shoulders reared the wicked head of a cat.

Courageously he'd stumbled forward, hands outstretched. He was in such a mood to attack angels and devils alike. He reached out—and for a second time the concerns of Bostock and Harris crossed the purpose of the headmaster's son.

The brutish Jupiter flew at the intruder in the darkened room, savaged his face and fled, hissing with alarm; nor was Bostock far behind. Ralph Bunnion shrieked and fell with a sound like thunder. The house shook, and the wanderers in the night came rushing upon the scene before there was any chance of escape.

They found him lying drunkenly beside Tizzy Alexander's tumbled bed; and even in the uncertain candlelight it was plain there had been further damage done to his unlucky face. Denial—even if he'd been in a condition to make one—would have been hopeless, and the little Academy quaked in the grip of confusion, anger and fear.

Events which, by skill, compromise and goodwill might have been halted, were now whirled out of all sensible men's control on their fatal course of calamity. Dr. Bunnion could no longer uphold the innocence of his moaning, bleeding son; and Major Alexander did not see how he could avoid avenging his daughter's honor.

Shortly before dawn, when Mr. Brett had at last managed to forget his own wretched situation sufficiently to fall into a light sleep, he was awakened by yet another knocking at his door. Savagely he cried out, "Go away! For God's sake, leave me in peace! All of you, go to Hell!"

Outside the door, poor, bewildered Tizzy Alexander sobbed quietly and went away.

Chapter Six

THE BELLS of St. Nicholas's wrinkled the morning air as they summoned the town to prayer. Dully the two distressed households understood it to be Sunday and they must needs carry their griefs and perplexities to church to thank God for being alive.

"Let us pray," suggested Mr. Hudson, the vicar, when the time came; and the congregation knelt—some opening their hearts for relief from private anguish and others endeavoring to close them against the prying eyes of the Almighty. Chief among the former were Mrs. Harris and Tizzy Alexander; and chief among the latter were Bostock and Harris.

Not even God can help me now, thought Harris, as he peered round the well-filled pews for a sight of Ralph Bunnion who, it turned out, had been the last living soul to clap eyes on Adelaide and had left her only he knew where. After the night's disaster, it was plain that Adelaide was not in the school. Harris had some confused notion of throwing himself on the school hero's mercy, confessing all (or nearly all) and imploring his aid. But Ralph Bunnion was nowhere to be seen.

Sadly Harris glanced sideways to where the sturdy Bostock knelt with closed eyes and open mouth. He envied his friend his slow, simple mind that was not tormented with dreadful thoughts. Though Bostock might never reach the heights that he, Harris, sometimes knew, he would never plummet to the depths that he, Harris, was now in.

A great loneliness fell upon Harris as round about him prayers of all descriptions rose in silence to the church's roof. He felt himself to be the outcast of creation against whom every man's hand was raised. Then he looked at Bostock again and was briefly consoled. Bostock was his companion and friend; he was just as involved as Harris himself and would, therefore, be bound to suffer at his side. At once Harris felt less lonely and more a part of the common fate of mankind.

Mr. Hudson nodded to his flock. He was a shaggy man with large hands and large feet and, as he began to snap and bark his sermon from the pulpit, was the very image of a pious sheepdog with a sharp eye for strays.

As the town was becoming quite fashionable of late by reason of an interest in sea-bathing, Mr. Hudson thought it necessary to touch on the extreme difficulty of rich men entering the Kingdom of Heaven unaided. The poor were all right— here he smiled encouragingly at the fisherfolk at the back— but the rich—here he frowned at the private pews—stood in need of assistance. Though he didn't say it outright, he implied pretty strongly that they weren't likely to get such assistance from God direct; their only chance lay through the proper channels. That was what churches were for. And St. Nicholas's in particular. They were not likely to do better elsewhere even though the actual building stood in need of repair. Exposed as it was to the winds from the sea, even the house of God was subject to the elements. The roof leaked. Money was required to restore it. And where should such money come from? From those who would benefit. From this very congregation who prayed and expected their prayers to be answered.

Here Mr. Hudson paused so that the equity of the arrangement might sink in. Harris felt in his pockets and wondered how much he could afford on the chance of a quick return. He had reached the final pit of despair in which anything was worth trying.

He had a shilling and a sixpence. Strenuously he wrestled with his conscience, arguing that Mr. Hudson would never know that if he gave the sixpence, a shilling had been withheld. But God would know, said a pious voice within. "Yah!" snarled Harris, whose faith was a rubbery commodity and tended to shift out of the way under pressure. "Who cares?"

He fished in his pockets and came upon a battered brass button that a horse had trodden flat. He mused; why the sixpence when the button would make as good a noise in the collecting box? After all, it was the thought that counted—and Mr. Hudson would certainly think it was money.

When the service ended, Harris frowned and dropped the button in the box. The vicar smiled and wagged his clasped hands behind his back; and Bostock, seeing Harris's gesture, sighed and put in a shilling, which was all he had.

"Well!" said Harris, challenging the great host of heaven. "Now show me You're really there! Where's Adelaide?"

The congregation had left the cool shadows of the church and were out in the pagan sunshine.

"Answer me!" muttered Harris, looking up defiantly at the golden pastures of the universe. "Or You'll be the loser!"

Thus Harris barbed his soul and aimed it at the sky—to bring down an angel; or nothing. That he himself had not been absolutely honest in this trial of faith did not disturb him in the least. On the contrary, he argued with Jesuitical subtlety, the Almighty now had every opportunity for displaying His vaunted understanding and forgiveness.

He waited while round about he heard the clatter of gossip and the salty grumbling of fisherfolk as the Sunday town, in homespun and starfish ribbons, jostled him out of their homeward way. But nothing came to him from the invisible God. Instead, sturdily stamping across the graveyard, came Bostock. He had left his family, gone out of his way to raise his hat, with furious blushes, to the wild slender Miss Harris, and come to join his friend.

Harris, who was at the very crisis of belief, looked depressed, and Bostock wondered how he might cheer him up. He did not like to see Harris miserable.

"I expect she'll turn up somewhere, Harris," he mumbled, and laid his hand timidly on his friend's narrow shoulder.

Harris turned. "Bosty, old friend," he whispered. "There ain't no God."

The words struck Bostock like a blow in the stomach. They were so strange and unexpected.

"The sky's empty, old friend," went on Harris grimly. "There's just us, Bosty."

"What, you and me?" Bostock was shaken to the depths of his soul.

"No," said Harris irritably. "Mankind. All of us down here. We're all there is, Bosty. The rest is—is air."

"Are you sure, Harris?" asked Bostock pleadingly. He knew he hadn't the intellect to question his friend, but at the same time he did not want to abandon his own beliefs without a struggle. They meant a great deal to him, and had it been anyone else but wise old Harris who'd shaken them, he'd have clouted him without more ado. "How—how do you know?"

Harris frowned. He did not care to admit that his reason

was chiefly that he'd received no answer to his gift of the brass button.

"But there *must* be a God," urged Bostock desperately.

"Why, old friend?"

"Because—because of everything. Look about you, Harris! All the grass and trees and different animals and flowers. Who made them if not God?"

"Somebody else," said Harris bleakly. The friends stared at one another, Harris as still and somber as the headstones among which they stood, and Bostock swaying slightly as if rocking in a sea of doubt. Bostock turned his small, fierce eyes from side to side, ranging the wide landscape as if trying to see in it some other light than the bright sun's. Painfully he stared from the soft, silken sea to the green, velvet folds of the Downs. Not two miles off he saw the tiny village of Preston clustering like a brood of kittens about the wise gray church whose square head watched over the cottages, ready to call them back if they strayed into danger. Bostock's eyes began to fill with tears. Passionately he struggled to reject Harris's grim philosophy and to bring his friend back into the warm, motherly world.

"Look, Harris—look!" he muttered, pointing to the village but unable to put his thoughts into words.

Wearily Harris looked. "What is it, old friend?"

"The—the church," said Bostock incoherently, and hoped Harris would understand.

Harris gazed at the aged building that looked, from where he stood, to be no better than a child's toy. "Poor, poor Bosty," he whispered pityingly. He was half sorry for the damage he'd done his friend, but nevertheless the truth was more sacred than anything else; nothing was worse than worshiping a lie. Just how Harris, whose mind was furtive in the extreme, managed to believe in this philosophy, was a mystery as deep as life; but then he was a scientist.

"Yes, Bosty—another church."

He stopped. His heart quickened. *Another* church. In his mind's eye he saw once more the horseman and the baby of the previous night, and in a blaze of understanding he guessed what had happened. Ralph Bunnion, with Adelaide in his arms, for some reason or another must have ridden *past* St. Nicholas's and on to the church at Preston!

The lights came on in his eyes. He thumped Bostock on the back. "*Now* I know, old friend!"

"I don't want to hear it," said Bostock bitterly—thinking Harris had shifted the heavens still further afield.

"He took her to Preston," said Harris. "*That's* where Adelaide went!"

"Oh," said Bostock. "I thought you meant God."

"What's God got to do with it? Come on, Bosty!"

He set off at a smart trot towards Preston and Bostock followed after. All questions of faith and belief had vanished from Harris's mind. He left the gates of Heaven swinging open, so to speak, for God to resume. His leasehold until he, Harris, chose to foreclose again.

When the friends reached Preston, Harris's inspiration was confirmed. Ingeniously they fell into conversation with a boy and learned that a baby had indeed been left in the church on the previous night. But almost at once their lifted hopes were dashed to the ground. They were too late. The baby had already been taken to the poorhouse in Brighton.

As they walked back in the deepest dejection, the fleeting thought struck Harris that had he put his shilling, or even his sixpence, in the collecting box instead of the brass button, they might have been in time. Then he shook his head. No god could be *that* petty.

"At least we know where she is," said Bostock hopefully, and secretly considered the shilling he'd sacrificed in church had been money well spent. Of such strange material is faith built, unbuilt and built again—in ever-changing designs.

By the time the two friends drew near their homes, they were buoyant again. Harris's eyes were gleaming and Bostock watched him admiringly. He knew that Harris's large brain was fairly humming to devise a plan to rescue Adelaide from the poorhouse. He did not anticipate any further problems.

They shook hands at the corner of Harris's street and parted, each confident that their troubles were all but at an end. Harris was whistling under his breath and, as he entered his house, his spindly, wrinkle-stockinged legs did a jaunty, doorstep jig.

"This is my son, sir," said Dr. Harris wearily as Harris entered the parlor, and the stranger smiled.

He was shortish, stout and quietly dressed. He wore a neat bagwig and had soft, large eyes. With an unaccountable chill, Harris saw he had a clubbed foot whose grim black bulk seemed to belie the gentleness of his expression.

"This is Mr. Selwyn Raven," said Dr. Harris to his suddenly pale son. "He has come to get at the truth about Adelaide."

Chapter Seven

"A SAD affair, my young friend," said Mr. Raven. Harris nodded warily, his eyes moving from Mr. Raven's mild face to his unnatural black boot.

"I don't wish to pry, young man, into any of your private secrets, but a few questions, if you'd be so kind, eh?" He nodded to Dr. Harris who looked momentarily distressed—as if on his son's behalf—then hurriedly left the room.

Harris felt curiously abandoned. He did not know what to make of Mr. Raven who kept shifting his wicked boot as if to draw attention to it.

"You are interested in such things?" asked the inquiry agent, observing Harris's fascination. "But of course! Being a physician's son such deformities must seem commonplace."

Harris nodded and smiled casually. Or believed that he did.

"Would you care to see it?" offered Mr. Raven eagerly. He bent down as if to remove the boot.

"No!" said Harris quickly. He had been seized by a sudden dread that the deformed foot might have been something altogether frightful. Mr. Raven looked mildly surprised and apologized for embarrassing the young gentleman. He had not intended to do any such thing, but when one had such a misfortune it was difficult to judge its effect. He himself had always found it was better to be open with it... not to attempt to hide it, or even to pretend it wasn't there. After all, it was an act of God and one didn't deny God—

"You do believe in God, young man?" he asked anxiously; and then, before the startled Harris could reply, he smiled and added, "But of course. You've just come from church. When did you last see your sister?"

"I—I don't remember," said Harris faintly. The abrupt change of direction made him break out in a sweat. Mr. Raven was an eerie adversary.

"I didn't mean to pry into your religious beliefs, young man," said Mr. Raven gently. "But I like to know where we stand." Again he moved his horrible boot as if, having discovered exactly where Harris was standing, he intended to flatten him under it. "Did you see any stranger in the neighborhood yesterday? A woman, perhaps?"

Again the abrupt change of direction; but this time Harris was ready. "Yes!" he said quickly; he was anxious to transfer Mr. Raven's attention to someone else.

"Interesting," said the inquiry agent; but strangely did not pursue the point. Instead he rapped his boot sharply with a stout stick that had been leaning beside his chair. He chuckled disarmingly and explained that the deformed member was inclined to "go to sleep," and he liked to wake it up from time to time...

Harris began to feel sick. He longed for Mr. Raven to go; he was morbidly terrified of him. Now Mr. Raven was asking him if he knew of any enemies the household had; a dismissed servant, perhaps...? Fiercely Harris retreated within himself. You're a genius, Harris! he screamed in his heart.

And he's a—a madman! You are more than a match for him. Outwit him! Be calm! Smile! Answer him; don't be rushed! For God's sake, be careful! None the less, in spite of the certainty of his own intellectual superiority over this man, Harris could not keep down a terrible desire to confess to Mr. Raven and so get rid of him. I took her! he longed to shout out. Bostock and me! We took her!

He felt the words rattling in his throat. He coughed and swallowed to keep them to himself.

"This strange woman you saw," said Mr. Raven smoothly. "Can you describe her?"

"What woman?" said Harris, bewildered by the suddenness of the question.

"Oh nothing. I must have been mistaken. Only I thought you said you saw such a one in the neighborhood. I must have misheard you. Pardon me."

Harris bit his lip. He'd slipped. The devilish Mr. Raven had caught him out. All desire to confess vanished under a flood of panic.

"No matter," murmured the inquiry agent, hobbling to his feet. "I shall be at the Old Ship Inn. If anything occurs to you—if you remember anything you think might interest me—come and see me. I shall be waiting, my young friend... any time, any time..."

With that, he clumped from the room and was presently out of the house.

The inquiry agent limped along the street, his stick and his great boot tapping and thumping inquisitively on the ground, as if searching for a weakness or a symptom of rot. Mostly he kept his eyes downwards, but from time to time he glanced at the houses he passed and then up to the splendid sun. And, as always, his eyes remained mild, and his expression innocent. It was only his boot—his monstrous boot—that suggested Mr. Raven was a formidable man.

He was deeply acquainted with the darknesses of the human soul, and he knew too well the terror of the guilty spirit as it twists and turns to escape. Suspicion was second nature to him; and he had no first. Wearily he brooded on his last interview—with the boy Harris whose spirit had fled almost visibly for refuge to his boots.

The inquiry agent shrugged his shoulders. He was all too used to being greeted with fear and guilt. Where was innocence? A dream—a milky idea in the noddles of fools, and nowhere else. It was not even in the hearts of children, all of whom had their corrupting little secrets which they struggled to hide from the light of day.

What had the boy Harris been trying to hide with his frowns and grins, his rapid, sideways eyes and his dismal attempts at honesty of manner? A theft from a neighbor, perhaps? Or a furtive tryst with some sluttish maid, et cetera?

The expression "et cetera" was a very necessary one to Mr. Raven. It was like a great black bag in which he tumbled men's thoughts and deeds when he sensed they were too deep and foul for other words.

Mr. Raven knew it all. Nothing surprised him anymore. Guilt was in every heart; even infants in their cradles tended to look fearful and evasive when Mr. Raven stared mildly down on them. The gypsy child in the Harris's usurped cot had crumpled its face and turned from the inquiry agent's bland eyes as if suddenly conscious of the original sin that had dealt it, like the Ace of Spades, into the frightened household's hand.

"Yes, my young friend," Mr. Raven had whispered. "You know—and soon, very soon, so shall I."

At length he reached the Old Ship Inn where he asked for a mutton chop and a pint of sherry to be sent up to his room; the Harrises had not seen fit to ask him to luncheon. Not that the omission rankled particularly, but Mr. Raven had noted it. He sat by his window and stared out on to the smooth Sunday sea and considered the strange affair of Adelaide Harris. Or, rather, the strange affair of the mysterious baby that now lay in her place; it was glaringly clear that Adelaide had only been removed to make way for it. The Harrises were ordinary folk and, however they might have rated themselves, Mr. Raven knew they were of no consequence in the world; so their infant could have been of no consequence in the world; so their infant could have been of no value to anyone. Its only possession was the space it had occupied—its cot; and this it was, rather than the infant itself, that had been stolen. For the dark one ... for the dark one ...

The importance of the black-haired baby fascinated and tantalized him. "What secret lust begot you, my young friend?" he murmured to himself. "And what shameful womb nourished you, et cetera? Discover that, and we discover all!" He rapped his boot with his stick as if seeking confirmation.

Indeed, it was almost as though he conversed with his monstrous appendage and received from it answers as black as itself. "Was it your mother or your father who passed on the telltale gypsy blood?"

Before there could be an answer, his sherry and mutton chop came in at the door on a tray carried by the boot-boy since none of the maids would venture into Mr. Raven's room.

The boy put the tray down and glanced inquisitively at the inquiry agent's boot and wondered if he ever took it off. Night after night there was only the commonplace right one left out to be cleaned. The great ugly left boot never appeared but on

Mr. Raven's foot. The boy went out and Mr. Raven ate his chop and continued to worry at the problem.

Two things were plain. The gypsy baby must have been important enough for it to have been laid in a private cot rather than entrusted to the stony mercy of some church night; and there must have been a traitor in the Harris household to have opened doors—and closed them afterwards.

The inquiry agent washed down the mutton chop with the sherry and returned to staring out of the window from which he could see the quiet sea endlessly unrolling on the shingle like some wide, secret document displaying itself, then drawing back with a whisper before it could be read.

"What is it saying?" murmured Mr. Raven, tapping his boot.

That there is nothing so black as the human heart, came the answer. Under the sea lie poisoned bones and ribs all chipped by knives. Bullets roll inside skulls and ghastly captains lash long-dead cabin boys with whips of trailing weeds, et cetera. Yet the sea's surface is as bland and fair as a baby's cheek...So plunge deep, Selwyn Raven, and deeper yet till you reach the gloomy depths where human motives coil and strike. For every action there is a foul motive—and this it is your sacred task to find.

"Alas!" whispered Mr. Raven, gazing down on his boot with a mixture of fear and repugnance. "Were it not for you I might not be cursed with such bitter knowledge. I too might be blind like other men and not be burdened with such truth. Before this affair of Adelaide Harris is done with, great families will totter and guilty souls will plunge into Hell. Murder may be done, et cetera..."

So it was that, with these thoughts in his mind, he clumped from his room and went downstairs to the back parlor where

sherry and claret were loosening devious tongues and un-
locking tangled hearts. Secrets black, secrets gray, all came to
the ears of Selwyn Raven as he sat and listened and distilled
them into the bitter draft of guilt.

Chapter Eight

RALPH Bunnion, having risen at last from his bed and taken a cautious lunch, was on his way to meet a friend. He walked carefully, for the effects of the calamitous night had not entirely worn off. His face was deathly pale and the double scratches had gone black and venomous-looking—as if some dissatisfied artist had made an attempt to cross him out. None the less he was dressed with his usual care, wearing a dark blue coat cut away to display a lavish waistcoat embroidered with the yellow and purple flowerets of love-in-idleness. Maggie Hemp had stitched it for him during a lull in the first weeks of their passion and had woven her name into the design.

Sunday walkers, crossing his path, glanced curiously at him but he returned a look of dignified aloofness and glided on. In his own way, Ralph Bunnion was something of a hero. Though he knew Major Alexander's accusation to be false and the challenge therefore unjust, he scorned to say so . . . partly because he knew he wouldn't be believed and partly because the notion of a duel was grandly romantic.

A great many noble and even tragic ideas thronged his brain and he tended to look on the passing landscape as bidding its last farewell to the gay and dashing Ralph. Already he'd determined, if he should fall, that he would bequeath his collection of waistcoats to Frederick.

Frederick was the friend he was meeting, and it was he who owned the pair of dueling pistols. Ralph would certainly have preferred swords, but in the end it turned out that he didn't know anybody who had a pair and it seemed undignified to hire them. So pistols it was to be, with Frederick as his second.

Or one of his seconds. Ralph frowned. His father had gone and saddled him with that sly, sour fellow Brett as the other. Ralph disliked Mr. Brett, and it was humiliating to be seconded by him. But there was no help for it now. Brett was to fix up about the surgeon, and there again his father had interfered. Sometimes Ralph wondered who it was who was supposed to be fighting the duel. His father insisted on having Dr. Harris whose brat was at the school. He fancied this might keep things in the family, as it were, and prevent them from getting out all over the town.

An expression of melancholy contempt came over Ralph's face. What good could even Dr. Harris do when the glorious Ralph lay quiet and still with only his red blood moving, moving away from a hole in his breast?

Ralph's heart beat rapidly. Why did he always think of himself as being dead? Was it an omen? "What will be, will be," he whispered philosophically—and entered the Old Ship Inn.

There were few people in the dim back parlor where Ralph and his friends delighted to hold court and sing and drink the night into day, but good old Frederick was among them. He was thinner than Ralph and would need to fill out before the waistcoats would fit him. Ralph shivered as once again his thoughts implied his own death.

"Arternoon, Mister Ralph, sir," said the landlord affably. "Pint of the usual?"

"Half," said Ralph quietly. "Just a half, landlord."

"Night on the tiles, eh?" chuckled the landlord; then, observing Ralph's savaged face, guffawed loudly as the full extent of his own wit reached him. "He—he! I sees you been tom-catting again! Lord, Mister Ralph, you'll have the town on your tail afore long!"

Though privately the landlord detested Ralph Bunnion and his gaudy friends, they were entitled to his courtesy as they drank well and kept the parlor from being lonely. Ralph smiled feebly at the landlord's tribute, then joined the negligent Frederick at a table by the fireplace.

"Rattlin' fine mess your face is in, old dear," said Frederick, yawning sympathetically. "Tell us all. Your uncle Fred's all ears." This last was not entirely a figure of speech. He did have rather large ears—or else a very small face—and they stuck out from under his wig like loosened coach wheels. Otherwise he was presentable enough, being the son of a successful livery-stable owner.

"Fred," said Ralph with a seriousness that caused his friend to abandon his smile, "I need your pistols—"

Suddenly Ralph stopped. He had become aware of a stranger watching him. He frowned, and the stranger's innocent eyes seemed to drift away under pressure of his own. This stranger was a stoutish, plainly dressed man; he was quite ordinary, even pleasant-looking, but for his left foot which was encased in a gigantic black boot. Ralph shuddered. There was something horrible about that boot and the way it seemed to crouch beside the commonplace right one like some silent, evil hound.

"What's up?" asked Frederick. Ralph shook his head, then went on talking but in a much subdued voice. The stranger half closed his eyes and leaned forward imperceptibly. From time to time Ralph glanced at him with a kind of fearful disgust—at which the stranger would ease himself back and seem to transfer his attention elsewhere, where it would be equally unwelcome.

"So that's how it stands," muttered Ralph, having explained the whole wretched story as he saw it, and confided his fears for the immediate future. "If I don't do for her cursed pa, sure as anything the brute will do for me. But come what may, I won't be blackmailed into marrying his tatty little slut."

Ralph was very violent against Tizzy whom he blamed for everything. He swallowed down the remainder of his claret and the landlord, unasked, sent his boy to replenish it. Ralph, feeling rather warm, removed his coat and Frederick gazed with gloomy admiration at the splendid waistcoat. Even the clubfooted stranger seemed impressed by it and Ralph lounged back carelessly. The stranger peered, and smiled...

The parlor door opened and a newcomer entered. He was slim, no more than twenty-eight, with a thin, worried-looking face. Though not fashionably dressed, his linen was clean and neatly mended. He glanced about the parlor uneasily.

This, thought Mr. Selwyn Raven, is a man who is haunted by a secret. Mr. Raven, to the landlord's disapproval, had been in the back parlor for some hours over a single glass of brandy and water. During that time, a little world of mean sins and cheap corruption had passed in review before him. Silently he'd sat and listened as they'd come and gone: faithless husbands, dishonored wives and false friends, all winding in and out of their tapestries of lies. But what he sought still eluded him. Then the haunted newcomer had come in and Mr. Raven had shifted his ominous boot. This man carries a load of guilt such as Judas Iscariot must have carried, thought Mr. Raven idly. His eyes widened as he saw the newcomer make

for the two young men who'd mentioned pistols and blackmail.

"Why if it isn't Mr. Brett," said Ralph Bunnion sourly, and
introduced Frederick to his other second.

Mr. Brett sat down with a furtive glance round the parlor as
if expecting Major Alexander to appear and confront him
with his wretched duplicity. He'd had an abominable morning in which he'd flitted from room to room in the school to
avoid the Major and the Bunnions. Luncheon had been worse,
with the headmaster saying grace as if it was a graveside
prayer over the invisible body of his son or his Arithmetic
master; then had followed a silent meal laced with such looks
as might have cut the beef far better than the knives. Next,
Major Alexander had caught him in the privy and earnestly
reminded him of his obligations as his second, claimed his
loyalty, his honor, his soul and, it seemed to the unhappy Mr.
Brett, his eternal life—and told him that the duel, unless anything happened to prevent it, would take place upon the following Saturday. He didn't see how he could postpone it any
longer.

Shortly after that the Bunnions, father and son, had trapped
him in the passage outside his classroom and, looking threat-
eningly over him, had claimed much the same degree of loyalty as had the Major before them. The one had followed so
closely upon the other that it seemed extraordinary to Mr.
Brett that the Bunnions couldn't still hear the Major's words.
At last, by desperate nods and reckless promises he'd escaped
them—only to see the fiery little Major beckoning him from
the stairs.

"When you call on Bunnion's second," he'd urged, "tell
him we're open to reason!"

Bunnion's second. That was him. "My principal's open to
reason," muttered Mr. Brett to himself in a quiet corner—and

half waited on a reply. To his overwrought mind it seemed that there must be at least two James Bretts; but alas, neither was an improvement on the other. Too well he knew that all his separate selves were made of the same weak clay.

Then he saw Bunnion *père* shambling towards him, his enormous eyes gleaming with *second* thoughts. Panic seized Mr. Brett. The school seemed full of Bunnions and Alexanders. Wherever he turned they appeared, from corner, door, stair, from the very shadows; smiling, beckoning, plucking at him, drawing him nearer and nearer to that moment of exposure when he would be revealed as an object of universal contempt and distrust. And in that universe would be Tizzy, her eyes out-flashing a sky-full of stars.

The headmaster was almost upon him when he saw Sorley, the fat boarder, passing on his way to the kitchen. "Sorley!" cried Mr. Brett, and clutched fiercely at the boy who stared from master to master with slow alarm. Dr. Bunnion patted Sorley on the head. Not for worlds would he have brought up the scandal of his son and Major Alexander in Sorley's presence. Mr. Brett knew it and for the next hour or so took to following the baronet's son everywhere, thus driving the fat boarder into a truly pitiable state of guilt for he knew not what.

"We must be discreet!" said Mr. Brett as he seated himself between Ralph and Frederick and gazed from one to the other in a dazed kind of way. Dr. Bunnion's last words to him had been concerned with the overwhelming need for discretion. Ralph's whole future was in the balance; a word out of place could wreck it. After all, the Sorleys of Cuckfield would scarcely be pleased to connect themselves with a scandal. It was more to Frederick than to Ralph that Mr. Brett addressed his words in the hope of impressing him with Dr. Bunnion's fears and Ralph's marital hopes. "Because of the Sorleys, you understand," murmured Mr. Brett.

"The Sorleys," mused Frederick. "Ain't that Sir Walter Sorley of Cuckfield?"

In his father's livery-stable business, Frederick had made himself master of a real directory of titled names. It was his only intellectual accomplishment and he was fond of displaying it.

"No need to shout," said Ralph, uncomfortably aware of the stranger with the club foot whose large, innocent eyes seemed fastened to his magnificent waistcoat, like buttons on abnormally long threads. "I suppose the other second will be calling on you any time now," he went on, turning to Mr. Brett who nodded eerily. "And then you'll be seeing about Dr. Harris? What the—"

Suddenly there'd come a sharp scraping noise from the direction of the stranger. His boot had moved forward and remained, swaying slightly, as if straining on a leash. Then the stranger, observing all eyes upon him, smiled apologetically, finished his brandy and water, and clumped out of the parlor.

"Good riddance!" muttered the landlord under his breath.

Mr. Selwyn Raven's vigil had at last been rewarded. He had heard what he'd been waiting for: the connection between one secret and another. He had found the telltale thread that, sooner or later, would lead him to the center of the weird labyrinth in which the mystery of Adelaide Harris was concealed. He went back up to his room to fit the pieces of the puzzle together in his mind.

One tiny thing, the unguarded mention of a single name, had illuminated everything. Dr. Harris. The inquiry agent sat down by the window and patiently recalled the fragments of talk he'd overheard. Blackmail, pistols, forced marriages, a Sussex baronet and then, like a key turning in these dark wards, the single name of Dr. Harris; the fatal connection.

"Tom-catting again, Mister Ralph?" The landlord's words recurred, and with them, the image of the young man, lounging back in his chair, displaying his ridiculous floral waistcoat. "Maggie Hemp!" whispered the inquiry agent, as he remembered the name woven into the design. "Maggie Hemp." He tapped his boot. The mystery of Adelaide Harris was growing clearer.

For a long while there was silence in the little room during which Mr. Raven stared across the sea. Then he began to fumble in his pockets and bring out several folded pieces of paper. One by one he opened them and smoothed them out till he found one of a suitable size. Then he settled down to write with a pen that seemed to writhe and strike at the paper like a serpent.

He wrote names: Adelaide Harris, the gypsy baby, Mister Ralph, the Sorleys of Cuckfield, Maggie Hemp, Dr. Harris— and et cetera. He was not such a fool as to imagine he knew everything yet. There was always the et cetera—the dark spider who would be at the center of the web.

But they were all connected somehow; that much he did know. He smiled rather grimly to himself when he reflected how quickly he had involved the seemingly innocent Dr. Harris in the fine mesh of deceit. In view of this he was relieved he'd not taken luncheon with the Harrises. He would not have eaten with them now if they'd begged him on their bended knees.

For a moment he had been sorely tempted to put Dr. Harris's name in place of the unknown spider, the et cetera of the web; but an obscure sense bade him hold his pen. It was this quality that made him the formidable man he was and ever prevented him allowing personal resentment to cloud his pursuit of truth. After all, what did it matter that they hadn't asked him to lunch?

He left the central portion of his plan empty, folded the paper and replaced it in his pocket.

"No matter, they are all monsters, one way and another." He stood up, his face clouded with the anguish of triumph; there was always anguish in Mr. Raven's triumphs, for his was a nature that looked for goodness but found only the spots that rotted it away.

He rapped his boot. "Beside them, even you are a thing of beauty." Then he stumped out of the room and down the stairs in search of necessary fresh air.

As he left the Old Ship, the distant bell of St. Nicholas's chimed six o'clock and, shortly after, a baby began to howl; then another and another, till a thin, despairing anthem filled the fishy air. It came from the poorhouse: a tall, black building that lay behind the Old Ship Inn. The foundlings—of which at present there were five—were hungry. The inquiry agent nodded. "Howl," he whispered bitterly. "Howl your little agonies and curses—till you are grown enough to take your revenge on this vile world. And then in your turn suffer again."

Tap-thump...tap-thump...The inquiry agent passed under the high windows of the poorhouse. But now his ears were shut to the sad howling. He was brooding on another actor in the drama of which the disappearance of Adelaide Harris was but the first scene. There was still the man with the secret; the man who had ignored him so completely that even Mr. Raven's clubfoot had not been honored with a glance.

"Brett," muttered the inquiry agent. "What manner of a monster are you?"

Tap-thump...tap-thump...

Chapter Nine

A BOY APPEARED at the corner of the building; a burly boy, though looking quaintly small in a cut-down sea captain's coat that was still too large; a red-faced boy with fierce little eyes that Mr. Raven recognized as violent and savage.

Tap-thump...tap-thump...The boy stiffened and glared at the advancing inquiry agent. Terror, confusion and guilt were written all over him. Mr. Raven smiled; he was used to that. The boy licked his lips, glanced towards the poorhouse and whistled. Almost at once another boy appeared. This newcomer was somewhat stunted and malignant-looking. Mr. Raven knew him; he was the son of Dr. Harris.

"Good evening, my young friend," said Mr. Raven affably.

"Meet Bostock!" said Harris rapidly, and gave a little hysterical laugh. "My friend Bostock. Bosty, this is Mr. Selwyn Raven what I told you of." He thrust Bostock between himself and the man with the horrible boot.

So, thought the inquiry agent with weary contempt, you have been attempting to rob the poorhouse. Perhaps you've already done so? But no matter. Boys will be thieves...and then they'll be men and fouler still. But outwardly he maintained his look of affability. He was not a man to waste his time on little crimes. He preferred them to bloat and fatten before he pricked them to let the poison out. None the less he saw the boys were petrified with fear and guilt and would, most likely, oblige him with their grimy little souls if he kept their secret.

"Up to mischief?" he chuckled. "Well, well! Boys will be —he!—he!—boys! But I'll not say a word, my young friends! I too was a lad, once!" He thumped his boot with his stick. "Weren't we, eh?"

"That's very decent of you, sir," said Harris; and, to Bostock's undying admiration, gave a careless smile. Bostock knew it was a careless smile because it was quite different from Harris's ordinary smile. Harris was a real marvel; he, Bostock, was quite dried up with terror, having been warned of the clubfooted devil.

"Brett," said Mr. Raven abruptly, after talking idly about this and that, as was his habit to put the boys at their ease. "Do you know a man called Brett?"

Harris looked at him in utter astonishment. What on earth was Mr. Brett to do with anything? The inquiry agent, observing this astonishment, which was plainly genuine, felt a sudden pang at his heart. Whatever trifling crime the boy might be carrying on his soul, there was no doubt he was innocent of the terrible darkness that lay beneath the affair of Adelaide Harris. It moved the inquiry agent strangely to have stumbled on this little patch of innocence in the wide, crawling desert of sin.

"Mr. Brett's a master at our school—Dr. Bunnion's," said Harris; and another huge piece of the puzzle fell into place in Mr. Raven's mind. Another connection. The school. The innocent son of Dr. Harris...and Mr. Brett, et cetera, et cetera! Snap, snap, snap went the links of the chain; in his remarkable inner eye the inquiry agent saw all the actors in the drama like spectral dancers weaving across some ominous shoulder of the Downs, fettered to one another by lust, hatred, vengeance and greed, et cetera. But who was it who led the dance and dragged it on to his chosen perdition? Mr. Raven could hardly wait to get back to his room and embark on a larger piece of paper; but there was still more he needed to know. He had to be sure...

"Tell me about this Mr. Brett," said the inquiry agent gently. "What manner of—er—gentleman is he?"

At once Bostock and Harris obliged with all they knew and suspected of Mr. Brett. They talked very freely and eagerly, which amused Mr. Raven as he guessed it was to distract him from their private concerns. Though he was a sinister and even frightening man, he was also a man of honor. It was perhaps this that made him truly terrible; he could laugh with one part of his mind while the other continued to gather all those materials with which he built the vaults of human hell.

So he smiled and nodded while Bostock and Harris told him of Mr. Brett's pallors and tremblings at every knock on the door, his fearful looks when asked even about historical murders, his strange reluctance to leave the school for so much as an afternoon, and his most certain guilt of some unspeakable crime, most likely in the north.

When they were done, Mr. Raven thanked them gravely, flattered them by calling them his assistants, then tapped and thumped his grim way towards that tangled nest of cobbled alleys called by some The Twittens and, by others, The Lanes, where there was a shop that sold paper of the larger size.

◆

Bostock and Harris, much shaken by the encounter, walked along beside the whispering sea.

"I think you got the better of him, Harris," said Bostock shrewdly.

Harris nodded. "But he's a clever man, Bosty. Don't under-estimate him. That question about Mr. Brett was a real banger."

"Why's that, Harris?"

"Sparta, Bosty. If he'd got on to that talk of Mr. Brett's about Spartan infants being exposed, he'd have guessed and it would have been all up with us."

Bostock halted and whistled at the narrowness of their escape. Harris patted him on the shoulder. "One needs a long spoon to sup with gents like Mr. Raven."

They walked on again, picking their way round the drying fishing nets above which flies wove glinting puzzles in the stinking air. The failure of their recent attempt to rescue Adelaide from the poorhouse weighed heavily on the friends. They had been so very near to success. Harris had actually got into the room where the foundlings were kept. No one else had been there at that moment. The poorhouse keeper must have gone to the privy or something. It had been a remarkable piece of luck such as happened once in a lifetime. Harris had been laughing at the ease of it all.

"And there she lay, Bosty: my sister. Right at the end of the row. I think she knew me, Bosty. She gave a sort of smile. Just another minute and I'd have had her. Then you whistled..."

Bostock scowled and, picking up a stone, hurled it into the sea. "He was coming, Harris. I had to warn you."

Harris nodded. The friends halted and gazed mournfully back towards the poorhouse. They dared not return; yet it seemed unbearable not to.

"There's only one thing to do," said Harris at length.

"Own up?" said Bostock faintly. "Tell the truth?"

Harris looked at his friend with a universe of pity in his face. Bostock's simplicity touched him and made him feel curiously protective. He wondered how long Bostock would have survived in this stern world without his Harris.

"The truth?" he said gently. "What is truth, Bosty? There ain't no such thing, old friend. There's no truth in nature, Bosty; and that's where it counts. Everything has to hide to survive. Truth in the wild means sudden death; and truth at home ain't much better. And anyway," he added, "it's too late to own up now, old friend."

"What then, Harris?" whispered Bostock, another bastion of his innocent young soul cracked and tottering from this last intellectual blow of his friend's.

"A letter, Bosty. An anonymous letter to my pa. It's the only way. A letter informing him where Adelaide really is. Then he can go and fetch her and no one will be any the wiser."

Bostock sighed. "You're a genius, Harris."

Then the friends shook hands and dispersed to their homes.

There was a quiet on the Harris household; there was an aimlessness, also, as if certain invisible threads that had held the family in order and regulation had been severed and so exposed the bleak loneliness of souls. Private chasms of fear had opened in every heart ... and grinning calamity squatted in the hearth.

The Harris sisters were in the kitchen with the servants, picking at a vague dinner of cold mutton and cheese. Dr. Harris was out, and Mrs. Harris, the distraught mother, was crouching in the nursery where the strange baby still lay like a nightmare in Adelaide's cot.

Morgan, the nurse, was certain the infant was a changeling, an uncanny creature left by those malignant sprites who were the fallen angels of some ancient faith. There was no other explanation. She reminded Mrs. Harris that, against all advice, Adelaide had been christened in the goblin font of St. Nicholas's with its ugly pagan carvings grinning in the stone. Angrily Mrs. Harris had told her to hold her tongue, but Morgan, who was Celtic and wise in country ways, could not be silenced. She went on and on until Mrs. Harris had bowed her aching head and allowed Morgan to consult her elder sister who was even wiser.

So Morgan had gone off to call on the Hemps where her sister had once been nurse and was now the cook. Both the sisters had come from Aberystwyth as quite young girls in search of fortunes and husbands; but, having found neither, had settled in the Hemp and Harris households to which they'd brought a touch of Celtic magic.

The sisters talked long and hard over a glass of cordial and Morgan then returned, with a parcel of strong herbs, through the devious Lanes at about half past six. For a few uneasy moments she'd fancied she heard the sound of unequal footsteps—a tap-thump...tap-thump—as if she was being followed, but soon she outdistanced them and reached the Harris home with her wild garlic, coltsfoot and sheep's sorrel safely under her arm.

The changeling was asleep, but its face clearly lacked the smooth innocence of a mortal babe. There were shadows and creases across it that hinted of weird dreams and dark passions a-brewing; and its little mouth was shut in a line of cruel pink.

"I got 'em, ma'am," breathed Morgan; and Mrs. Harris raised her tear-stained face uncomprehendingly. So Morgan, seeing the poor lady was beyond clear thinking, laid a strong hand on her shoulder and set about making a fragile ring of herbs round the cot. This done, she opened wide the window and bade Mrs. Harris repeat after her the Celtic rune her sister had told her.

At first Mrs. Harris, who was a God-fearing woman, was quite repelled and would have nothing to do with it; but at length she was worn down and haltingly pronounced the eerie spell. Though she did not understand it, it was a call into the darkness of the lost faith—a command to the invisible goblins and demons whose ghostly bishops, on midsummer nights, crossed the moonlit lawns of those churches and abbeys that had usurped the ancient shrines. The uncanny words demanded the presence of the bringers of the changeling.

As they died away, a breeze sprang up and billowed out the curtains; then the door blew open with a sharp sound. And Harris came in. There was a look of intolerable curiosity on his face.

"For God's sake, go away!" cried his unhappy mother. "Haven't I enough to bear?"

Harris stared in bewilderment at the circled herbs and silently withdrew.

"He's gone and spoiled it, ma'am," said Morgan bitterly. "Just like all else he sets his hand to."

For the remainder of the evening and several times during the night, Harris had a strong smell of herbs in his nostrils and an overwhelming desire to go again into the nursery; but the memory of the bitter words from Morgan and his mother rankled in his heart, and, with difficulty, he conquered the impulse. Instead, he lay awake and composed the anonymous letter he had determined to send to his father, the letter that would bring the whole terrific affair to a quiet and sensible conclusion.

Simple, brief and to the point. Bostock would write it. No

one knew Bostock's writing; indeed, there were very few who knew Bostock could actually write. Bostock would write it during Monday's school, and it would be delivered on the same day; poked under the door at half after five. Harris sighed and smiled as he drifted on the tide of sleep. Why hadn't he thought of it before? Tomorrow...the poorhouse... Adelaide...home at last...

Chapter Ten

SORLEY, the fat boarder, driven half out of his mind by guilt on account of Mr. Brett following him everywhere, had at last come to terms with his conscience and taken a stolen veal pie out of concealment, scratched "Sorley is sorry, sir" on the crust, and placed it in Mr. Brett's bedroom. This done, he was able to pass into an untroubled sleep from which he awoke wretchedly hungry but spiritually refreshed.

Mr. Brett, on the other hand, awoke to considerable bewilderment and discomfort. He had not expected the pie—which Sorley had laid by the end of his bed—and had trodden in it. Thus all traces of its origin were obliterated and Mr. Brett was left, standing on one foot, much puzzled by the broken mystery.

At last he decided it must have come from Tizzy's mother, Mrs. Alexander. There was good reason for his supposing this as, for some time now, he had been giving Tizzy lessons in Classical History when school was over. Whether his passionate love for Mrs. Alexander's daughter had begun with the lessons or just before them, was no longer possible to say; but there was no doubt the lessons aggravated it. As he sat in the empty classroom, waiting for her gentle knock, his heart thundered so that he almost jumped out of his skin when at last it came.

It had been Mrs. Alexander herself who had suggested the lessons—her German heart lifting to a scholar—and in return for improving her daughter—as if I could improve *her*, thought Mr. Brett with a sigh—she mended his linen and had promised to make him a shirt. "For your veddink, Herr Prett," she'd added with a sentimental smile. "Veneffer it shoot pe."

Mrs. Alexander's English had once been much better, but the longer she lived with her husband, the fiery Major, the further she retreated into the tongue of her childhood—as if striving to recapture the illusions she'd had when she'd never understood a word the Major said.

Mr. Brett sat on his bed, wiped his foot and smiled. He liked Mrs. Alexander and would have gone to thank her directly; but the damage done to the pie, he thought, would make him look awkward and ungrateful, so he waited till breakfast and contented himself with smiling meaningfully at her across the table whenever the occasion offered. At first Mrs. Alexander was frankly puzzled; but then she smiled back as if with a suddenly kindled optimism.

"You giff Tizzy her lesson today?" she murmured as they left the table. Mr. Brett nodded warmly. "Goot! Better than anythink, it takes her mind off this shtoopid business vit that Relph Bunnion."

"Very decent of you to take trouble with my gel," muttered the Major, brushing between his wife and Mr. Brett. "Improving a gel's mind is as good as giving her a rich dowry, I always say. Whoever gets her ought to be grateful to you, Brett. Take it as a personal favor. We don't say much, eh? But friendship between men…hoops of steel and all that."

The Major hurried away leaving Mr. Brett to gaze after him with a feeling of hopeless anger. Major Alexander always succeeded in infuriating him into silence. Friendship between men was not something that was uppermost in his thoughts; nor deeper down, neither. He frowned and went towards his classroom.

Major Alexander did not follow suit. Instead, by devious and almost underground ways, he went to Dr. Bunnion's study where he appeared with the somewhat quizzical air of a man gauging how much powder would be needed to bring down everything in sight. Dr. Bunnion looked at him uneasily. The Major compressed his lips and closed the door.

"My dear sir," he murmured, appearing to examine the walls, "a few minutes of your time is all I ask."

Dr. Bunnion nodded helplessly and the Major, having satisfied himself about the walls, fixed his eyes on the headmaster's desk. "Strictly speaking, sir, it's my—um—second's place to be here; but for good reasons—very good reasons, I might say—I've come myself. I'm not a bloodthirsty man. Your military men rarely are. It's your damned civilians who are always so keen on blood. What I want to say, sir, is that this unhappy affair is not of my choosing."

"The challenge was yours, Major Alexander," said Dr. Bunnion bitterly.

"No choice," said the Major. "My child's honor and all that; and a gel's honor, I need hardly tell you, is a delicate flower. Had to act as a father, you know. But now I've come to see you, man to man, to discuss what might be done about avoiding bloodshed. A parley, you might say, sir."

He laid his hands on Dr. Bunnion's desk and leaned forward, staring very confidentially at the headmaster's cravat. "To be open and aboveboard, sir, I'm fond of your boy. He's a fine fellow and I'd have been content to have him as a son-in-law.

In a way, you might say that I love the lad as a son—and that's why I don't aim to stand in his way." Here the Major gave a little skip sideways, as if to illustrate his point. "I understand your ambitions for the lad. Good God! What father wouldn't? But there's me family's honor which is, and always will be, dearer to me than blessed life itself."

The Major gnawed his lip and, having finished with Dr. Bunnion's cravat, looked searchingly at his fingers. He leaned forward still further till the headmaster could make out the powder in the Major's military wig, and also a few cake crumbs. "But there is a compromise, sir," breathed the Major, and went on to mention that, in addition to his daughter, he had a son.

Dr. Bunnion laid his fingers together and pursed his lips. He knew of the Major's son—and of the Major's difficulties in finding a situation for him.

"I understand he's in a monastery," murmured the headmaster cautiously.

"It didn't suit," said the Major. "He—ha-ha—he couldn't acquire the habit! Truth of the matter is, he wants to teach. I think he's got a talent for it."

"But—" began Dr. Bunnion hopelessly.

"Brett," breathed the honorable Major. "No good, you know. Sly; secretive. I can't bear underhand men. If Brett goes, good thing for the school; then my boy Adam comes. Even better. What d'you say, sir?"

The Major skipped back and stared at the headmaster's waistcoat as if to divine what was going on within. In addition to being honorable, the Major was a reasonable man. Though he would have preferred to marry off Tizzy to Ralph, he was quite prepared to settle for the chance of planting his son Adam in the Bunnion stronghold and so increasing his grip on it. If the headmaster agreed, at one stroke the Major would have avoided the duel, ridded himself of the contempt-ible Brett, who, he always felt, looked down on him, and acted in the best interests of his family.

Dr. Bunnion was silent. As a father, the Major's offer ap-pealed to him; but as a man he shrank from it. He did not at all like the idea of being outnumbered by the Alexanders in his own establishment, and he felt awkward about dismissing Mr. Brett who was, after all, acting as his son's second.

"Thought it best to have a word with you," said the Major, smiling cunningly at the headmaster's left ear and deciding to let his offer simmer for a day or so. "Man to man. Though we don't say much, deep down I fancy we understand each other. Real friendship... silent... strong... hoops of steel and all that. Settle it out of court, eh?"

Whereupon the Major withdrew and made his way to-wards his own classroom. He went by way of the kitchen as he thought it best, in everyone's interests, that he should not be seen coming from Dr. Bunnion's study. It was thus that he happened to see a maidservant gossiping at the side door with a stranger.

Inquisitively the Major halted. He peered over the maid's shoulder. The stranger had a pleasant, innocent-looking face; but he was burdened with a clubfoot.

"Yes," said the maid. "We do 'ave a Mr. Brett. Quiet gent, but a bit crafty if you ask me."

"Indeed, I do ask you," said the stranger gently. "What makes you think he is crafty?"

"He ain't as honest as he pretends," said the maid who had, that very morning, come upon the ruined veal pie in Mr. Brett's bedroom and recognized it as having been stolen from the larder.

At this point, Major Alexander, feeling that he could be more helpful about Mr. Brett, interposed with a curt "good morning," and proceeded to set the stranger to rights about Mr. Brett.

It really was a stroke of extraordinary good fortune. The Major guessed at once that the stranger was an inquiry agent out for Mr. Brett's blood. He'd had experience of such men before. Whatever Mr. Brett was suspected of, the Major had no idea, but he'd have laid odds on its being something pretty unpleasant. Thus he was able to look on the blackening of Mr. Brett's character as being in the way of a public duty. The Major was really a very scrupulous man. He prided himself on never having performed a mean or underhand act in his whole life without honor, duty or family love being mixed up in it somewhere. In the present instance he believed he could trace the presence of all three.

Mr. Raven listened gravely. What he'd heard fulfilled his hopes, but did not surprise him. But even yet he was cautious. There was nothing impetuous about the inquiry agent. He needed to make doubly and trebly sure before he could be committed to a course of action. He could not afford to be wrong. He took out a grubby pewter snuffbox and snapped it open, with the idea of distracting the Major into an unguarded admission.

"Hemp," he said quietly. "Does the name Hemp mean anything to you?"

As Mr. Raven had intended, the Major was momentarily nonplussed; then, becoming aware of the snuffbox which gave off a very sour smell, he was reminded of a campaign among the docks at Deptford, and a queer pipe of tobacco…

"D'you mean Indian hemp?"

"I would have thought more gypsy," said Mr. Raven carefully, as he thought of the baby in Adelaide Harris's cot.

"Could be," said the Major, thinking of the swarthy seaman who'd offered him the interesting smoke. "Or even Lascar. But gypsy or Lascar, they're all queer customers not to be trusted. I don't know much about them myself, of course."

"Oh, but I do," said Mr. Raven, thinking of the name embroidered on Ralph Bunnion's waistcoat: Maggie Hemp.

"But I'll tell you one thing," said the Major, anxious to return to the subject that interested him. "I'd trust a gypsy before Brett any day."

With that, he left the clubfooted stranger and continued to his classroom, resolving as he walked that he'd write directly to his son, bidding him come to Dr. Bunnion's where there would shortly be a vacancy.

"Brett," muttered Mr. Raven as he clumped away from the school. "As we thought…the Prime Mover…Brett." Here the inquiry agent brushed so near to the truth of the Adelaide affair that the very angels in heaven spread their wings and prepared to flee.

"And Hemp with the gypsy blood…But Brett is the one. What is his real name? De Brett? Viscount Brett?" Mr. Raven preferred to look in high places for his corruption. The nobler the structure, the louder the uproar when he brought it tumbling down.

Tap-thump…tap-thump…He passed along the morning streets where women avoided him and fishermen spat. There was a briskish breeze coming off the sea and the distant waves wore scabs of white. The inquiry agent halted and stared across the water.

A strange exultation filled him as he sensed how close he was to understanding all parts of the mystery. So intricate was it that the smallest movement of each thread set up shiverings across the whole unsavory web. Only the previous evening he had observed Morgan, the Harris nurse, visiting the Hemps and hurrying guiltily away. Thus the connection between the two households had been confirmed and noted down. But who had sent her and on what desperate errand?

The inquiry agent scowled and shook his head. He suspected the affair was approaching some sinister climax. Perhaps his own presence was the cause? He walked on, much troubled by certain tiny aspects of the affair that still eluded him.

He was by the poorhouse and the morning wailing of the five foundlings mingled with the harsh laughter of the swooping seabirds. He leaned in the narrow shadow of the poorhouse wall, seeming to listen intently to the wordless misery the seagulls jeered at. Then, as if making a certain decision, he rapped his boot and clumped off out of the sunshine into the dark parlor of the Old Ship.

He settled himself in a corner, called for brandy and water, and then, making sure he was the only customer, took out a piece of paper from his pocket that unfolded almost to the size of the table top. "Brett," he whispered, studying the extraordinary design that reached now to the paper's edge, "the next move is yours, my friend." He turned the paper round. "What will it be, eh? No matter…no matter…we will be watching. And then, my friend, we will strike with a thunderbolt, et cetera."

While the inquiry agent was so engaged, his great adversary—Mr. Brett—was struggling with Ancient History in his classroom at the Academy. Fiercely he tried to pull over his head the paper layers of time and escape from everything. But wherever he turned in the Ancient World he seemed to be confronted by images of his own plight—encircling enemies and hopeless love.

In the back parlor, Major Alexander, though he now had every hope that the duel would not take place, was none the less uneasy that something might go wrong and he found himself setting his pupils terrific problems concerning the speed of bullets and the cost of coffins in English shillings and German marks.

Not even Dr. Bunnion himself was able to escape the shadowy fears that beset the school. As it was close to the end of term, the headmaster had planned to describe the building of Solomon's temple, right down to the last half cubit of an ornamental angel's wing, so that any boy, with skill and industry, might construct it for himself during the holiday. Instead the troubled father found himself brooding aloud on the sacrifice of Isaac. In his mind's eye he saw himself as Abraham, poised above the sacrifical stone on which lay the hapless Ralph. "And the angel of the Lord called unto him out of heaven...lay not thy hand upon the lad." And the angel spoke in the secret, clipped voice of Major Alexander. "And Abraham lifted up his eyes, and looked, and behold, behind him a ram caught in a thicket by its horns..." And the ram had the gentle, long-suffering face of Mr. Brett. "And Abraham went and took the ram and offered it up...instead of Ralph."

The class looked up in surprise; and Dr. Bunnion flushed and corrected himself. But the notion of sacrificing Mr. Brett to Major Alexander's honor gathered strength in his mind and tormented him throughout the day.

Just before luncheon, being unable to bear the weight of the problem any longer, he confided in Mrs. Bunnion who looked at him in amazement. To her there was no problem at all. He must close with the Major's offer and get rid of Mr. Brett directly. What right had Dr. Bunnion even to think of keeping Mr. Brett and so endangering Ralph's life? She had never heard of anything like it in all her born days! He was to stop behaving like a weakling and send Mr. Brett packing at once! Really! Who was he afraid of?

Mutely Dr. Bunnion gazed at his dignified wife who, though not as tall as he, morally overtopped him by a good six inches. So after the meal he made several attempts to corner Mr. Brett and at last succeeded in catching him at the foot of the stairs.

"Well?" began Dr. Bunnion harshly, seeking an opportunity of losing his temper and so dismissing Mr. Brett in hot rather than cold blood. "I suppose you haven't bothered to see Major Alexander's second?"

Mr. Brett nodded uneasily. He had. Dr. Bunnion looked taken aback. "What then? What did he say?"

"Saturday," said Mr. Brett. "In the morning."

"But that's the end of term! Good God! Couldn't he have waited till the holiday?" The headmaster stared at Mr. Brett in horror. "What an idea! Don't you know the parents will be here? What d'you imagine they'll think when they find my son bleeding to death—perhaps already dead—and my Arithmetic master in jail for it? What kind of a school d'you suppose they'll think I conduct? Saturday! You must be mad, Brett—"

"But it wasn't up to me, sir—"

"Couldn't you have explained to Alexander's second? It was your duty!"

Feebly Mr. Brett shook his head.

"Saturday!" repeated Dr. Bunnion savagely. "I'll tell you one thing, Brett"—at last he felt his blood to be heated enough to obey Mrs. Bunnion—"before Saturday comes you'd—"

"—Sorley!" cried Mr. Brett, seeing the fat boarder pass by. "Come here, boy!" He reached out and clutched him by the shoulder, then turned back to Dr. Bunnion in desperate triumph. "I—I interrupted you, sir."

"You'd better—er—see about Dr. Harris," muttered the headmaster, thwarted by the presence of the baronet's son. Then he shambled away, his blood cooling in defeat.

Mr. Brett, still holding on to Sorley, gazed after him. How much longer could he hope to survive in this dangerous world? Till Saturday, perhaps? "Come, boy," he whispered. "Soon it will be Saturday... and the end."

He walked slowly to his classroom together with the fat boarder who kept staring up at him piteously. But Mr. Brett had no eyes for Sorley. He was thinking of Tizzy Alexander and how soon he was fated to leave her. The look on Dr. Bunnion's face had been unmistakable. His time was running out. His days in the school were numbered; and the headmaster had decided on what the number was to be. His last chance had come. He would have to tell Tizzy he loved her—or resign himself to never seeing her again.

His eyes filled with tears at the very thought of living without her. He would risk all and tell her that very afternoon. Good God! He was a grown man—not a tongue-tied lovesick child! And if he kept silent he'd lose her for certain. James Brett, you fool—take her firmly in your arms, look into her eyes and say, after me, "I love you, Tizzy Alexander; with all my heart and soul, I love you, my dear..."

These thoughts so filled his imagination that the afternoon lesson went by as in a dream. His twelve pupils threw ink pellets, tormented Sorley and buzzed and hovered from place to place; but they troubled him no more than the antics of the classroom flies.

It was during this time that Bostock, under Harris's anxious guidance, wrote the letter that was to inform Dr. Harris, anonymously, of the whereabouts of his lost daughter, Adelaide. He'd had several attempts at it that, for one reason and another, had been abandoned, but eventually it was completed almost to Harris's satisfaction. Afterwards, Mr. Brett remembered vaguely having seen Bostock writing something with Harris, his evil genius, bending over him. But he'd had too much on his mind to be more than remotely curious; and in a little while the memory faded altogether.

"Just think of it, Bosty," said Harris cheerfully as the friends walked home. "Tonight we'll have Adelaide back again."

Chapter Eleven

THE INQUIRY agent, despite his immensely active mind, was a man of great patience. Though this quality had at first been imposed on him by his deformity—which prevented rapid movement—he had cultivated it until it had become perhaps his most formidable attribute. He could wait a life-time, if necessary, to trap and destroy his prey. But when at last he moved, the unhurried tap-thump of his stick and boot was as relentless and terrible as the approach of the angel of death.

He sat in the back parlor of the Old Ship awaiting word of the move he knew must come. The only other occupant of the parlor was Ralph Bunnion's friend, Frederick. From time to time Frederick glanced at him with nervous amiability; Mr. Raven fingered his glass and smiled deprecatingly at his boot.

"Poor bastard!" muttered Frederick impulsively. At bottom he was a generous and even kindly young man. Mr. Raven looked up and Frederick reddened and hid his face in his tankard.

"Indeed, you're right!" said Mr. Raven eagerly moving

closer. "I *am* very narrow in my means—and certainly might be considered poor next to you and your friends. And, as for the other, there's no doubt about it. I was a foundling, you know. But it's all God's will, young man. He knows best."

"I—I—" began Frederick, then breathed a sigh of relief when he saw Ralph Bunnion enter the parlor. But the damage had been done. Having been neatly trapped into extending sympathy to the man with the clubfoot, he could not get rid of him when Ralph came to sit down. Not that the horrible fellow seemed to push himself forward; it was just that he wouldn't move away. He sat, too close for comfort, meekly silent and staring at his boot in the most pathetic manner imaginable.

"Saturday," muttered Ralph at length, seeing further privacy was impossible. "It's to be Saturday. Brett told my pa yesterday; so you'd better get the you-know-whats oiled and ready."

"I've got 'em here, old dear," breathed Frederick, producing the case of pistols and endeavoring to conceal them from the club-footed man's innocent eyes.

"Not now. Saturday, I said."

"Where?"

The stranger bent forward with involuntary interest. Frederick stared at him with hostility. An unwise expression; Mr. Raven made a mental note to enmesh him in the design. The inquiry agent was a dangerous man to cross.

"Brett will tell you," said Ralph.

"Brett—Brett!" exclaimed Frederick peevishly. He was hurt and angry that Mr. Brett seemed to be supplanting him in an affair where he, of all people, should be standing closest to Ralph. After all, he was Ralph's friend, and he was providing the pistols. "It's always Brett these days, ain't it! Anybody would think he'd arranged the whole thing!"

"They would indeed," breathed Mr. Raven, finishing his drink and heaving himself upright. "They would indeed, my friend." He nodded politely to the two young men and clumped out of the parlor to make certain additions to the architecture of his plan.

The Harris household had spent a grim day. Mrs. Harris could not be persuaded to leave the nursery and Dr. Harris had given instructions that she was not to be left alone there for more than a few minutes. Her grief had shown no signs of diminishing and the doctor had very real fears that she would do the mysterious gypsy baby an injury.

Even when the wet nurse came to perform her duty, it was only under the haggard eyes of the forlorn mother and, as she confided in Morgan the nurse, "It's a wonder me milk don't curdle into cheese."

The wet nurse came in the afternoons at about a quarter after five. Dr. Harris himself let her in and took her upstairs; he was a humane man and did not want the unknown baby to suffer. Thus when there came a knock on the door at the expected time, the doctor was rather put out to find that it was Mr. Brett from the school, wanting a word with him.

"I'd be obliged if you'd be brief, Mr. Brett," he said, remaining in the hall. "As you must know, we have great family troubles..."

Mr. Brett nodded. He didn't know, but on the other hand he had enough troubles of his own without being burdened with Dr. Harris's.

"Dr. Bunnion would be grateful, sir," he said, coming directly to the point, "if you would attend a duel on Saturday morning."

Dr. Harris gaped at him; and Mr. Brett explained matters as

briefly and discreetly as he could. The doctor sighed and shrugged his shoulders. At any other time he would have been amazed and fascinated; but the loss of Adelaide so dominated his mind that all else seemed trifling. "You understand that I am a physician, Mr. Brett; not a surgeon—"

"But Dr. Bunnion was particularly anxious, sir—"

At this point Dr. Harris heard the unmistakable shuffle and flop of the wet nurse's step. "Very well—very well," he muttered agitatedly. "Let me know the time and place. Now, if you please, good day to you, sir." He opened the door to let Mr. Brett out and the wet nurse in. "Duels—duels," he grunted. "Has all the world gone mad?"

Mr. Brett, who had expected all manner of difficulties to be put in his way and had been fully prepared for failure and the consequent anger of Dr. Bunnion, could not help smiling with happy triumph at the ease of his success. It gave him unexpected confidence in himself and made him think that perhaps he possessed a more powerful personality than he'd supposed. He broke into a brisk trot as he made his way back to the school and his beloved Tizzy.

The world was suddenly a beautiful place and he seemed as light as the bright warm air. Seagulls flew like angels above him and he looked upward as if he was on the point of soaring among them. He did not see the man with the clubfoot who happened to be standing at the corner of the street.

"It is beginning," muttered the inquiry agent, grimly noting Mr. Brett's rapid pace and triumphant smile. "The end is beginning. When the Devil runs, can Hell be far away?"

There was a coolness between Bostock and Harris. The delivering of the anonymous letter was partly to blame; the rest was on account of a bouquet of wildflowers Bostock wanted to give to Mary Harris, whom he particularly admired, as it was her birthday.

"Give 'em to her tomorrow," Harris had said impatiently. "Another day won't signify." He did not want Bostock, who was ink-stained from writing the anonymous letter, appearing at his house on the same day as the letter itself.

"They'll have faded," said Bostock obstinately.

"Who cares?" said Harris with more than a touch of irritation; then, seeing that Bostock looked offended, he instantly regretted his tone. He sensed that his friend was affected by that soft passion that he, Harris, knew to be as disrupting as it was unscientific. He smiled at his scowling friend who was grasping the bouquet like a weapon.

"I know how you feel, Bosty," he murmured kindly. "You fancy you're in love with Mary."

Bostock reddened; Harris was uncanny.

"But I'm afraid there's no such thing as what you call love, old friend."

Bostock braced himself, and Harris continued. "It's only an instinct, old friend; nothing more than that. It's like—like blowing your nose; you have to do it, and you feel better when you've done it."

Bostock stared mournfully at the bouquet he had so laboriously gathered. If Harris was right—and he always was—he should have got Mary a pocket handkerchief.

"We all have these instincts, Bosty," went on Harris. "Generally we get them when we're thirteen or thereabouts. I'll be getting them myself, any day now. You see a female and right away you want to have carnal knowledge of her."

"Carnal knowledge?"

"Poke her," explained Harris. "It's the law of nature, Bosty."

Bostock thought of the wild, slender Miss Harris—and blushed to the roots of his soul. He looked down at the little forest all jeweled with tiny blossoms that he was clutching. "Is that really all it is, Harris?" he asked sadly.

"That's all, Bosty," said Harris compassionately; and, to his relief, Bostock let the flowers fall. Who'd have thought Mary would so nearly have come between them?

"Five minutes after six, Bosty," went on Harris after a pause to allow his friend to bring his mind to the matter in hand. "That's the time to do it. Poke—er—push the letter under the door and then go like the wind."

Bostock nodded and Harris held out his hand. Bostock hesitated.

"Old friend," said Harris. "It all depends on you." Bostock sighed and the friends shook hands.

Harris made a good deal of noise as he entered his house so that the time of his arrival should be generally known and not confused with the arrival of the letter. He went up to the nursery and engaged the wet nurse in conversation while she, poor soul, all but suffocated the black-haired baby under her shawl as she modestly tried to hide her breast from Harris's inquisitive gaze.

At five minutes after six Harris's heart began to beat violently. The time had come. He strained his ears, but he heard nothing. Bostock must have been as silent as the air.

"Well, that's all for now, you gutsy little darlin'," said the wet nurse, returning the baby to its cot and her breast to her gown. She nodded to Morgan and went downstairs. Harris followed her. He stared towards the front door. There was no letter. Dismay seized Harris. Had Bostock deserted him? After all he'd said, had love really deprived him of his friend?

The wet nurse shuffled down the last stairs—when something white flew from under the door with tremendous force and vanished under the wet nurse's skirts. It had been the letter. Bostock, ever faithful to his friend, had kept his word;

but resentment at the shattering of yet another illusion had caused him to be over-strong.

Dr. Harris, hearing the wet nurse in the hall, came out of his study to pay her. Harris the younger glared at the ragged hem of her gown. She took the money, lifted her dress to stow it away in her petticoat—and saw the letter.

She picked it up and gave it to the doctor. "It's yours, sir," she said and, jingling slightly, she shuffled out of the house.

Dr. Harris opened the letter and read it. Harris watched his father's face in an agony of expectation which, however, he concealed under a mild interest.

"W—what is it, Pa? Anything...important?"

The doctor frowned. "The impudence of it! Sending that wretched woman with their begging letters! Don't I do enough for charity as it is?" Wearily he showed his son the paper on which Bostock, after so many attempts, had at last revealed the whereabouts of Adelaide. "Dear Dr. Harris," he had written. "Think of the poorhouse."

The doctor fumbled in his pockets. "Here, son," he said. "Take this down to the poorhouse with my compliments."

He gave the dazed Harris a handful of silver, crumpled up the letter and trudged upstairs to the nursery. Harris stared after him in an agony of rage and disbelief. There were tears in his eyes. Everything seemed against him; even his own father...

He left the house and slammed the door behind him as if he would shake his home to the ground. Though Bostock was ever a great comfort to him, he was glad that his friend was not at his side. Harris doubted whether he could have re-strained himself from blaming Bostock for the horrible fail-ure of the scheme. Bostock had pushed the letter so unnecessarily hard that if the back door had been open it would most likely have gone clean through the house. There was no doubt that everything now rested on Harris's shoulders; and he felt they were cracking.

Bitterly he counted up the money his distraught father had given him: nineteen shillings. In the old days, such a sum would have filled him with wonderment and joy. But now it weighed him down. He walked on towards the poorhouse while the sun, sinking in an irony of crimson, orange and gold, served only to deepen the private night of his despair.

He would have to give the money to the poorhouse. His father might meet Mr. Bonney, the keeper, at any time and mention it. But on the other hand, so large a sum as nineteen shillings would be sure to startle Mr. Bonney into mentioning it of his own accord. Then the affair of the letter would be bound to come out; and then everything else.

Harris moaned. Then he frowned; then he half-smiled. Why hand over all the nineteen shillings? What was wrong with five? He paused and completed his smile. He rubbed his hands together. Mr. Bonney would accept five shillings gratefully and not think twice about it, Harris nodded shrewdly. All problems, however great, yielded to a little thought. Five from nineteen left fourteen shillings. A handsome sum. Harris brooded. Quite by chance he seemed to have hit on a remarkable way of making money. When the affair of Adelaide was cleared up, he and Bostock might work on a grander scale . . .

"Good evening, my young friend."

Harris almost jumped out of his skin. The hateful Mr. Raven, who had been taking the evening air outside the Old Ship, suddenly accosted him.

"I didn't mean to startle you," said the inquiry agent apologetically. "You must have been quite lost in thoughts. Were I a rich man, ha-ha! I'd offer you a penny for them."

Harris smiled feebly.

"Come, let me guess. A young lady perhaps?" Mr. Raven gazed slyly down at his boot. "Are you on your way to a tryst?"

Harris laughed lightly. "Just to the poorhouse, sir. My pa asked me to give them some charity money." Harris was honest enough to be truthful when he didn't see that it could do any harm. "A very charitable man, my pa."

"Very," agreed Mr. Raven, and waved the boy on his way. He watched him disappear into the poorhouse, then shook his head and returned to the frontage of the Old Ship where he set about wondering if there was a space left for the poorhouse keeper in the frightful web of which Mr. Brett was the center and Adelaide Harris no more than a single, unimportant thread.

After a few minutes the brilliance of the setting sun reflecting on the sea distracted him and irritated his sensitive eyes; so he went to take his brandy and water in the gloom of the back parlor. His heart was heavy; the more he considered the complexity of the affair he was engaged upon, the more depressed and disgusted he became with the vileness of mankind.

Mr. Bonney, the poorhouse keeper, was away, but his wife, who liked to be called the matron, greeted Harris in his stead. "A real Christian," she said as she pocketed the five shillings Harris gave her. "No matter what 'is domination may be, I call 'im a real Christian and I'll say so to 'is face. And you're a little one, Master H. God bless you—on be'alf of our five 'ungry mouths."

Harris, after vainly peering over Mrs. Bonney's high shoulder for a sight of Adelaide, bowed and withdrew. On the dark, narrow stairs, he passed the wet nurse who, smelling of gin, was on her way to do her duty by the foundlings. She looked at Harris sharply, shrugged her sturdy shoulders and continued on her way, leaving Harris to meditate on the irony of the same milk feeding both Adelaide and the alien baby in her place.

Upstairs, Mrs. Bonney waited for the wet nurse to settle herself down before going across to the Old Ship. Five shillings was a largish sum to hand over to her husband without subtraction. Two and sixpence would be more than enough... and very nice too for the poor little mites. Which left a further two shillings and six-pence for brandy which was altogether healthier and more genteel than gin.

"Evening, Mrs. Bonney," said the landlord affably. "And how's them sinful brats of your'n?"

"It ill be'oves a publican to talk of sin," said Mrs. Bonney with dignity. "A large brandy, if you please; and a half of gin to cool it down."

The landlord smiled. He was too sensible a man to take offense at anything save a bad debt. He dispensed Mrs. Bonney's brandy and gin and took her money.

"From the charity bag, ma'am?" he murmured with a good-natured wink. "Ah well, them poor mites wouldn't have much use for strong waters, eh?"

"A decent Christian," said Mrs. Bonney, tasting her brandy, "don't mock the unfortunates of this world." Then she settled down and was much surprised and gratified to find herself admired by a gentle-looking stranger who suffered from the inconvenience of a clubfoot.

"You look after the poorhouse, ma'am?"

Mrs. Bonney nodded. "In a manner of speaking. I'm the matron."

"Godly work," said Mr. Raven.

"A vessel of charity," said Mrs. Bonney, cooling her brandy with a mouthful of gin.

"Charity," said Mr. Raven wistfully. "How little there is in the world."

"Oh, I don't know," said Mrs. Bonney thoughtfully. "It comes and goes."

"Now that lad I saw calling on you just now—Master Harris, wasn't it?" said Mr. Raven earnestly. "Do you often receive charity from the young?"

Mrs. Bonney looked at him sharply. "That were from 'is pa, sir," she said carefully. "And it were private. For Mr. Bonney. Nothing to do with charity." She had no intention of letting the stranger imagine she spent charity money on herself. She had a position to keep up. Being matron, she felt she ought to be above suspicion.

"A private—er—donation, then?" murmured the inquiry agent, almost to himself.

"Call it what you like," said Mrs. Bonney, becoming suddenly aloof. "It were something between Mr. Bonney and Dr. H. of which I am totally ignorant as God is my witness."

"Indeed, indeed," said Mr. Raven and gave such a smile that Mrs. Bonney was chilled to the bone and wondered who or what she had betrayed. "Pray to God it ain't you, Mr. Bonney," she whispered. She did not know that in her aloofness she had betrayed not her husband but herself. A space had just been found for her...

Chapter Twelve

ONCE AGAIN Mr. Brett had failed to tell Tizzy Alexander that he loved her madly and could not see his way clear to living without her. He had arrived back at the school from his successful visit to Dr. Harris still full of confidence in his powers, to discover that Tizzy had been waiting in the empty classroom for all of fifteen minutes. His mood being high and feeling his personality to be equal to anything, he'd put on an air of negligent gallantry and made a joke of his lateness. Unluckily Tizzy, who was somewhat on edge on account of the coming duel and her own responsibility for it, had not thought it funny to have been kept waiting and so was distinctly cool. Whereupon Mr. Brett made a further error of judgment by attempting to explain, a shade too carefully, what had kept him.

"It is of no importance," she'd said, not listening. "I understand quite well that many matters must come before me. You don't have to find excuses, sir. It's perfectly all right with me if you choose to meet someone else in the town. These things happen, you know. Only I abhor excuses...so please don't trouble yourself. After all, when all's said and done, I know I'm only the Arithmetic master's daughter!"

With that she'd opened her book, fixed her shining eyes upon it—and Mr. Brett's soaring spirits had dipped. The words of love he'd so dearly prepared were once again wrapped up and put away in his heart's bottom drawer for some more propitious occasion. He fixed his mind on Ancient History and tried to sail off into that golden time; but something warned him that Tizzy was in a different boat, so to speak, and, from time to time, pupil and master glanced at each other with sad, puzzled eyes.

After the lesson he left the classroom in a mood of angry gloom—and collided with Major Alexander at whom he stared with absentminded savagery.

"To me son," mumbled the Major awkwardly. He was holding a letter and was sure Mr. Brett had seen it and read the address. It was the very letter in which the arrangements for Mr. Brett's dismissal were mentioned and the Major's son invited to hasten to fill his place. Consequently the Major was particularly anxious not to invite interest by appearing too furtive about it. "Setting me affairs in order, y'know," he explained, staring uneasily at Mr. Brett's clenched fists. "Saturday. If I should fall, and all that...Sentimental nonsense, of course; but one never knows. Last farewells, eh?"

"Yes...yes...Saturday," muttered Mr. Brett, and hurried on his way.

For several moments the Major remained, staring after him. He had never seen Mr. Brett look so angry and he could not help wondering if somehow he'd got an inkling of the private discussion with Dr. Bunnion.

He shook his head. He didn't see how that was possible. If Brett had really suspected anything, the Major felt sure that he'd have been rude enough to have mentioned it. The trouble was, the Major was too sensitive a man. People didn't realize how easily their chance expressions affected him; and he had so large a conscience that there was always something on it.

For the sake of his peace of mind he decided to postpone the sending of the letter until the following morning. He kept it under his pillow for the night. Next morning, after breakfast, he handed it, firmly sealed, to his wife for prompt dispatch.

Mrs. Alexander, large, fair and sad, read her husband's letter with a sigh that stretched from first word to last. Then she replaced the seal with a spot of melted tallow—an accomplishment she had come by in her years with the Major—and called for Tizzy to take the letter down to the town for the post.

When her daughter had gone Mrs. Alexander frowned and her eyes glimmered with tears. So, she thought bitterly, it's all arranged. Herr Brett is to go—and Adam is to come. What an exchange! And so soon! On Saturday, even. She blinked, then straightened her ample shoulders and went into Tizzy's room where, with rapid hands, she set about rummaging the shifts and petticoats to see what needed mending...

Tizzy, brightly pretty in her yellow spotted muslin and flower-embroidered cap, went down into the town like a butterfly. There was always a coachman or two in the yard of the Old Ship who'd carry a letter to Southwark to oblige a girl like Tizzy.

It was now nearly a month since Adam Alexander had been waiting at Southwark after leaving the monastery at Basingstoke at the abbot's request. "Burn me!" had shouted the Major's son, passionate for martyrdom, for the young man was something of a firebrand, having inherited his father's temperament. "Why don't you burn me at the stake, then?" To which the abbot had wearily replied, "I'd be glad to, young man—but I rather fancy you're too wet to make a worthwhile blaze." So Adam had shaken his fist at the abbot and the dust of the cloisters from his sandaled feet and made his way to Southwark where he languished till his father should find him another situation.

Tizzy handed the letter to an ancient coachman and rewarded him with a shilling and a smile in place of the kiss he'd asked. Then, with the smile still about her—for to be asked for a kiss is a marvelous curver of the lips—she left the yard in time to meet with Ralph Bunnion who was on his way into the Old Ship's back parlor.

Aroused by Tizzy's beauty and tortured by the memory of what it had brought him to, Ralph halted. "It's all your fault!" he snarled. "When blood flows on Saturday, it'll be on your conscience forever! I hope you're satisfied." Then he said, "Murderess!" and stalked into the inn in a blaze of peach velvet and a flash of love-in-idleness.

Tizzy stared after him, her eyes stinging with tears at the injustice of it all. For a moment she wished with all her heart that Ralph Bunnion would indeed be slain on Saturday; but she repented instantly as that would have made her father a murderer. So did she wish her father killed instead? Again she recoiled from the thought. She began to walk away with downcast eyes and the ancient coachman who'd asked her for a kiss gazed after her and fancied she was limping, as if she'd stumbled and been bruised against one of the world's sharp corners.

"Charming young woman," murmured a stranger with a clubfoot.

"A lass and a half," agreed the coachman. "Sweet as a lane in May."

The inquiry agent smiled. Quite reasonably he had taken Tizzy to be Maggie Hemp as there seemed no purpose in introducing a newcomer to the scheme at this late stage. The threat of blood on Saturday and the terrible taunt of "Murderess" had further confirmed him. Cautiously he craned his neck to read the name on the letter the coachman still held. "Adam Alexander." Mr. Raven's brain reeled. Was there no end to the complexity of the affair? Were its hideous tentacles reaching out to yet another victim?

Every impulse bade him follow the young woman in the yellow dress; but his foot ached from the constant dragging from place to place. He groaned with frustration and heaved himself up to his little room where he spread out his paper and, in a few minutes, was calmed by studying it.

Blood on Saturday. At least he had until then. Everything indicated that Brett would hold his hand until that fatal day. "But on Saturday," he whispered to his boot, "we will forestall him and strike with a thunderbolt!"

Tizzy Alexander, after thinking miserably about casting herself from the top of Black Rock and so ending her young life on a romantic full stop, had decided to give the world just one more chance and had arrived back at the school before lunch. As she passed slowly before the front parlor window, she heard Mr. Brett talking about the infant Perseus being abandoned to the sea in a fragile ark. Strange how often babies seemed to be abandoned in the Ancient World as well as the modern. Dreamily, for Mr. Brett's voice always made her deliciously dreamy, she caught herself remembering the little baby she'd found on the Downs on that hateful afternoon when everything had begun. Between her other troubles, she'd thought of it often since it had been whisked away in Ralph Bunnion's lumpish arms. She'd wondered what had become of it and whether it was now being as loved as she'd have loved it if she'd been given the chance. Now she wondered how it would have been—with the baby of course—how it would have been if she'd gone walking with Mr. Brett instead of Ralph Bunnion. She remembered the last lesson—and sighed. He'd have talked of Ancient History all the way there and all the way back.

She peered through the window at the twelve large, clumsy boys who sprawled and huddled in their places like heaps of old clothes. It won't be long before they're lovers and husbands, she thought with amazement; even those two awful ones in the front...what were their names, now? Bostock and Harris. Her gaze shifted. And there's that poor, fat child, Sorley. But he looks so pale; and thinner. I must mention it to Ma. Perhaps he needs some physic?

She stopped. One by one the boys had turned and were staring at her. They were grinning. Alarmed, she looked to the front of the class. Mr. Brett was also staring at her. His eyes were enormous and his face was pale as death. He half raised a hand towards her—when she went as red as a poppy and fled into the school.

"Vy must you frighten the vits out of me, child?" said Mrs. Alexander angrily as Tizzy burst in upon her. "A leddy shoot knock." Then she shoveled away a large piece of white material into her workbox and shut the lid on it as if it were alive. Tizzy frowned.

As always, Bostock and Harris walked home together. The coolness between them had gone; theirs was a friendship that was strengthened by disaster. It was now as firm as a rock. Harris had confided in Bostock the misfortune that had overtaken the anonymous letter and had been generous enough not to blame his friend for it. Bostock had listened, staring at Harris in mute and terrified sympathy. He had never known Harris to fail in anything so many times. Bostock felt that it was fate; but he didn't like to say so as he knew Harris didn't believe in fate. None the less, there seemed no other explanation and Bostock, in his heart of hearts, was sure that Harris and he were opposed by a power that was beyond them. Genius though Harris undoubtedly was, there were still things in heaven and earth that even a genius might not overcome. He stole a mournful glance at Harris and wondered how he might tell him that it looked like Adelaide was gone for good.

But he couldn't bring himself to do it. He saw that Harris was battling with a new idea. Truly there was something heroic about Harris. In the face of all calamity, he fought indomitably on.

"There's fourteen shillings left," said Harris, brooding as if over a great distance. "And fourteen shillings could go a long way."

Bostock nodded and wondered how far Harris was considering going with it.

"Now if we was to invest it, little by little, in that Mrs. Bonney at the poorhouse..."

"Yes, Harris?"

The lights were beginning to flicker in Harris's eyes and, in spite of himself, Bostock couldn't help being excited.

"If we was to go each day with a shilling or two for the foundlings..."

"Yes, Harris?"

"So that our comings and goings would seem natural and aboveboard..."

He paused and looked inquiringly at Bostock for another "Yes, Harris," which somehow he seemed to need. "Then sooner or later she won't be there, Bosty. It happened before and it'll happen again."

"Yes, Harris?"

"So we lift Adelaide, Bosty, old friend! Easy as kiss your hand! Don't you see? It's as good as done! A little patience, a little money—and it'll all be over!"

Once more the lights were fully on in Harris's eyes. He was all triumph.

"And—even if it don't work again," said Bostock, striving to prepare his friend for the inevitable worst, "we'll have done a real charity with all that money for the foundlings!"

"Charity?" said Harris mockingly. "What's that, Bosty? My poor old friend, there ain't no such thing as charity." He laughed sardonically and Bostock steadied himself to have yet another support of his youthful soul knocked away.

"Hypocrisy," said Harris. "Nothing more, Bosty. Self-interest rules us all. The man what gives to the poor is only doing it to be well thought of by the world."

"But what about them that give secretly, Harris?"

"Worst of all," said Harris contemptuously. "They're the ones that spill it all out in their prayers to buy themselves a seat in Heaven. Sniveling in their pews: Look God, haven't I been good today? You'll remember, won't you, when the time comes?"

"But you said there wasn't any God—"

"Then more fool them and it serves them right when they find out they've done it all for nothing. No, Bosty, old friend— all your saints and philanthropists only give to satisfy themselves, else they wouldn't do it. Stands to reason. Hypocrites, every last one of 'em. Charity's a snare and a delusion, Bosty."

"But it's supposed to be Christian, anyway."

"What's that, Bosty? Mark my words, old friend, if there was such a thing as a real live Christian—which there can't be as nature's against it—he'd be honest enough and truthful enough in his own heart never to sink to your sneaking charity. He'd be a man, no matter how many poor he came across, no matter how they yelped and whimpered for bread, who'd not demean himself by giving anything away. He'd be a man who'd scorn to puff himself up with goodness. That's what I'd call a real Christian, Bosty! None of your sniveling hypocrites!"

Bostock stared at the ground. He was thinking of the shilling he'd put in the collecting box on Sunday; and he was deeply ashamed.

Mrs. Bonney, having drunk away the two shillings and sixpence of yesterday, was feeling the effects of it. Mr. Bonney was still away so she still had the remaining money and she was sorely tempted. The stranger with the clubfoot had put the fear of the Devil into her—else she'd never have drunk so freely. Now her temper was at its worst and she knew she was being harsh with the foundlings when they howled. But she couldn't help it. Gin and brandy was the only thing that would put her to rights. In a way, if she spent the remaining two and sixpence at the Old Ship it would be as much for the foundlings' benefit as for hers. Her temper would be sweetened and once more she'd be as an angel to them. So surely it couldn't be sinful to aim to be kind?

She was thus fidgeting with her conscience and the two shillings and sixpence when Bostock poked his fierce head round the door and gave her a further two shillings for the poor.

"Bless my soul!" said Mrs. Bonney, patting Bostock's inky hand. "Another little Christian!"

"No I ain't," said Bostock sadly. "I'm a hypocrite, Mrs. Bonney."

"I don't care what domination you may be, Master B.," said Mrs. Bonney. "You're a real Christian to me."

Chapter Thirteen

SORLEY was ill. Mrs. Alexander had noticed and mentioned to Mrs. Bunnion that the boy was sickly pale and showed signs of wasting away. Mrs. Bunnion had told her husband, but he had refused to believe it—as indeed he refused to believe anything of an unpleasant nature. Then he saw with his own eyes that the boy took no breakfast on the Wednesday and scarcely touched his lunch.

At once the headmaster plunged into an extreme of anxiety. Though a sensible and respected man whose scholarly accomplishments no one would have questioned, he was much given to extremes of alarm. They arose from the very weakness of his nature that caused him to ignore disagreeable matters. He knew this weakness and he despised and dreaded it; but he could not help it. He happened to be squeamish about omens of disaster. Thus, by the time something was actually forced on his notice, it had generally swollen to the gravest proportions.

In a matter of moments he had convinced himself that Sorley was dying. All the tangled troubles of the school and the duel sank away into idle dreams before the stark reality of Sorley's approaching death. He dispatched Ralph for Dr. Harris, even though he feared that the baronet's son was already beyond the physician's skill.

"I can make nothing of it," said Dr. Harris after he had examined the listless Sorley. "Everything seems in order—yet...?" He prescribed one of Mr. Parrish's powders to stimulate Sorley's appetite and departed, leaving Sorley in nature's hands.

Dr. Bunnion saw him to his carriage and asked if he should inform Sir Walter of his son's condition. Dr. Harris, obsessed and distracted by his own strange tragedy, looked at the headmaster vaguely, at first nodding and then shaking his head. "Forgive me," he said, seeing the headmaster's bewildered look, "but I have troubles at home. As you must know, we have lost our youngest child."

Dr. Bunnion, who naturally took "lost" to mean the child had perished, expressed sympathy; but at the same time felt a pang of uneasiness. If the physician had been unable to save his own child, what hope was there for Sorley? It was exactly as he'd feared; Sorley was doomed.

He hurried back and administered Mr. Parrish's powder with his own hands, saying to the pale and haunted-looking boarder, "Never mind, boy—I will send for your father." He had no intention of sending for Sir Walter, as the thought of that great man terrified him; he had only meant to comfort the boy. Then he left the room, closing the door reverently behind him. When he returned, some two hours later, Sorley had gone.

The fat boy was running. At first he made for the town; but the sight of people frightened him and he turned towards the great green Downs. Sweat ran off him in streams and his cheeks shook and jumped till he felt they would tear away from his face.

He had been driven half mad with guilt. Mr. Brett had been following him everywhere, not letting him alone for an instant. Always the figure before him—always the hand on his shoulder, clutching tight. He did not know what it was he'd done, and that made it a thousand times worse. Had it been some particular crime he could have confessed it—as he'd done on the crust of the stolen pie; but it hadn't been the theft of the pie at all for the pursuit had gone relentlessly on. The very uncertainty of what it was about tormented him like a mortal disease. Sleep deserted him and food—his chief pleasure—tasted rancid in his mouth. What had he done? What had he done?

In anguish he dredged up every mean and petty act he'd ever committed, every paltry crime and dishonesty that crawled in the dark of his brain. He would confess them all. But there were so many! Every moment more came creeping out. Sins of the day, sins of the night, dark and unwholesome...How vile he was! To confess all was unnatural, impossible. Naked he trembled in his mind's eye, covered with misdeeds that scaled and erupted all over him like a leprosy of the soul.

His fat flesh seemed gummed to his clothing as the sweat congealed. He collapsed on the grass high up on the Downs and drifted into a terrified half sleep that was worse than no sleep at all.

He was not strong, clever nor brave, and in his deep self-examination he had wretchedly failed. The threat of his father coming to the school hung over him like a nameless sword. He dared not go back. If only—if only he'd had a friend! Even at home in Cuckfield he'd never had one. His mother scorned him for his absurd appearance, and his father despised him for his dread of all the great dogs and high horses that flashed yellow sneers at him wherever he went. The school had been a haven; Dr. Bunnion and his wife had been kind . . . so kind . . .

Extremity of distress drove Dr. Bunnion to extremities of discretion and he succeeded in concealing the loss of Sorley until after five o'clock when the day pupils had gone. There was nothing to be achieved by panic, he told himself over and over again.

Nor, on the other hand, was anything achieved by the lack of it. Despite immense searches—in the confines of the school and among the half-built houses nearby where pits and trenches gaped with horrid blackness, laced with jagged teeth of rubble—Sorley was not to be found.

"You must send for Sir Walter at once," Mrs. Bunnion urged; but the headmaster, clinging desperately to the notion of a schoolboy prank, kept shaking his head. "He is coming on Saturday, my dear. He has promised. What can it serve if he comes now? Why distress him prematurely?"

So the search continued with an energy and urgency that, had he known of it, would have moved the lonely, fat boy to tears. But then men, like teeth, are only valued when they've gone, and it takes a gap in the family, like a gap in the mouth, to sharpen the heart.

Major Alexander, seeing Dr. Bunnion's total absorption in the loss of Sorley, instantly feared his own concerns would go by the board and the as-good-as-promised dismissal of Mr. Brett would be forgotten in the general confusion. Thus Saturday's duel would become inevitable; honor demanding that he would have to face Ralph if his private condition was not met.

"Brett is to blame, sir," he muttered, whenever he had the opportunity. "He should have kept a closer eye on the boy. No good for the school. Negligent . . . negligent . . ."

Though the Major spoke sincerely, he was not to know that it had been the very closeness of Mr. Brett's eye that had done the damage. Nor was Mr. Brett himself aware of this as his only concern with Sorley had been to clutch on to him as a shield against any possible unpleasantness from Dr. Bunnion.

"Perhaps he's gone home?" Mr. Brett offered, timidly attempting to ease the headmaster's mind; but Dr. Bunnion only shook his massive head in which there was rooted the irrational dread that the angel of death had come for Sorley and had taken him, lock, stock and barrel.

After two and a half hours the search was halted for dinner, during which time the fat boarder's empty chair exercised a terrible fascination over all present and provoked in every breast fresh fears and thoughts that, often, had very little to do with Sorley but were concerned with the wider and more frightening business of living. Major Alexander thought of the sharp pains of violent death, and Mr. Brett thought of the sharper pains of severed love; while Tizzy Alexander found herself thinking of children left alone and remembering yet again the abandoned baby on the Downs.

Thus the disappearance of the fat boy took its place as yet another wave proceeding from the pebble that Bostock and Harris had cast into the sunshine calm of the previous Saturday afternoon.

And still Bostock and Harris went steadily on. Like a pair of cats intent on their prey, nothing deflected them as they moved through the long week towards its end . . . inadvertently drawing after them a tangle of threads that, minute by minute, became more and more hideously entwined.

They were on their way back from the poorhouse after

having donated a further two shillings to the Foundlings. Mrs. Bonney had been there, but to Harris's interest she had been looking quite glazed and gave off strong whiffs of brandy. The extreme pleasure with which she'd fallen upon the new donation had suggested a great deal to Harris, and his hopes rose cautiously to the skies.

"Did you notice, Bosty?" he murmured to his friend. "She was hardly with us. It's my opinion that another five shillings will see her awash altogether. And then——"

But Bostock said nothing. Too many setbacks had lamed his spirit and injured his faith in his wonderful friend. And indeed it was possible that Harris had miscalculated. Mrs. Bonney was a large and seasoned lady and, though brought to the water's edge, so to speak, it might well have taken more than Harris estimated to get her afloat.

Although when Bostock and Harris called she had indeed been shining with spirits, her glaze wasn't so thick that she couldn't see through it. She still waited for the wet nurse's arrival before floating downstairs and across to the Old Ship. And she remained sufficiently in command of herself to be chilled by the sight of the stranger with the clubfoot. She was aware that brandy made her affectionate and talkative and was sensible enough to be uneasy of what she might say; so before she touched a single drop, she gave the inquiry agent an unmistakably hostile stare which said quite plainly that there would be trouble if he attempted to take advantage of her. Whereupon Mr. Raven—who shrank from all scenes not of his own making—rose uncomfortably to his feet and clumped outside.

Sorley stood up. The sun had gone from the sky. It was almost dark and new terrors seized him as the loneliness of the

Downs crept upon him like a ghost. He felt hungry. Mr. Parrish's powder was doing its work. Even as he stood, staring longingly towards the little lights that had begun to wink and gleam about the bulky town like netted fireflies, his hunger increased until he began to feel quite faint and lightheaded.

Home! He would go home after all. He would catch a coach—he would go down to the Old Ship Inn. There was sure to be a coach going to Cuckfield. And if not, somebody would feed him. After all, they were all human...He could eat a horse. Maybe they'd give him one...an old one ready for the knackers? I must eat, thought Sorley desperately. I must eat or I'll die.

He began to walk—then to stumble—then to run. He leaped the little hillocks and sprouting tufts of nettles; he went like the wind and puffed the air as if to drive great argosies before him. He rushed upon the town in an ecstasy of hunger. Through street after street he pounded, towards the busy sounds of horses and harness and grumbling wheels and men's cheerful voices and the maddening, all-pervading smell of mutton and onions that the fat boy dreaded might be in his mind alone.

"Hungry—hungry!" he grunted. "Must eat—"

"And why not?" murmured a voice that seemed to come from the night itself. "And why not, my young friend?"

He stopped, falling almost to his knees. A figure was standing in his path; a sturdy, squarish man with a large, black clubfoot. "Sorley!" moaned the fat boy, by way of explanation for everything—his circumstance, his tragic appetite and his right to pity. "I'm Sorley—"

"*Sorley?*" The voice contained a thrill of excitement.

"Hungry—food—for the love of God—please!"

"What are you doing here?"

"Mr. Brett—always after me—no rest—don't know why—

help me—help me—must eat!" The boy was almost incoherent with his unnatural hunger and exhaustion; lights danced in the air and among them were the stranger's eyes. He swayed as if he would fall.

"My poor, poor boy!" whispered the inquiry agent, putting out a hand to support him. "I never thought—I never guessed he would act so soon! Come—come!"

He led him through the front parlor of the inn and up the front stairs, thus avoiding the more popular back. Mr. Raven was trembling uncontrollably at this terrific turn his adversary had taken, and at the thought of how fate had directed his steps to intercept it.

Once in his room, he ordered a plate of mutton and onions for Sorley and laid him on the narrow bed to rest until his supper came. Then he sat and watched him while working away to accommodate him more precisely in the close-woven design.

At last there came a knock on the door to announce the mutton was outside.

"Here, my poor friend—eat," murmured the inquiry agent.

Once or twice, almost timidly, Mr. Raven asked him questions, skillfully innocent questions of nothing in particular—and of Mr. Brett. But it was of no use. Mr. Parrish's powder had so multiplied Sorley's appetite that the boy could do nothing but eat rapidly, fiercely and to the total exclusion of the world. So the inquiry agent held his peace till Sorley was done; then he asked him with great gentleness if he had anything to say, to confess. The word "confess" was very important to Mr. Raven as he'd always found its very softness tended to unlock the most obdurate lips.

Sorley stared at the stranger from the night who had taken him in and fed him. He peered about the little room and heard the faint jingle of harness from below. All seemed dreamlike, and most of all the stranger himself with the great black boot that put a period to his short left leg. Perhaps there was something nightmarish about him; but Sorley could not think ill of anyone who gave him food.

Confess...confess. The word ran round his brain like oil; then the dreadful memory of his flight to the Downs rose up within him and he remembered his multitude of guilt. It pressed against his chest like a banquet of sin. Confess...confess...

The stranger, sitting quietly by the window, outlined against the dark sky, seemed like a graven image. Such of his face as Sorley could make out, seemed gentle and innocent... so Sorley confessed.

At first he was hesitant, bleating only of little pilferings at home, then he grew bolder and gave up larger misdeeds. They seemed to keep each other company, his sins, for they ventured forth quite easily when together. They lost their shyness and came tumbling out. Sins of the day, sins of the night—everything, everything!

Sorley panted with excitement as he ridded himself of all his burdens. The sense of lightness and perfect freedom was intoxicating and, had he been able, he would have invented fresh crimes for the joy of confessing them. At last he came to the end. There was nothing more left. A great tiredness came over him and, at the same time, a vaguely nagging sense of shame. Uneasily he peered towards the still figure of the stranger in the window. To his relief and joy there was no revulsion on his face, no anger, even. There was only a small, sad smile. So Sorley sighed and went to sleep.

The inquiry agent stood up and crossed, very quietly, to the bed. He looked down on Sorley. This young human being had emptied out the contents of his darkest heart without restraint. Mr. Raven shook his head in bewilderment. Was it all so little—so trifling? Was there nothing blacker than this mere blush of gray? Was there no—et cetera?

For some minutes he stood, looking down; then he covered Sorley with a blanket and settled himself down in the uncomfortable chair to pass away the night. In a little while he too was asleep and their snores mingled harmoniously.

Chapter Fourteen

MRS. BUNNION had taken it on herself to write to Sir Walter that his son had run away. She had seen that her husband's sense of discretion had so gone to his head that even when the boy failed to return that night, he still hoped to avoid a scandal by keeping the affair within the confines of the school. So, early next morning, she quietly sent a servant to hire a horse and ride over to Cuckfield with her letter. This done she settled back with the cool satisfaction of a wife who has done her husband's duty for him. She adopted an air of unshakable calm and in that way became a tower of strength to the headmaster.

"I don't know what I would have done without you," Dr. Bunnion was moved to say on more than one occasion. "If not for your support, my dear, the news of this tragedy would be all over the town by now—perhaps even in Cuckfield."

Mrs. Bunnion patted her husband's arm and smiled. If nothing else, the calamity of Sorley's disappearance had served to draw the headmaster and his wife closer together than they'd been in years.

But the effect on the other husband and wife in the school had not been so happy. Major Alexander had become very agitated and irritable, and the continuing sight of his wife calmly sewing while the world went up in flames, enraged him.

"And what the devil are you making now, madam?" he muttered, as Mrs. Alexander shook out the shapeless yardage of white linen she was stitching at. "A shroud for your husband on Saturday?"

"*Bitte?*" said Mrs. Alexander, firmly retreating into her native tongue.

Baffled, he turned away and stared at himself in the long glass that Mrs. Alexander used for studying the effects of her dressmaking. In it he saw a face seamed and shadowed with fear and distress. The mine he had so cunningly laid was in terrible danger of exploding beneath him. The cursed duel loomed ahead and there seemed to be nothing that would now avert it.

Honor—honor! What quagmires and pitfalls it led him into! Because of honor he could not withdraw his challenge unless Dr. Bunnion met his condition and got rid of Brett. Now the vanishing of Sorley had put paid to that. Brett, furtive and underhand as usual, had made himself indispensable. Because he'd been hanging about Sorley these last days, Dr. Bunnion clung to him as to a brother. Plainly he imagined that Brett had some special knowledge of Sorley's habits that would lead to his return. So long as the baronet's son was missing, there was no chance at all that Dr. Bunnion would dismiss Brett.

The man in the mirror was trapped, and bleakly the Major recognized himself as this luckless victim of honor. Even supposing there were other conditions he'd settle for—and, in his present state, the Major could have thought of hundreds— his own impetuous nature had rendered them out of the question. He had already written to his son. Tomorrow night, most likely, Adam would be presenting himself, loud with the news of Mr. Brett's dismissal—which would not have taken place—and louder still in his expectation of being employed in his stead. He knew there would be no keeping Adam quiet; not even the abbot at Basingstoke had been able to do that.

The Major bowed his head and Mrs. Alexander, taking advantage of the space, held up her stitching to the mirror to study the way it fell; thus when the Major looked again, it seemed for a moment there was a ghost over his shoulder—the ghost of himself.

"For God's sake, keep that thing out of my sight!"

"Bitte?" said Mrs. Alexander.

Brokenly the Major realized his only hope lay in pressing on vigorously with the duel until the headmaster came to his senses and cried a halt.

At the first opportunity, which was later that afternoon, he took Mr. Brett on one side and, reminding him earnestly of his duties as a second and a friend, instructed him to inform Ralph Bunnion's second that the duel would take place at eight o'clock on Saturday morning on the seashore opposite the Old Ship Inn. He chose this somewhat public place in the melancholy hope that Dr. Bunnion, when he heard of it, would be so alarmed at the prospect of the entire town's turning out to watch, that he'd accede to anything to prevent it. The more the Major thought about it, the more optimistic he became; he felt sure that in this way honor could at last be satisfied and he could live with himself on terms of mutual satisfaction and respect.

Soon after Mr. Brett had gone on his errand, which was about an hour before dinner, the Major seized the opportunity of remarking to Mrs. Bunnion that it seemed a shade negligent and even casual of Mr. Brett to leave the school when everyone was so concerned. Mrs. Bunnion nodded and said that she had every confidence that soon Mr. Brett would be leaving the school for good. Whereupon the Major reflected that honor, if pursued with sufficient industry, might still bring its own rewards.

Mr. Brett hastened through the town to get his unwelcome errand done with. A strong wind was blowing off the sea. The gulls were flying inland and it was possible to see a great distance over water. Plainly the fine weather was breaking up and Mr. Brett felt a sharp uneasiness for Sorley if he should be out in it. Indeed his concern for the fat boarder almost drove everything else out of his mind. Though he himself had suggested that the boy might have gone home, in his heart of hearts he didn't really believe it. He had once met Sorley's father.

The thought of fathers reminded him bitterly of the errand he was upon. So it was to be at eight o'clock on the seashore, with all the world looking on, that James Brett was to be revealed as the furtive scoundrel who had been acting for both the opposing parties in an affair of honor. No doubt there would be many who would imagine he had egged them on. Dully he wondered if Ralph Bunnion or the fiery Major would shoot him for his duplicity, or merely be content with kicking him out of the town. He thought of the bright contempt in Tizzy's eyes, and that was worst of all.

"O God!" he whispered. "Let the sun fall down from the sky before those eyes of hers turn as hard as stone! But what can I do? If there's a god in heaven—Zeus, Jupiter or Jehovah, I don't care which!— tell me what I can do?"

He paused, and the sea wind seemed to blow fiercely right

through his head as if to clear it of rubbish and weeds for some new seeding...

He entered the back parlor of the Old Ship at about a quarter after seven. It was uncommonly noisy and he recognized the matron of the poorhouse exchanging loud unpleasantries with everyone present. In particular she seemed very angry with a man with a clubfoot whom Mr. Brett had seen several times before. She kept accusing him of trying to take advantage of her and he looked horribly embarrassed. The rest of the parlor, being temporarily spared, were clearly enjoying his plight and Mr. Brett felt quite sorry for him as he was no match for the lady in her high mood. He wondered why the man didn't leave; but it turned out he was waiting for a plate of mutton, while the landlord, who wasn't hurrying himself, kept winking with pleasure at each of the lady's verbal thrusts. Then the man with the clubfoot happened to catch Mr. Brett's sympathetic eye. Inexplicably he paled and muttered, "Pity from you of all people!" Mr. Brett shrugged his shoulders and concluded that the man was weak in the head; then he saw Frederick sitting in a corner and nursing his mahogany pistol case. He began to make towards him.

"Two-faced!" shouted Mrs. Bonney suddenly; and Mr. Brett stopped in his tracks as the chance remark struck home.

"Not fit to be in company with decent Christians!"

The man with the clubfoot gave a sickly smile and attempted to murmur something to the landlord who grinned and nodded but did nothing more.

"There 'e goes!" warned Mrs. Bonney. "Watch 'im! Says one thing to your face and another be'ind your back! A Christian gentlewoman don't know where she is with 'im. Oo's drunk me brandy? Bleeding thieves! Oh, Gawd, where am I?" She sat down heavily and peered about her. "Where are you, Mr. Bonney? I can't wait 'ere all night!"

Then she became quiet, but continued to gaze about her with some anxiety—as if she was worried she was waiting in the wrong place.

Mr. Brett stared at her; an idea was stirring in his mind. An idea not unconnected with the coming duel and the expression on Mrs. Bonney's face.

Sorley was starving again. His extraordinary benefactor seemed to have been gone for hours. All day he'd remained in the little room, waited on hand and foot by the curious Mr. Raven. Whenever he'd asked to go out, Mr. Raven had warned and begged him to remain where he was as he was in great danger. Mr. Raven never said what this danger was, but his manner put the fear of God into Sorley. He had known all about the visit of Dr. Harris to the school, and when Sorley had told him about the powder he had been given, Mr. Raven had looked very troubled and grave.

This seemingly supernatural piece of knowledge had alarmed Sorley still further and he obeyed Mr. Raven willingly. Though people might have called him a fool, he certainly wasn't foolhardy; and anyway, Mr. Raven treated him so well. Sorley had never known such gentleness and even deference before. Towards afternoon he began to gain in confidence and quite put on airs. He found himself rather enjoying lording it in this little kingdom with its view of the sea. It tickled him no end to see Mr. Raven clump about on menial errands so readily.

That was why he began to feel alarmed and desperate when Mr. Raven was gone so long for his supper. It wasn't like him to keep Sorley waiting.

Sorley scowled and went to the door. The loud, angry voices he'd heard before had now subsided into a murmur.

He opened the door. He remembered the way he'd come up. He wouldn't be so silly as to risk those stairs. He smiled cunningly—and went down the back stairs.

"*Sorley!*" roared Mr. Brett. "Come here, boy!"

Chapter Fifteen

DESPITE the vigor of the gale that rattled the windows and buffeted the doors, the relief and joy on Sorley's return produced a burst of sunshine in almost every heart—Mrs. Bunnion and Major Alexander alone having slight reservations.

Though she would certainly never have wished Sorley ill, his untimely return presented Mrs. Bunnion with an unpleasant problem. Uncomfortably she watched her husband congratulating himself on the narrowness of his escape from an awkward and painful situation. Unfortunately, though he did not at present know it, he had not quite escaped. The servant who had taken Mrs. Bunnion's letter to Cuckfield had returned to her with the murmured news that Sir Walter Sorley would be arriving tomorrow. She sighed. She did not care to think how her husband would take what he would surely regard as an unwarranted going behind his back. Like all weak men— and Dr. Bunnion *was* a weak man—he was not apt to be indiscriminate in his anger and not pause to think.

Though considering the matter narrowly, Mrs. Bunnion was willing to admit that she *had* gone behind her husband's back; but it was only because, at the time, he'd been facing the wrong way. After all, he should have written the letter himself and not left it to her sense of fitness and duty. Supposing the worst had happened and Sorley had not been found; what then? Where would the headmaster have been if his wife had not written her timely letter? And now, because of the merest chance on Mr. Brett's part, Dr. Bunnion would never appreciate what a treasure he had in his wife. Anger would blind and destroy his judgment.

If only Mr. Brett had had the decency to wait another day, even...The more she thought of it, the harder she found it not to dislike the interfering way he'd come between husband and wife; much as she despised Major Alexander, she couldn't help agreeing with him that the sooner Mr. Brett went the better it would be for the school.

As for the Major himself, he was bitterly disappointed in the lack of resolution shown by Dr. Bunnion who now showered such esteem and gratitude on Mr. Brett that the Major felt quite sickened by it. Like all sly, furtive and underhand men, Mr. Brett had a gift for ingratiating himself at the expense of his betters.

"Very well done, Brett," said the Major warmly during the evening. "Delighted it should have been you who found him. Couldn't have happened to a nicer man!"

No matter what he thought privately of a man, the Major always believed in giving praise where it was due; or even where it wasn't, for that matter, so long as it served a worthwhile purpose.

The Major was fighting desperately to save his honor, and if at times he suspected that his conduct did not appear entirely straightforward, he knew it was because honor was the hardest of taskmasters and demanded the cruelest of sacrifices. As Mr. Brett was the particular sacrifice he still had in mind, he did not spare himself in his efforts to catch him unawares.

Mr. Brett smiled gratefully. He was in that state of mind when all the world was goodness and every man a friend. Had Tizzy Alexander come in his way that evening, he would undoubtedly have swept her up in his arms and put out the lights in her eyes and the fire in her lips with kisses that extinguished only to rekindle. But Dr. Bunnion kept plying him with port and congratulations till gradually he sank beneath both.

Then Dr. Bunnion went once more to reassure himself that Sorley's return was not a dream; after which he retired to bed, where Mrs. Bunnion overwhelmed him with such tenderness and affection as he had not known since the first nights of their marriage. "My dear," he murmured. "Life is so good..."

Mrs. Bunnion, veil-eyed in the dimness, smiled enigmatically, and trusted that her efforts would have kindled such a flame in her husband's heart that no unpleasantness to come would quite put it out.

Certainly it lasted through the Friday morning. Though the sky was full of dark clouds scudding towards London like black coaches stuffed with letters of dismay, Dr. Bunnion went his ways in a private sunshine. Not even the thought of the morrow's duel overcast it as much as it might have done. The vanishing of one shadow from his life went a long way towards dispelling the other; and he promised himself that he would apply himself vigorously to halting the whole insane venture—after lunch.

On his way down from Religious Instruction—which he'd left for the few remaining minutes in the charge of the most trustworthy pupil—he came upon Mrs. Bunnion who was unaccountably lingering in the hall. He twinkled his eyes with an almost mischievous knowingness. Life was so good...

Mrs. Bunnion smiled back with all the sweet mystery of a

lovely woman whose powers are about to be put to the test. She had, at that very moment, seen Sir Walter Sorley dismount from his steaming horse and make for the door.

Fleetingly she wondered if she ought to prepare her husband for the blow that was about to fall; but before she could decide, it fell. The baronet had knocked, been admitted and called Dr. Bunnion a damned scoundrel who needed horse-whipping.

It had all been frighteningly sudden. Who had let him in was not very clear to Mrs. Bunnion. Perhaps she'd done so herself? He stood in the hall, panting and sweating slightly from the healthful exercise of his ride and demanding that a servant should attend to his horse. He did this with a directness that implied pretty strongly that if no one else was available, Mrs. Bunnion herself should oblige.

He was a strong, upright looking man, not so tall as Dr. Bunnion, but broader across the shoulders. His brow also was on the massive side, and his heavy, almost handsome, face had an expression of natural authority. He was, in truth, what he was always proud to call himself: an English country gentleman of the old school. It may not have been a very good school, but all such gentlemen seem to have gone to it.

"Bunnion! I trusted my boy to you—and now you've betrayed that trust! What the devil are you doing about finding him? Answer me, sir! Don't just stand there!"

Mrs. Bunnion looked to her husband in alarm. Although he was, as Sir Walter observed, standing, he was swaying slightly—as might some tall forest tree that has received the fatal stroke of the woodman's ax and totters before crashing to its ruin. A glazed and terrified look was in his eyes and he passed his hand across them.

Who had done this thing to him? Incredulously he stared at the baronet. How had the news reached him? Who had betrayed him? Some venomous servant, perhaps? Someone who ached for his destruction? Someone who hated him with a cold and implacable hatred?

All this Mrs. Bunnion read in her stricken husband's face; and her heart almost failed within her. How—how could she reveal to him that the vicious traitor was his gentle lover—the companion of his days and the comfort of his nights? That the hand that had written the fatal letter was the selfsame hand that had so sweetly caressed him? How could she strike him to the ground when he was in most need of support?

She could not do it. There comes a time when truth is no longer the shining sword of the angels, but rather the arrogant ax of the butcher. So Mrs. Bunnion trembled and held her tongue and prayed for a miracle to save her from discovery.

"My dear Sir Walter—my dear Sir Walter," moaned Dr. Bunnion, "I—I—" Then he was spared further explanation as the pupils came out to lunch. They roared and tumbled and thundered from their several classrooms and united in a single stream of immense force that flowed towards the wooden extension of the kitchen where the day boys ate.

"Papa!" shouted Sorley; and Sir Walter stared in angry bewilderment at his son.

"He—he was recovered yesterday," mouthed Mrs. Bunnion faintly above the din.

"Then why the devil wasn't I told?" The baronet's anger had taken another turn. Though no one could have questioned the depth of his feelings for his son, this sudden sight of him had thrown the baronet quite off course. During his great ride he had worked himself up into a state of pleasurable anticipation at the thought of browbeating the Bunnions. He was, at heart, a simple man and had simple pleasures. Now the unexpected sight of his son thwarted him and made him feel unnecessary and foolish.

Dr. Bunnion tried ineffectually to explain that it had all been a schoolboy prank...no cause for real alarm...in fact one of his own people had brought the boy back quite unharmed...everything all right now...and what pleasure and indeed an honor to have Sir Walter visit, even though, as it turned out, unnecessarily...would he care to stay to lunch?

"So you panicked, eh?" said Sir Walter, glancing contemptuously from husband to wife as the last of the boys eddied round him like a small ripple round an old pile. "Thought you'd lost your prize pig, eh?" Here he nodded to the portly Sorley who remained beside him. Suddenly he grinned. "Shouldn't wonder if you filled your breeches, eh, Bunnion?" He laughed, then observing that Mrs. Bunnion had gone very red, added, "Saving the lady's presence, eh? But I expect she knows what's what!"

Mrs. Bunnion curtsied feebly in acknowledgment. There was no doubt that Sir Walter, despite his rough exterior, was one of nature's gentlemen. In the farmyard anyone might have told him apart from the pigs; it was only in company that there might have been some difficulty.

He stayed to lunch. There was enough to eat as Mrs. Bunnion had no appetite. The discovery of her treachery had not yet been made and she had felt quite ill with apprehension. Once or twice her husband had muttered to her, "Who could have told him? Who could have been so vile?" but she'd shaken her head and had been unable to answer him; so Dr. Bunnion had lapsed into a state of listless despair in which the only consolation seemed to be that matters could get no worse.

But here he was mistaken. Sorley was stabbing him in the back. In order to ingratiate himself with his sport-loving father, the fat boy was telling him about the approaching duel. Despite all the headmaster's efforts, it had proved impossible to keep the affair from the pupils. Major Alexander had discovered that wagers were actually being laid among the boys; and he had been mortified to learn that the odds were heavily against him.

Now Dr. Bunnion was forced to sit and listen in helpless shame as Sorley acquainted his father with the affair in all its sordid details. He was amazed how much the boy had found out—and how his miserable brain had retained it all.

Dr. Bunnion knew he was done for. Nothing could survive such a scandal. The school would have to close. God knew how he would make a living. Not even an obscure curacy in some dingy parish would be open to him after this. The scoundrel who'd informed Sir Walter had done his work well. He was ruined beyond recall. But who—who could it have been?

He stared stonily down the table, and chanced to see Mr. Brett smiling to himself as if some private dream was about to come true. What dream? Then he saw Major Alexander frowning at Mr. Brett distastefully. Suddenly he recalled how the Major had warned him about Brett being furtive and sly.

"Brett!" he whispered to his wife. "It must have been Brett!"

"Oh no!" breathed Mrs. Bunnion. "I'm sure—he couldn't— oh, never! I can't believe it! Not Mr. Brett?"

"Brett!" repeated Dr. Bunnion bitterly; and Mrs. Bunnion, feeling it hopeless to argue with her husband in his present mood, shrank back and let matters take what course they would.

In her heart she knew she was acting unwisely—that no scapegoat could or even should save her; but she was drowning and when a straw hove into view, she was inclined to clutch at it regardless of its propriety in holding her up.

"And where's that young stallion Ralph?" asked Sir Walter amiably. "A good lad even if he is only a schoolmaster's son."

Sir Walter did not mean to be offensive. He honestly liked

Ralph and was well aware of the Bunnions' hopes concerning the lad and his daughter Maud. Frankly, he wasn't opposed to the match. Though a baronet, he was not a rich man and could spare little in the way of a dowry for his child. In fact, whoever took her off his hands would have to take her as she stood, with nothing but her shift and his noble name. If that was all right by the Bunnions, it was all right by him. Sir Walter, whatever faults some might have seen in him, was no snob. God in Heaven! He'd sent his son to be educated alongside a riffraff of tradesmen's brats! If his daughter married beneath her, he wouldn't break his heart; and the lad was well set up and would, most likely, breed clean.

Ralph was sent for and Major Alexander excused himself. Since the challenge it had not been thought discreet for the antagonists to sit at the same table. It would have created an embarrassment. This gentlemanly behavior had been proposed in the first place by Mr. Brett—to each of the principals separately—and had helped tremendously in keeping his own extraordinary situation from general discovery.

The baronet greeted Ralph kindly and hoped all would go well on the morrow. Had he known of the affair, he would have been pleased to act for Ralph himself as, being a gentleman, he had some knowledge of such sporting events. Then he went on to give Ralph sound advice on where and how to stand so as to present the smallest target. If the ground sloped, it was an advantage to be lower down as landscape offered a more confusing background than sky to one's opponent. Also, he said with a smirk, it was better to be hit above rather than below the waist.

"Ha—ha! We don't want you gelded, eh?" He stared round. "Saving the ladies' presence, eh, but I expect they know what's what!"

"*Bitte?*" said Mrs. Alexander.

"Bitter," agreed the baronet, grinning broadly. "Very! You've hit the nail on the head, ma'am! Bitter for his bride. Like a mare being served by a feedbag instead of with it!"

He laughed immoderately at this and only subsided when he saw the ladies were not joining him. "Mealymouthed lot," he grunted and returned to the business of powder and shot, but continued to look round hopefully whenever he had occasion to mention balls.

The duel was now inevitable. In spite of all Dr. Bunnion's intended efforts, the fatal event was to take place. The headmaster's spirits, briefly raised by the baronet's unexpected pleasure in the wretched business, had collapsed when the full enormity of it struck home. By tomorrow his only son would be either a murderer or a corpse. This was the reality.

"And yet it serves me right," he whispered to his wife in the privacy of their room which they were preparing to vacate for Sir Walter to sleep there that night. "It serves me right for being so meek and gentle. Believe me, my dear—oh, believe me—when the meek inherit the earth, I fear it's only six feet of it. O God, if only I'd listened to that well-meaning, honorable fellow Alexander and got rid of Brett days ago!"

"But—but is it too late?" murmured Mrs. Bunnion, an unworthy hope stirring.

"How can I dismiss him when everyone knows it was he who fetched Sorley back?"

"And—and if he stays there's really no hope of saving our son?"

"I couldn't approach Alexander again. The man has a fanatical sense of honor. He won't budge an inch...and then it will be all over the town...his wretched daughter...no!"

"Perhaps you could—put it to Mr. Brett? Surely he'll be human enough to listen? I'm sure he's a good man at heart. There is a kindness about him..."

Mrs. Bunnion was a deeply honest woman. She was doing her very best for Mr. Brett; and, short of owning up directly to her own unfortunate treachery which had not yet been discovered, it was hard to see how she could have acted more generously. Had anyone suggested she was deceiving herself she would have been rightly indignant.

"The man is a viper! He is furtive, underhand, sly! Never forget it was he who brought Sir Walter here! Never forget it was he who has ruined us!"

"Until he is proven guilty, my dear, I shall continue to believe in his innocence."

"You are too good and trusting, my love."

"Perhaps I am," said Mrs. Bunnion uneasily. "But I am a mother and have a mother's heart. I'm more inclined to forgive than you are, my dear. Whatever Mr. Brett may have done, I still believe in the goodness of his heart. If you choose to think the worst of him, I cannot prevent you. It is because you are a man and look at the world more sternly. To you, everything is either right or wrong. But to me there is no real wrong, only sadness and mistakes and things done for the best. All I can do is to try to soften you ..."

"My love! If only I had such a heart as yours!"

"You have—you have!" whispered Mrs. Bunnion with a wistful smile. "I will go to Mr. Brett myself. I will plead with him for Ralph's sake. He will listen—I know he will listen."

"Be careful—be careful! I fear you are no match for him!"

A steely glint came into Mrs. Bunnion's eyes as if the very thought of Mr. Brett's being too much for her was insulting. "My dear," she said firmly, "even Mr. Brett has a mother; and it is as a mother I shall plead."

Chapter Sixteen

WHEN MRS. Bunnion left her husband she had no fixed idea of what she should do. All she knew was that Mr. Brett must leave and somehow or other she must bring it about. She was prepared to go to any lengths to achieve this as she had by now fully persuaded herself that any sacrifice on her part was to save her son. Mothers throughout the ages had performed prodigies of heroism for their children, and she would not lag behind. Nature and custom sanctified her; and love lent a dignity to her intentions. She would exploit the full range of a woman's means to gain her ends, and no woman, so prepared, has ever failed. From the soft warmth of her mature charms to the icy force of her contempt, from anguished pleading to cataracts of reason, she would use all the weapons at her command. The prospect both excited and inspired her. She felt herself to be every-woman—all things to all men: lover and flail, mother and bride...Such was the concern of this woman for her child.

At no time at all was she ever directly moved by the consideration that, if she succeeded in getting rid of Mr. Brett, the blame for having written the unlucky letter might go with him as an uncustomed item in a general baggage of guilt.

While Mrs. Bunnion was thus troubled with thoughts of her child, the other mother in the distracted household was similarly occupied in this, the deepest business of nature. Mrs. Alexander, having at last finished her sewing, was attempting to guide the gentle torrent of Tizzy's black hair.

"Up, Ma. I like it up."

"A vooman's peauty is in her hair, *liebchen*. So vy make it look like a puddink? Ma knows best vat suits her child. Ah— like silk..."

And so it was; Tizzy couldn't help smiling in the glass.

"Look up, *liebchen*. Keep still..."

"Oh, Ma, I can't see a thing when you put them drops in my eyes."

"A vooman don't need to see, but only to be seen, *liebchen*. Ach—it makes your eyes look as deep and vide as the River Elbe at Hamburg."

"Really, Ma?"

"A man might fall in and lose his heart forever, *liebchen*. Ach! Vy vear your bodice so high? It vill choke you!"

"But, Ma—it won't be decent if it's any lower!"

"Decent? Decent? Vat's decent? *Liebchen*—I made your bodice; but Gott made vat's under it. So vy talk of decent? Ain't Gott's vork better than your ma's?"

"Oh, Ma!"

"So pink your cheeks! Like flowers!"

"I'm blushing, Ma."

"And how else should a man know ven he's kindled a fire? Gott is kind. Make a kiss with the lips, *liebchen*, and ve turn them into a rose."

"Not the lip rouge, Ma! It tastes like physic."

"And so it is, *liebchen*—but not for you! Now look in the glass and see how your ma knows best!"

Tizzy looked, but her eyes were misty from the belladonna, so she took her mother's word.

"And now, *liebchen*, it's time for the lesson; and may both of you learn."

As Tizzy rustled out of the room, Mrs. Alexander stared after her with tears in her worn blue eyes. They were tears of pride and hope, of memories and regrets. Then she turned back to the glass and gazed at her large, sad self. But her eyes were misty, too, and it seemed to her that the mirror still held Tizzy's reflection. "Gott is kind," she whispered. "Something sveet has come out of it all!"

Tizzy heard from somewhere the murmur of voices, then the loud laughter of Sir Walter Sorley. She bit her lip, tasted the lip rouge, made a face and attempted to hurry down the stairs. But cautiously. She could not see very well; and light made matters worse. Even a glimpse of the dull afternoon sky through a window provoked a rush of tears and turned the Academy into a house under the sea where stairs swam and walls were drifting and vague.

"Oh, Ma," she muttered as she stumbled and all but fell on the bottom stair, "a woman ought to be able to see where she's going!"

At last she found the classroom door. Will it be Ancient History all over again, she wondered with a quickly beating heart? Or will he see at last that there's something wonderful in the world today? She knocked.

"Come in."

Mr. Brett was standing. Little points of light seemed to be

all over him. Tizzy could hardly bear to look at him, he was so splendid.

"Sit down," he said; and Tizzy thought she heard a tremble in his voice. She lowered her eyes and found her place in the front row where Bostock sat during the day.

The seat and desk were on the small side and her yellow muslin gown overflowed and streamed to the floor like a pool of dappled sunshine. She tried to arrange it becomingly, and knocked down a book. Mr. Brett moved to pick it up but Tizzy inadvertently forestalled him. She looked up, and his face glimmered large. She wasn't sure whether he was looking at the book or at her. She blushed and didn't know whether to bless or blame her ma. But either way there was something about Mr. Brett that had never been before... and, for a moment, Tizzy really fancied he was drowning in her eyes.

"Where were we?" he said, resuming his place. Tizzy's heart misgave her; was it really to be Ancient History again? She braved the light and turned her eyes to where she dimly saw his face.

Just then a corner of the sun broke through the thick sky and sent a dusty golden shaft down into the room. The flies danced like tiny jewels and Mr. Brett dissolved in glory.

"Did I tell you of how Jupiter loved Io?" asked Mr. Brett softly.

"And turned her into a cow," said Tizzy, thinking of many marriages and with tears welling helplessly out of her eyes.

"Did I tell you how Leander loved Hero?" murmured Mr. Brett.

"And was drowned for it," said Tizzy, smiling sadly at Mr. Brett through her salty veils.

"Did I tell you how Antony loved Cleopatra?" whispered Mr. Brett, moved powerfully by Tizzy's emotion.

"And killed himself," nodded Tizzy. "And then she did, too, and they were buried in the same grave."

She tried to make out how Mr. Brett was looking—if he was smiling or serious. But she could not be sure; her drugged eyes had changed him into something dreamlike. His wig seemed turned to a silver helmet with a nodding plume, and the face beneath seemed carved out of the softer parts of sleep.

"Did I tell you of how Romeo loved Juliet?" breathed Mr. Brett.

"And did himself in like Antony before him?" whispered Tizzy. "Poor Juliet, poor Cleopatra, poor Hero! Is love always such a widowing thing?"

"Did I ever tell you," sighed Mr. Brett, now fathoms deep in Tizzy's eyes, "that your eyes are like mysterious, twilit pools, and your lips are a pair of kissing cherries?"

"No," whispered Tizzy. "You never did."

Then his face grew perfectly enormous and she stood up to meet him and hoped he could see better than she, the nearest way to a kiss.

For an instant she wondered if the lip rouge would put him off; but it didn't—not in the smallest degree. Oh, Ma, thought Tizzy, through a gap in her joy, you was right after all!

"I've loved you for so long, Tizzy Alexander!" murmured Mr. Brett, drawing breath for another kiss. "With all my heart and strength!"

"Then why didn't you say so before?" said Tizzy. "Because I've loved you, James Brett, for at least as long as you've loved me!"

Then they kissed again while the classroom flies danced in the shaft of sunlight and the world spun idly like a child's toy, a million miles below.

◆

"Mr. Brett!" The voice came like a sword between them, and severed, they fell apart.

"For God's sake, Mr. Brett—and you, girl—have you no shame?"

Mrs. Bunnion stood in the doorway, her eyes flashing and her fine bosom heaving. "And in a classroom, too!" Fully prepared to sacrifice herself, she had come gently to Mr. Brett, thus her sense of outrage at the scene that confronted her was quite sincere. She was appalled. "I don't blame you, sir. I blame that—that Miss Alexander. First my own son—now you. But you must understand, sir, I—we cannot have it! Not in the school. You must leave, Mr. Brett. At once!"

In every way Mrs. Bunnion was an exceptional woman. Her sense of justice never deserted her. She could still defend Mr. Brett's character even though, at the same time, she was able to urge his departure for the good of all. No one could have said that the thought of private advantage had moved her in the least.

"And as for you, miss," she said, staring bitterly at the tearful and disheveled Tizzy, "I shall spare your mother and father what I have just seen. Not for your sake, but for theirs; they have suffered enough on your account. I trust that you, Mr. Brett, will also be discreet. Please go quietly. Leave a note; say you have been called away on family affairs. I will support you, sir—and also respect you for sparing us all any further unpleasantness."

Here the quality of Mrs. Bunnion's virtue proved more than its own reward. If Mr. Brett did oblige and leave as discreetly as she proposed, then her own somewhat high-handed dismissal of him would never come out. Being human, she couldn't help feeling a distinct sense of satisfaction at the convenience of it all.

"Go?" said Mr. Brett palely. "Now? After I've——?" He glanced at Tizzy as if the sight of her loveliness was more eloquent than further words. Mrs. Bunnion shrugged her shoulders.

"No!" said Mr. Brett suddenly—to everyone's surprise and his own most of all. "I will not go. Let your husband dismiss me himself. And let him find a better reason—if he can— than my love for Miss Alexander. You may shout the house down, Mrs. Bunnion—but I won't go!"

Mrs. Bunnion stared at him. There was amazement and even terror in her eyes. A fly buzzed and settled on her pale cheek; but she seemed not to notice. Then, as if awakening from a sudden dream, she turned abruptly and left the room. She had been shaken to the depths of her soul. Mr. Brett's refusal had been like an earthquake in which the firm pavements of her existence had cracked and yawned asunder. Mr. Brett's departure had been her only hope of avoiding the discovery of her damning letter. Now that hope was gone. Her marriage, her life itself would be laid in ruins.

She did not return to her husband. She was not able to face him. Instead she went to their bedroom and looked about it with inexpressible anguish. She remained thus for several minutes till at last, dully surmising that life must go on to its bitter end, she set to work gathering together such intimate belongings as she and her husband would require for the night. Since they were obliged to make way for Sir Walter, they had fixed on sleeping in Mr. Brett's room and Mr. Brett was to be with the boarders. Mechanically she plucked at the pillows and opened and closed drawers without understanding or even seeing anything that lay within. How—how had it all come about, she wondered miserably. In a few days—no more—in a few days her brisk and comfortable world had been plunged into despair. How had it happened?

Bostock and Harris, in a mood of tense exultation, were on their way to the poorhouse. Bostock was wearing his over-sized blue coat and was carrying an embroidered quilt from his mother's bed as the evening was windy and Adelaide might catch cold.

Yes; at last the time had come. On their last visit to the poorhouse Mrs. Bonney had been in so advanced a state of oblivion that Harris was convinced a mortal frame could withstand no more. Success this evening was certain; Bostock's waning confidence in his friend was quite restored, and Harris pointed out that when it was all over they would still be eight shillings in pocket.

"We could lay two shillings on Ralph Bunnion for tomorrow," said Harris shrewdly. Bostock nodded. Like everyone else, he was on the school hero's side. The heavy odds on Ralph Bunnion's victory in the coming duel was really no reflection on Major Alexander's ability. It was the expression of a general hope rather than a certainty that the best man would win. Had the Major been the deadliest marksman in all the land and Ralph the poorest, such hearts as Bostock's would still have wagered all on Ralph's success; and so, too, would Harris's—though a shade less impulsively.

"Here we are, Bosty, old friend," whispered Harris as they reached the scratched and battered door of the poorhouse. "If Mrs. Bonney ain't in the Old Ship, she'll be in her bed as bran-died as a butterball."

The two friends entered the gloomy house in which the unmoving air was ripe with the smell of babies, gin and fish.

They crept upstairs to the long, low room where the found-lings bubbled and slept.

"There she is, Bosty," breathed Harris triumphantly. "Down at the end."

Bostock advanced, his coat unbuttoned and ready, and flap-ping gently like the grubby plumage of some ancient bird. He had actually laid the embroidered quilt across the bleak little cot when...

"Gor' bless me! If it ain't me two little Christians come to cheer me Friday night!"

Mrs. Bonney, veiled in brandy, had risen from her bed. She stood in the doorway, blinking and swaying, but unmistak-ably awake. Her frame must have been more than mortal. Six shillings' worth of spirits had done little more than dent her.

"All donations is welcome," she said and stumbled down the room with hands outstretched. Even in her present state, charity was uppermost in her mind.

Harris, whiter than Bostock had ever seen him, fumbled in his pocket.

"Here, ma'am!" he croaked. "For—for the poor!" In a panic he gave her the whole eight shillings.

"If only there was more like you," said Mrs. Bonney moistly, "this ol' world would be a 'appier place. You'll go straight to 'eaven, Master H. You'll gallop right through them gates in a coach and four! And so will you, Master B.— right alongside of 'im!"

She had seen the embroidered quilt. She took it up and pressed it to her glassy cheek. "All donations is very wel-come..."

"My ma took three years to make that quilt," muttered Bostock in the street outside, overcome by his misfortune. "What'll she say when she finds it's gone?"

"What's a quilt compared to a live baby?" said Harris with the weary bitterness of one plagued by trifles. "We ain't got Adelaide, either."

"Three years," said Bostock, hurt by Harris's attitude. "And it don't take as long as that to make a baby, Harris."

Harris, a shade unnerved by the unusual workings of Bostock's mind, looked at him almost with respect. "Bosty, old friend, we can't give up now. We're so near to it. As sure as my name's Harris, eight shillings' worth of brandy'll pickle her cold. Tomorrow morning, Bosty. Early. We'll try for the last time. I promise, it'll be the last time."

Bostock thought, then shrugged his shoulders and sighed. After all, they were friends. "We'll miss the duel, Harris."

"We've got nothing left to bet with, Bosty. And anyway, my sister comes first. Poor little Adelaide! She must be wondering what's happening."

Mrs. Bonney, divided between taking the beautiful quilt up to grace her bed and going straight to the Old Ship, decided on the latter. She fancied she'd heard Mr. Bonney come in so it wasn't as though she was leaving the foundlings untended.

"Evening all," she said to the little parlor at large, and sat herself down to a night of very good cheer indeed. God alone knew she'd earned it. Nobody but a lady in a similar walk of life could know the trials of charitable work. With high satisfaction she observed, out of the dim corner of her eye, that the brute with the clubfoot had taken himself off into the shadows to avoid her. Good riddance! He crowded her; and once in her cups, Mrs. Bonney liked plenty of room to swim.

Mr. Raven went up to his lonely little room. There was an ache in his heart as he stared at the forlorn and empty bed. He remembered Sorley and the warmth of confession. He remembered looking after him...until that devil Brett had taken him away. He, Raven, had been powerless to prevent it. His strength was all in his mind; he would have been no match for a man like Brett—and his wry foot put pursuit out of the question. But tomorrow he would hurl his thunderbolt!

He went over to the table and took the papers out of his pocket. He spread them out and studied the affair of Adelaide Harris. The ever-increasing complexity had now extended over two large sheets, and the inquiry agent had some difficulty in remembering how they fitted together.

The whole conspiracy was represented by a tremendous number of lines, crossing, joining, dividing and intertwining to form the pattern of a spider's web. At various points of intersection, names were trapped like helpless flies: Dr. Harris and his wife, the Bonneys, the Bunnions, the entire Hemp household, Morgan the nurse, the gypsy baby, Adelaide Harris, Frederick and the landlord of the Old Ship who always said "good riddance!" whenever Mr. Raven left the parlor. But right in the middle of this diabolical plan, like the terrible spider he was, crouched the inquiry agent's great adversary, Mr. Brett.

Long, long he brooded over it, careless of the fading light. He moved his finger from place to place, murmuring, "Et cetera, et cetera," and drawing ever nearer to the vital spot that, once cut, would destroy the whole unclean thing and reduce it to a heap of meaningless threads; then, with nothing to support it, the deadly creature in the middle would come crashing to the ground to be squashed under the inquiry agent's avenging boot.

At last his finger halted. He had found the vital spot. "The thunderbolt," he whispered. "Who would have thought it?"

Chapter Seventeen

NIGHT, dark and impenetrable, seemed to collapse over Dr. Bunnion's Academy rather than fall in the usual way. Moon, stars and all the high paraphernalia of the heavens were utterly obscured by banking clouds that the wind had gathered in a great black rubbish dump above the town. Here and there uneasy candles gleamed out of windows as curtains were briefly drawn aside.

Major Alexander looked out often. His son Adam had not yet arrived and the Major clung to the frail hope that he would not come. Sometimes he fancied he glimpsed a striding figure in the dark; then he'd hold his breath and wait for a loud knock on the front door. But no such knock came and the Major concluded what he'd seen had been a trick of the shadows or a ghost.

Ghosts were much on his mind; twice he'd imagined he'd seen his own in the long glass in his room. He was not a superstitious man, but he felt there was something ominous in the air—an invisible iron curtain that was slowly shutting him off from the world of men. He felt horribly lonely and would have been glad even of his wife's company; but she was with Tizzy so he cursed her German soul. He should have married an Englishwoman; she at least would have understood him—and understood an Englishman's honor.

He paused in his pacing and gazed into the glass. He tended to examine his figure rather than his countenance, for it was an unfortunate disability of his that he was unable to look even himself in the face. In his military days, this natural drawback had given him an unlucky reputation for shiftiness, which no efforts on his part had been able to dispel.

Well—he was out of that now. He had kept himself to himself and no one but his wife thought ill of him... damn her German soul! If he died tomorrow he would die as the man of honor he really believed he was. It paid to be secretive and not to demean oneself with friends. It was decent strangers who took their hats off when a man of honor's coffin went by. Filthy friends would be all too apt to say, "There goes shifty Alexander. Caught at last!"

Inadvertently, his eyes met his reflection's. "Liar!" he whispered. "Liar, liar!" He had seen a face gray with dread, and lips that seemed to writhe over the terrible words, "I don't want to die! Please, Ralph, don't shoot me!"

The striding figure the Major had glimpsed in the night had not been a ghost. It had been Mr. Brett. The thought of sleep had been intolerable and the dark grandeur of the night had drawn him out. He looked up and was surprised how low the sky seemed; even the trees were not so tall as they'd seemed yesterday. Mr. Brett felt twice his old height, but very light and strong in his movements.

She loved him! Tizzy—enchanting Tizzy—Tizzy of the marvelous eyes and lips as sweet as ripe cherries—he could taste them yet! Glorious, blushing Tizzy in the sunshine of her dress whose bodice, try as it might, could scarcely subdue the pride of her breasts. She loved him and had said so. What more had the world to offer? Crowns, glory, fortune and even fine weather were but trumpery items, sops thrown to the millions to make up for not having Tizzy.

At last everything stood in due proportion. First things had finally come first, and Mr. Brett laughed aloud as he recalled his defiance of the awesome Mrs. Bunnion. Love was his general and Tizzy his flag; so inspired he could conquer the world.

But now he'd best go inside. It was coming on to rain and there was no sense in falling to a chill before he was more than love's lip servant. As he entered the school a vague memory of having been told something about the night's arrangements crossed his mind. He paused, frowning slightly in an effort to pin it down. No; he couldn't remember. Perhaps it would come to him later.

He went upstairs, light as a feather, and humming, slipped into his remote little room. Mrs. Bunnion was in his bed. She stared at him in terror.

"Oh my God!" said Mr. Brett; and remembered what he'd been told. He was to sleep with the boarders as the Bunnions were to have his room for the night.

"What do you want with me?" whispered Mrs. Bunnion. Her husband, after futile attempts to share the narrow bed, had gone down to the sofa in his study and left her alone.

"I—I forgot," said Mr. Brett uneasily, staring at the magnificent Mrs. Bunnion whose hair streamed across his pillow like the banners of yesterday.

"I thought—I hoped—I prayed you had come to—to say you had changed your mind."

"I'm sorry, Mrs. Bunnion."

Uncomfortably he saw her eyes were puffy with crying. Surely she couldn't be so concerned about the school? Or was it Ralph and the duel that was so distressing her?

"If it's Ralph—" he began; but she shook her head and her tears came on again. "Oh, Jack, Jack!" she sobbed.

"James," said Mr. Brett firmly. "It's James. But I don't suppose it matters now."

Mrs. Bunnion looked at him and managed a faint smile. She really was rather lovely—in a time-worn way, and Mr. Brett caught himself wondering by what declension she'd come to be the headmaster's wife.

"You must love Miss Alexander very much," said Mrs. Bunnion gently. He nodded. "She is a—a pretty girl."

Pretty? Mr. Brett was amazed at such a belittlement.

"All young girls are pretty, James. Even I was; once." Here she gave so sad a smile that Mr. Brett forgave her for undervaluing Tizzy.

"And so you are now, Mrs. Bunnion," he said gallantly. "Your husband is a very lucky man."

"My husband?" she whispered. "Lucky?" And then it seemed to the startled Mr. Brett that the gates of her heart burst open to a final flood of despair. At first she covered her face with her hands as if still seeking some privacy in her grief. Then she was forced to abandon this as she could not draw the great, broken breaths she needed to sustain herself, nor easily expel them in the long stairways of sobs down which she seemed to be tumbling and falling with frightened jerks of her shoulders and head.

Quite consumed with pity, Mr. Brett watched her, not daring to move or speak. Then Mrs. Bunnion told him why she wanted him to go. She confessed what she had done and how she had hoped his departure would carry away her guilt. She told him that she was no longer young, and that all her life meant was to be with her husband; that there was nothing else for her, and that to lose him would be to lose everything. Such love as there was between them was not like the love of the young. It was no longer a blaze from which many another brand might be lighted; it was a gentle, forlorn glow in a large and empty night. There were no other brands anymore; there was but the husband and the wife.

Mr. Brett remained silent. He did not know what to say. This scene of human fear and misery dazed him. Stupidly and irrelevantly all he could think of was that he would have to go to bed without his night things as it was impossible to start looking for them now. "Good night, ma'am," he mumbled, and left the room.

He went down to his classroom, the place of his triumph. He sat at his desk and stared over the shadowy seats that were unnaturally quiet. There were not even any ghosts to comfort him; he was utterly alone. What did his victory mean? Someone else's defeat. He frowned and rubbed his eyes. Must success always bankrupt another? Can nothing be won without inflicting despair elsewhere? Was this the only way of the world?

What if he agreed to take the blame for the letter? For a moment this seemed possible; then he shook his head. Dr. Bunnion would dismiss him in such a rage that Mrs. Bunnion would be compelled to confess.

He opened his desk and fumbled for paper and ink. There were two letters for him to write. One was to Dr. Bunnion, explaining that he'd been called away on family business; the other was to Mrs. Bunnion, begging her to look after Tizzy and tell her he loved her dearly and would send for her when he could. He did not really believe that such a time would ever come, but the essential gentleness of his nature made him offer this forlorn hope.

When the letters were written, he left one in his classroom and, after listening for sounds of Mrs. Bunnion and concluding she was asleep, pushed the other under her door. Then he returned to his classroom to gather such books as he kept there, and settled himself down as best he could and waited for the dawn. He would have to leave his clothes where they were, in the wardrobe in his room; but this extra sacrifice seemed to lend an added nobility to his renunciation.

Upstairs, Mrs. Bunnion had not been asleep. She had seen the letter appear under the door and had lain quite still for several minutes, not daring to take it up. Another crushing disappointment was more than she could endure. At length she could bear it no longer.

She read Mr. Brett's letter three times over, as if unable to believe it. Then she lay back on the bed and stared at the ceiling. "Thank God!" she whispered. "Thank God!"

Beside her the night-candle flickered wildly till, with a sudden splutter and gulp, it went out. But Mrs. Bunnion, the letter still clutched in her hand, was already fast asleep.

Chapter Eighteen

SATURDAY'S was a morning made for farewells. The rain was falling heavily, as if to hurry everyone on their way and then wash out all trace of them. From time to time there were vague flashes of lightning and distant, impatient grumbles of thunder. Major Alexander, who'd woken early, looked out on it all with melancholy satisfaction; at least such weather made the world not so hard to leave.

It completed also Mr. Brett's misery as he slipped out of the school and hastened through the teeming air. He was going to the Old Ship to get a coach to anywhere; and if he caught a chill on the way and died of it, so much the better—so much the better for all. He knew he was being noble, but he got no pleasure from it—and wondered if anybody ever did.

It was scarcely five o'clock and the town was still asleep, so he was surprised to see someone trudging towards him. At first he took the other to be an early washerwoman, then he saw it was a young man in a monk's gown. The young man was quite extraordinarily wet and his pleasant, innocent face with its crown of fair hair stuck out of his gown like a washed stick of celery poking out of a sack.

Taking him for a member of some charitable order, Mr. Brett wished him good morning and offered him a shilling. The young man thanked him, took it and squinted up at the glum sky.

"What we need, sir," he said surprisingly, "is a God for today."

"Indeed," agreed Mr. Brett; "if He'd stop it raining for us."

But this did not seem to be what the young man had in mind, for he frowned at Mr. Brett and continued on his soaking way. Mr. Brett smiled after him. There was something he'd rather liked about the wayward monk. There was something about his features that had reminded him of someone . . .

At last Adam Alexander, who'd had to walk a good part of the way from Southwark, drew near to Dr. Bunnion's Academy. The shilling he'd just been given would have been much more useful ten miles back; but then he was used to God being out of date and too late.

At last, there it was standing before him; his new home!

He approached the front door and was about to knock when it opened and his father appeared before him.

"Can't explain now!" muttered the Major, seizing his son's cassock with nervous violence. "But come round the back, lad. And for pity's sake, hold your tongue!"

Mrs. Alexander, whose ears were quite as sharp as her husband's, for the first time in many a long year had occasion to bless the arrival of her son. As soon as she was certain the Major was somewhere at the back of the house and occupied in silencing Adam, she left her room and went in search of Mr. Brett. He was not with the boarders so she suspected him of mooning in his classroom. But he wasn't there, either. She was about to leave when she noticed a letter on his desk. It was addressed to Dr. Bunnion, but trifles like that did not bother her. Where her daughter's happiness was concerned, she was capable of great feats of dishonesty. To be frank, Mrs. Alexander, deep down, was not a particularly honest woman; it was perhaps this quality that had first attracted the Major.

She opened the letter and read it. She scowled. She had half expected Mr. Brett to run away. In her experience all men—except her husband—tried to escape once they felt themselves to be entrapped. She sighed and shook her head. Not for nothing had she lived so long with the ex-Major of Engineers. She had made preparations. And anyway, she thought to herself as she hurried to her daughter's room, if he got away from Tizzy, he'd be caught by somebody else, and maybe by somebody not half so good as her Tizzy. So she was really doing him a kindness...

"Qvick, *liebchen!* Up! Dress! Ve'll cetch him yet! Hurry—hurry! Everything is mended and packed. Qvickly! Gott forbid you should be left behind and have to marry such a man as did your ma. He loves you—and you love him! It's natural! Vat more do you vant?"

When Mr. Brett reached the Old Ship there was no one about but a pair of horse boys playing dice under a projecting roof in the inn-yard. After some moments during which he became absently interested in their game, he asked them when the first coach would be pulling out.

"Where to, mister?"

"Anywhere...anywhere at all."

The boys grinned at each other. "Coach going to Southampton at about eight."

Southampton! A misty vision of ships sailing to forgetfulness filled his aching mind. "Is there anywhere I can wait till it leaves?"

"Not for an hour or more, mister."

"May I shelter here?"

"Suit yourself, mister; only don't get in the way of the dice."

Mr. Brett nodded and knelt down beside the players. After a little while he became fascinated enough to ask if he might join them. After all, what had he to lose, except money? The boys stared at one another, then grinned again.

"Suit yourself, mister—so long as you play fair. Remember, we ain't much more'n children."

So he began to play, at first winning and then losing so steadily that he began to wonder if there was more skill in the game than he'd thought. Sometimes he suspected one or the other of them to be cheating; but he couldn't see how it might be done. Besides, they always looked so childishly surprised when they won...

"Gawd 'elp us!" said one of them suddenly. "There's someone comin'! Thanks for the game, mister!" They grabbed their winnings and, with the speed of stable rats, scuttled away and vanished.

"So you have so much money you can throw it away, Herr Prett? Tizzy, *liebchen*, it's a gambler you are marrying!"

Then Mrs. Alexander broke down and cried her eyes out while her daughter was in her lover's arms. "And—and don't forget to give him the veddink shirt, *liebchen*! I finished it only yesterday, Herr Prett!"

◆

At about half past six a loud rattle of thunder awoke Mr. Raven. "Yes!" he whispered to the grim bulge of his boot under the blanket; then he stared through the filthy window to the thick sky. "And the day is made for it!" He left his bed and fetched in his other boot which he always left outside the door, though more as a gesture than anything else as it hadn't been cleaned for days. Then he dressed and clumped downstairs for his morning brandy and water.

The landlord was not yet about, so the inquiry agent wandered to a window that looked out onto the yard. He stiffened with excitement. He had seen them! Brett and the woman he had good reason to know as Maggie Hemp. Brett was smiling, laughing; he seemed possessed by a spirit of ruthless gaiety. He caught sight of the inquiry agent's terrible face. He waved and grinned and put his arm about the female, Hemp.

A nerve twitched and jumped inside Mr. Raven's huge boot so that it beat on the floor like an enormous wounded bird. The inquiry agent had seen baggage. The malevolent pair were on the point of escaping! This he had not expected!

"When does the first coach leave?" His voice trembled as he asked the potboy who came in, surly and slow, to take his order.

"Eight o'clock. Southampton."

"Eight o'clock!" The inquiry agent groaned harshly. Even the ordinary affairs of daily life seemed to work in favor of his adversary. At eight o'clock other matters would be afoot; matters of life and death and et cetera. What was he to do? For the first time he cursed the burden of his boot. He could not move quickly enough.

He closed his eyes. He must not panic. Panic was the death of thought. He looked out of the window again. He caught his breath. The baggage was plainly the female's. Brett had none. Mr. Raven smiled; he understood. Brett was not going.

Once more Brett's eyes met his—and this time the inquiry agent returned his cheerful wave with an ironic inclination of the head. How nearly the Devil had succeeded in panicking him, thought Mr. Raven grimly; but he was not to be bluffed. "Laugh and grin to your heart's content," he murmured. "But I know what I know, et cetera..."

Faintly he heard the potboy muttering to someone at the back, "Brandy an' water at this time in the morning! I tell you, he ain't human!"

But Mr. Raven was human; all too much so. In some men, being human was a sign of strength; in Mr. Raven it was definitely a weakness. He smiled at the potboy when his drink came and wondered whether it was too late to enmesh him in the web. He attempted to call up in his mind the immensely complicated tangle of intrigue to see if there was a space for the insolent potboy. But it was hopeless. No mortal mind could envisage that plan in all its tortured detail.

At length he could bear it no longer and the continuing sight of Brett and his paramour aggravated him terribly. He swallowed his drink and stumbled back to his room. With trembling hands he spread out the grotesque plan again and stared, for the last time, on the tangled lives and murderous plots that comprised the Adelaide affair. His finger moved from place to place, but it was in vain. The design was complete and the potboy would have to go to the Devil on his own.

Carefully he folded up the plan and thrust it into his boot. "You'll keep the secret, eh?" he chuckled. Again the nerve twitched and his boot shuddered. The plan, perhaps meaningless to a casual observer, fairly screamed to Selwyn Raven that a murderer was moving along one of the spidery lines towards a certain intersection where there waited the man to be murdered. But the inquiry agent had the measure of it all. Brett's bluff had failed and all the monsters were doomed. The time had come for Mr. Raven to launch his thunderbolt. He struck his boot to stop it trembling and then clumped unobtrusively out of the Old Ship and made his way towards the house of Dr. Harris, where he had not been asked to stay to lunch...

Chapter Nineteen

UTTERLY worn out by her night of grieving, Mrs. Bunnion still slept. Mr. Brett's letter had fallen from her hand to the floor. No one else in the house knew that he had gone.

In the kitchen extension, tragically unaware that the duel need now no longer take place, Major Alexander was making his peace with his son and apologizing for having brought him so far for nothing. There was no vacancy in the school; there was only approaching tragedy. Still, he was glad to see Adam for what might well turn out to be the last time. He felt that, of all people, Adam was the only one who understood him. They were very close.

"Come, Father," murmured Adam, embarrassed by the Major's display of emotion, "it's not over yet. There's still hope."

But the Major shook his head. All his elaborate schemes had misfired, and he was morbidly convinced his pistol would do the same. "Whatever anyone says of me, son—*afterwards*, you'll know I acted honorably. To know that will be a great comfort to me. It's all been only for your sister's good name. Perhaps I was wrong to put family honor so high, but such is my nature. And I feel yours is the same, son. I know, if you had been here, you would have done the same."

"I'll stand by you, Father!" said Adam impulsively. The Major thanked him, but couldn't help being a shade disappointed that Adam hadn't offered to stand for him, instead. The more he thought of it, the more this failure of Adam's depressed him and a slight cloud overcast their relationship. A lifetime's habits of suspicion were not so easily cast off, and the hapless Major found himself wondering if his son's eagerness to remain by his side was not prompted by the hope of another, more frightful vacancy?

The Major was a complex man, and suffered in a complicated fashion. But his opponent, Ralph Bunnion, was simple and did not suffer at all. Almost dressed, he was sharing a bottle of claret with the jovial Sir Walter Sorley. Indeed, his greatest concern seemed to be for what waistcoat he should wear for the occasion; thus he was in the tradition of all those heroes who love to show death more respect than life. The love-lies-bleeding he rejected on account of its unfortunate associations, while the love-in-idleness was stained. At last he fixed on an elegant creation of love-in-the-mist that Dolly Packer had done for him in the old days.

"Bleeding, idleness and mist," he murmured in an unusual mood of poetry. "It's like life, isn't it, Sir Walter. First the wound, then the resting, and then the uncertainty of it all."

Sir Walter sniggered and said it reminded him of marriage. Ralph frowned and put his waistcoat on. It was probably his most beautiful garment, having, in addition to the purple flowers, several finely woven silver plumes twining down towards the edges.

"Pretty, isn't it," said Ralph proudly. Sir Walter grinned.

"And witty, too," he chuckled. "Old man's beard, I fancy. Couldn't you keep up with her, lad?" Here Sir Walter fairly choked with laughter, spraying claret all over himself in a fine red rain.

"It's traveler's joy!" said Ralph indignantly.

"You know best," said Sir Walter, wiping himself dry. "You and the—the lady. Oh lord! Couldn't keep up with her! D'you get it? Must tell Maud and Lady Sorley!"

While the two men were thus preparing themselves for the fatal occasion, Dr. Harris, who was to attend one or the other of them, adjusted his wig and scowled at himself in the glass. The idiotic duel. As if he didn't have enough to worry about! Nearly a week had gone by and there was still no news of Adelaide. Though he had by no means given up hope, he was beginning to feel that gnawing dread at his heart that he always experienced when he knew a patient was dying. Bitterly he felt that Captain Bostock had failed in his duty; he had done nothing and had been content to leave everything to Mr. Raven. Dr. Harris's confidence in the inquiry agent had waned. He had already paid him twenty-five pounds and all the fellow seemed to do was to drink brandy at the Old Ship. And all the while the weird gypsy infant lay in Adelaide's cot.

Slowly the doctor packed his bag with such instruments as he might need. Privately he was convinced the two fools would miss each other; but he was cautious enough to go prepared for the worst. Bandages, forceps, scalpel, brandy... was that all? He fastened the bag and, observing the heavy rain, took out a cape. He would rather have waited for the wet nurse, but she didn't come till after eight. Still, Morgan would stay with Mrs. Harris and not leave her alone with the baby. There was no doubt his wife's hatred of the infant had become more acute in the last days. He went down the stairs. Damn Selwyn Raven! He would give the man until midday and then the gypsy baby would go straight to the Bonneys at the poorhouse. He had had enough!

He opened the front door. Bandages...forceps...scalpel... brandy...From force of habit he told off the contents of his bag to make sure nothing had been forgotten. He paused, shook his head; then, half humorously, he shrugged his shoulders and went back for a prayer book. "Just in case," he murmured. "Just in case..." Then he went out to his carriage which was already waiting.

Some two minutes after the doctor had gone, his front door opened again and his son emerged, carrying an old piece of blanket. He looked rapidly up and down the street, blessed the teeming rain that was keeping the townsfolk within doors, and hastened away to collect his friend. The change in the weather must mean a change in their luck, thought Harris; and he felt in his bones that all was set for success at last.

Unhappily no such optimism attended Major Alexander as he and his son set out from the school at approximately the same time as Harris met Bostock at the other end of the town.

"What about mother?" asked Adam. "Oughtn't you—we to say good-bye?"

"Much she cares," said the Major bitterly. "Damn her German soul!"

"And Mr. Brett?"

"We'll meet him there."

Ralph Bunnion, on the other hand, having no cause to be bitter with anyone save Tizzy Alexander, lingered to say good-bye to his father. Mrs. Bunnion, it turned out, was still asleep and the headmaster didn't want to waken her as he couldn't bear the thought of her distress at the parting scene. With

tears in his eyes he wished Ralph well, and then lapsed into
the apathy of despair from which he'd been disturbed. Thus
it was a good ten minutes after the Major and Adam had gone
that Ralph and Sir Walter Sorley set off confidently for the
fatal meeting.

"What about your seconds, lad? Your friend with the pistols and that fellow Brett?"

"We'll meet them there."

The rain lashed down on the town with unabated fury and
Frederick, walking briskly to the dueling ground with the
mahogany pistol case under his arm, prayed that the powder
would not get wet. He stopped and took off his cloak and
wrapped the case inside it. It would be horrible if one of the
weapons failed to discharge and someone was killed by the
other. It would make him feel like a murderer. In a few moments he was wet to the skin; but at least the pistols were
keeping dry and his friend would have a fair chance. He consulted the little silver and enamel watch that someone had left
in one of his father's coaches. The time was twenty-five minutes to eight; so he quickened his pace.

The inquiry agent had arrived at Dr. Harris's house. He had
been terribly hampered by his boot which was full of rainwater and so was twice its ordinary weight. Furiously he banged
on the door—and kept banging till a frightened maid appeared.

"Your master!" shouted Mr. Raven. "Where is he?"

"Gone out."

"Already—already? Fetch your mistress. Quick—quick!"

Mrs. Harris, hearing the commotion, had already come

down. The inquiry agent stared at her savagely. Her name was on the paper in his boot, caught in that frightful web. She was a guilty woman. All women were guilty.

"Give me the baby," he snarled. "I know everything, Mrs. Harris. *Everything!*" She stared at him, at first not taking in what he'd said. Then a look of joyous amazement lit up her face. Adelaide! He had found her!

"Thank God!" she wept. "Morgan—quick! Fetch the baby!"

Perhaps had her mind not been so distraught with anguish and had she not loathed the gypsy child so much; perhaps had her husband been at home, even, Mrs. Harris would not have been so hasty.

"Wait!" she pleaded. "Wait while I dress, Mr. Raven!"

"No!" he answered harshly. "There is no time. A life is at stake."

At twenty minutes to eight, with the gypsy brat stoutly wrapped and held in his powerful arms, the inquiry agent left the Harrises' house and stumbled through the rain.

So—at last, they were all out in the open and going their several ways: the duelists, the inquiry agent, the gypsy brat— and Bostock and Harris. The selfsame rain came down and soaked them all as if in a universal dismay at the prospect before them.

The baby had begun to cry, but all the world was crying and Mr. Raven told it so. Then it peered up at him through slitted eyes, and the inquiry agent shuddered at the inquity in them.

It was possible that at some time during this final journey he had doubts as to the course he'd determined on; but doubts at all stages of an enterprise are part of the human condition. He was right to doubt; he was neither a beast of the field nor a god. He was a man—and men may be wrong. A little higher than the beasts, a little lower than the gods, man is ever a double loser. For a pinch of divine understanding he has sacrificed his instincts; therefore a man should always have his doubts, and et cetera...

Fiercely Mr. Raven cast his mind back to the affair's beginning (while struggling to shield his burden from the rain); the bizarre appearance of the strange baby in Adelaide Harris's cot. Only an explanation as bizarre as the event itself would answer it. And there was no doubt Mr. Raven had provided such an explanation.

But then never knowing for certain how an event has begun, a man can only guide his understanding along the path of his own experience. Thus some men look up to the great sky and see God; others see but the blind and empty stars. Either way a man is condemned to build his tower on the shifting sands of doubt. The best he can do is to struggle as high as he can, then make his divine leap. Mr. Selwyn Raven nodded his head, and struggled on to make his divine leap.

Two other voyagers in the rain, namely Bostock and Harris, had reached the poorhouse. They were very wet and somber. Bostock's mood was partly due to the distress in his home at the loss of the quilt, while Harris's was because he felt he had reached the end of a road. All his courage, all his ingenuity—and all his money—had been staked on this last endeavor. If he failed and Mrs. Bonney wasn't dead drunk, then Adelaide was lost forever. So also would be the esteem of Bostock; and, in a strange way, Bostock counted for more than anything. Bostock was his friend and had always looked up to him. Where would Bostock be without him—and where would he be without Bostock?

Harris scowled. "This is it, Bosty old friend."

Bostock stared at him, and Harris fancied there was a coolness in Bostock's eyes. "This is it, Harris."

The friends shook hands and pushed open the poorhouse door.

Within, the air was curiously strong. The ordinary smell of fish, gin and babies was overlaid with something sharper and yet richer. It was not in itself the smell of brandy, and yet there was brandy in it. It resembled more than anything a heavy cake that had been burnt. It was very powerful on the stairs and grew more so as the friends mounted. At last they reached the room where the foundlings lay; and the smell was tremendous. Bostock and Harris stopped in the doorway. They trembled.

There was a chair at the far end of the room, and in the chair, wrapped in Mrs. Bostock's quilt, sat Mrs. Bonney. Her eyes were partly open but they gave no glimmer of recognition. The smell, now in great waves, was coming from her. As Harris had promised, the last eight shillings had done it. She was as brandied as a butterball and she stank like a vat.

"Christians," she mumbled weirdly as Bostock eased off his mother's quilt. "Darlin' Christians at it again…"

Mr. Raven had made his divine leap. With a last muttered, "And et cetera," he had laid the gypsy brat outside the house of the Hemps. *The Hemps?* Yes, the Hemps. Where else should the thunderbolt fall?

He had rapped on the door, then hobbled into concealment to a flash of lightning and a clap of thunder. Then he waited, his reputation at stake. If he was right—and still he was human enough to fear he might be wrong—then this one dramatic stroke would bring everything tumbling out of the cupboards of Hell and into the light of day. He fumbled in his boot for one last glimpse of his plan. He drew it out. It was sodden with rainwater. Every last name and line had run into a filthy pool of ink. No human being could ever have made any sense of it. It was lost forever. Mr. Raven cursed; then he grew still.

The door had opened. The elder Miss Morgan looked out, looked down. She screamed. Mr. Raven sighed with relief—and smiled.

The elder Miss Morgan crossed herself. Though she'd never clapped eyes on it before, she recognized the weird infant from her sister's account. The worst had happened; the fateful spell she'd given away had come home to roost. She screamed again. (Mr. Raven hugged himself.) The foul goblins had laid the changeling at *her* door. If it entered in the house, then all the hellish mystery of Celtic ghosts would be let loose to break the plates and drive everyone storybook mad.

Careless of the rain she knelt down, snatched up the wrinkled fiend and rushed away down the street. She would leave it where it could do nobody any harm.

Mr. Raven watched after her and wondered where she might be going. He would like to have followed, but he dared not. He was waiting for the murder. Very soon now, he had good reason to believe, Ralph Tomcat Bunnion would attempt to assassinate Indian or, rather, Gypsy Hemp. He hoped to God he would be able to prevent it.

Harris kissed his infant sister. He was sincerely glad to see her again; there were times when he never thought he would. Bostock looked on, deeply moved. Then the friends, watched by the insensible Mrs. Bonney, crept out of the room with the quilted Adelaide in her brother's arms.

"Harris," whispered Bostock as they were on the stairs. "What about the other one? What do we do about the baby at your house?"

Harris looked at him. He had entirely overlooked the other baby. He couldn't think of everything; but he wasn't going to admit it to his friend. Bostock's faith in him was in the melting pot. To confess to an oversight now would be to crack the mold and let Bostock's faith trickle away altogether.

"First things first, Bosty," he whispered, and continued down the stairs.

"Harris!" gasped Bostock as they opened the poorhouse door. "Oh, Harris, you're a genius!"

On the step before them lay the alien baby where the terrified elder Miss Morgan had deposited it a moment before.

"Christians," sighed Mrs. Bonney, as Bostock and Harris laid the gypsy child in the empty place. "Bleedin' Christians comin' and goin' like pink mice . . ."

Chapter Twenty

THE RAIN was beginning to give over. A stout sea wind was bundling the clouds towards London and a distant glitter of sunlight had appeared on the gray sea's horizon. Mrs. Harris, her daughters and Morgan the nurse, unable to bear the suspense of waiting indoors, had been scouring the nearby streets for some sign of the triumphant inquiry agent with Adelaide in his arms. Caped and hooded, they leaned and turned into every gust of wind with their garments whipping like broken wings. Mrs. Bostock, looking out from her window, saw them and begged them to come inside—at least until the worst of the wind had dropped. At first Mrs. Harris wouldn't hear of it; but when Mrs. Bostock declared that a physician's wife should know better than to court a severe chill, she saw the sense of it and, with her soaking family, accepted Mrs. Bostock's kind invitation.

It was while she was waiting there, sitting in Mrs. Bostock's parlor and drinking hot soup, that Bostock and Harris returned Adelaide to her proper place. The emptiness of the house—which had been left in the care of the kitchen maid who would never come out of the kitchen since Morgan had warned her about goblins—and the consequent ease with which the friends accomplished their task, prompted Bostock to declare once again that Harris was a genius.

"I suppose I must be," said Harris dreamily. "But, Bosty, old friend, it don't make me feel any different from you."

Bostock stared at him disbelievingly. Was it possible that Harris really felt as vague and puzzled by the world as he did?

"I get the bellyache just like you do, Bosty; and the rain makes me just as wet."

Bostock smiled and shook his head. Harris was having him on. "It's the way you think, Harris; high, like an eagle."

"It seems quite ordinary to me, Bosty. Honestly it does."

Suddenly there came a knocking on the front door that put a period to all meditation. "It's the wet nurse! Quick—the window! Help me down, Bosty!"

At five minutes after eight o'clock, Harris, strolling into his home from nowhere in particular, was greeted with the most astonishing news. Adelaide had been restored! She was back— his little sister had come home!

He was overjoyed. His real warmth of affection and great delight surprised even his sisters who were glad enough to answer his many eager questions as to how the miracle had come about. The wet nurse had been admitted by the kitchen maid, he was told, and taken up to the nursery. She had come out almost directly saying the baby had been changed and looked amazingly like a poorhouse brat of her acquaintance. At first the maid had pooh-pooh'd her, thinking her to be in gin and not able to tell one baby from another as she saw so many. Then the wet nurse had lost her temper and flounced off so the maid had conquered her fear of goblins and gone in to see for herself. "Adelaide!" she'd shrieked—and then tumbled straight out into the street shouting, "She's back! Miss Adelaide's come back!"

Actually it turned out that Mrs. Harris, drinking soup at the Bostocks', had heard the cry some moments before anyone else, but had not dared to say so for fear she should be imagining it; but then Morgan heard it, and then everyone did. They all rushed out in a terrific commotion—the Bostocks included—and sure enough, Adelaide was back!

All this was told to the openmouthed Harris at such a rate and with so many interruptions—for the sisters disagreed on details—that the poor boy was quite bewildered and kept staring round the room in helpless amazement.

"But who—" he managed at length, "but who did it?"

"Why that inquiry agent, of course. Mr. Raven. It was all his doing."

Harris nodded. Mr. Raven, of course...

"And Ma says you're to go down to the Old Ship and ask him to lunch. Go on, hurry up now. Adelaide'll still be here when you come back!"

But the inquiry agent was not at the Old Ship. Nor was he still outside the house of the Hemps. Eight o'clock had been and gone and no pistol shot had broken the morning air. The murder had been forestalled—as he'd hoped it would—so Mr. Raven had clumped off to Dr. Bunnion's school to pick up the traces of his archenemy Brett. But when he got there he found the school in an end-of-term confusion with no one willing or able to help him. Not a soul seemed to know where the devil Brett had gone. Mrs. Bunnion, who had at last woken up, had gone flying out in a hopeless attempt to prevent the unnecessary duel, and the headmaster himself was doing what he could to conceal his agonized fear that Ralph, now two hours gone, was bleeding to death from Major Alexander's merciless bullet.

"Of course you know," said Mr. Raven, irritated by his casual reception, "that Brett was at the bottom of everything?"

Distractedly Dr. Bunnion nodded. "That is exactly what I keep telling my wife, sir."

"You villain, James Brett! You terrible, crafty, shocking villain! If Ma had only known, she'd never have let me fall in love with you!"

The time was shortly after nine o'clock; the place was the warmly dancing interior of the Southampton coach, now well on its way. The speaker was Tizzy Alexander, and her place was in the arms of her Mr. Brett. The cause of her censure was that Mr. Brett had just confessed to her his unusual part in the duel—and just what he'd done about it.

She was looking at him with great severity, and frowning with all her might. But the corners of her mouth, do what she would, kept tugging and twitching, and her shoulders were beginning to heave and shake. "James Brett," she began; but could say no more. Laughter engulfed her, helpless laughter that came bubbling up and exploding in her eyes. She rocked with it, and the coach rocked with her; and then Mr. Brett joined in and the tears ran from their eyes in shining streams while an outside passenger nearly overturned himself in an effort to see what was going on.

"But what else could I do?" gasped Mr. Brett. "What else could I do?"

Tizzy only shook her head and, when she was able to speak,

all she could say was, "Do you think they're still there?" and then she was off again.

At a quarter to ten o'clock, Major Alexander and his son, Adam, cold, wet and ankles awash—for the tide was coming in—retreated from the seashore. "As I suspected," said the Major with grim satisfaction. "The fellow's a coward and won't face me!"

High on the Downs, near where Adelaide had been found, Ralph Bunnion and his party waited perhaps five minutes longer on account of not wanting to disappoint Sir Walter and to outface a small number of spectators who were beginning to jeer.

"I knew the swine was craven when I first clapped eyes on him," grunted the baronet. "All those damned military fellows are the same. Shoot your eyes out with a cannon, but not with a pistol. You have to get too close for that!"

Then they too left the dueling ground, with Frederick half glad his pistols had not been put to the test.

"And what the devil happened to that fellow Brett?" said Sir Walter as they walked along.

"And where was Mr. Brett?" said Adam Alexander to his father as they neared the school.

But it was not until the thwarted duelists met that they discovered Mr. Brett's duplicity.

"I told him that it was to be on the beach by the Old Ship," said Major Alexander furiously.

"He told me it was to be on the Downs," said Ralph Bunnion, equally annoyed.

"The man's a damned scoundrel!" said Major Alexander. "He has insulted an affair of honor!"

Mr. Brett had taken the only advantage possible in being second to both parties. He had arranged for them to meet some three miles apart.

"I warned you!" snarled the Major, glaring at Dr. Bunnion's knees. "I told you the man was furtive, underhand and sly!" Then he went off with Ralph and Sir Walter to Ralph's room where, heedless of gathering parents, the three men of blood and honor drowned their furious disappointment and humiliation in bottomless tankards of claret as red as their unshed blood.

Mrs. Alexander shrugged her ample shoulders and muttered something in her native tongue. Then her eye fell upon her firebrand son, Adam. She smiled sadly at him, and he, touched, laid his arm around her shoulders. Who knows, she wondered to herself in German, perhaps, in time, I might make something of him?

Mrs. Bunnion alone still had a good word to say for Mr. Brett; and whenever her husband recalled his treachery, she always defended him warmly and declared she couldn't believe it of him. Then Dr. Bunnion would smile and say, "What a heart you have, my love. Generous to a fault."

As for the headmaster himself, now that all his fears had proved groundless and nothing disagreeable had happened, he was more convinced than ever that nothing was to be gained by facing an unpleasantness but a nasty shock.

Mr. Raven did not have lunch with the Harrises on that memorable Saturday, even though they pressed him to stay. He had sworn that he'd not break bread with them even if they begged him on bended knees. He did not want their lunch and he scorned their hospitality. He suspected he'd have been asked to eat in the kitchen. Besides, his work there was done.

The return of Adelaide he took as a matter of course; he was pleased but not surprised. According to his plan, it had been bound to happen—and happen it had. The greater triumph was what had not happened. There had been no murder. This was indeed a feather in his cap; but alas, not the one he really wanted. Brett had escaped him. At the last minute he must have decided that the inquiry agent had come too close. So Mr. Raven was on his way to Southampton to track his adversary down. He and his boot would be the eternal pursuers, and Mr. Brett and his paramour would be the eternal pursued. To the ends of the earth he'd follow them, with his terrible tap-thump...tap-thump...

Had Tizzy and James been aware of this, they might indeed have been chilled; but the ship that took them to the crisp New World was too full of dreaming to let so lame a nightmare in; and the raven had no wings.

But back to that tremendous Saturday once more. One small mishap marred the general rejoicing in the homes of the Bostocks and the Harrises. Mrs. Bostock, returning unexpectedly from the Harrises, came upon her son attempting to dry out her quilt that had vanished mysteriously on the previous day and now appeared even more mysteriously. Despite Bostock's protests, she snatched it from him, and then she recoiled. It stank of fish, gin, babies and a very powerful odor that seemed to be compounded of brandy and burned cake. And so, Mrs. Bostock remembered, did the infant Adelaide.

She communicated this interesting fact to her husband who at once passed it on to Dr. Harris. The two fathers stared at each other. They grew very pale. Then, basely acting on suspicion alone, Captain Bostock thrashed Bostock with an old belaying pin he kept as a souvenir; but Dr. Harris, who was a more cultured man altogether, smote Harris with a volume of Harvey's *Circulation of the Blood*.

"Violence," said Harris the younger bitterly. "Personal violence. And only on suspicion, too."

"My pa said it was natural justice," mumbled Bostock, whose thicker feelings had not been so outraged.

"Justice? What's that? There ain't no such thing as justice, Bosty. It—it's just the calling card of brute force. Mark my words, Bosty; beware of the man who says he's just. He's the one who's out to get you if he can!"

Deeply impressed, Bostock nodded, and the two friends thereupon made a solemn pact to steer clear of justice in all its forms.

At the school Adam Alexander filled the vacancy created by the elopement of Mr. Brett, so Major Alexander's schemes at last bore a somewhat mottled fruit. Whether there was any justice in this or not is neither here nor there. It happened in accordance with the way of the world which is chiefly concerned with convenience.

The Night of the Comet

Chapter One

LOVE TURNS men into angels and women into devils. Take Cassidy, of Cassidy & O'Rourke, Slaters, Thatchers, General Roofers and Sundries. He was a liar, a rogue, and so light-fingered it was a wonder that, while he slept, his hands didn't rise to the ceiling of their own accord. Whenever there was a night without a moon, suspicion naturally fell on Cassidy.

Yet there he sat, in the back of the cart, as good as gold and singing of Molly Malone and her wheelbarrow, and cockles and mussels, alive, alive-o! While O'Rourke did all the work.

It was early on the Wednesday after Easter and four days before the comet. The sun was as bright as knives.

"There's somethin' in the air, O'Rourke!" said Cassidy suddenly, with a sniff like a gale going backwards.

"Fish," said O'Rourke. "Stinking fish."

Cassidy shook his head. He sniffed again and went as pale as it was possible for one of his complexion, which had something of brick, something of slate, and a good deal of the weather about it.

"'Tis the place!" he whispered. "I feel it in me bones,

O'Rourke. What's the name on the signpost? For pity's sake, tell me, O'Rourke!"

It wasn't that Cassidy was hard of seeing. Far from it. In the old days he could have picked out a silver sixpence in a farmer's fist fifty yards off. It was just that he traveled propped among bundles and sacks with his face pointing backwards, so it would have been a great effort for him to sit up and turn around.

"Brighton," read out O'Rourke, a long, bony, melancholy man, with hands and feet the size of spades.

"Brighton!" repeated Cassidy with a sigh, as if that one word encompassed all the hopes of journey's end.

A year and a day they'd been going, in their old green cart with a pony that looked as if it had come through a storm of dapples and never been wiped down.

They'd jerked and jingled down every street of every town and village from Liverpool all the way around to here and now. They'd stared up into every window and knocked on every door, looking and looking for a girl by the name of Mary Flatley, who'd made an honest man of Cassidy by the contrary means of stealing away with his heart.

She'd gone from Dublin one fine day (that was the blackest in Cassidy's life), with bag and baggage and left not a word behind, except, "Tell that smarmy villain Cassidy I'm gone to England to make me fortune and get a husband who'll not gawp and drool at everythin' in skirts! Tell him I'm done with him—the dirty philanderin' rogue!"

She must have loved him dearly to have had such a devil of a temper where he was concerned.

"In Dublin's fair city, where girls are so pretty," sang Cassidy, regardless of the fact that such a state of affairs had been his downfall.

"I first set me eyes on sweet Molly Malone!"

While O'Rourke, who was strong on Sundries, boomed, "Tiles and slates! Chairs to mend! Pots, kettles, and pans!"

The cart turned down a little street of flint-cobbled houses that sparkled like trinket boxes in the sun. Cassidy gazed up at the windows, but O'Rourke stared down at the ground.

Such was his nature. He was a gloomy man, whose very name sounded like a raven's croak: *O'Rourke! O'Rourke!*

Every night, while Cassidy slept, he went around the grave-yards with a lantern, reading the tombstones in the hope of not finding Mary Flatley under one of them.

Many was the sexton and late-night walker who'd seen the bony figure glimmering among the inscriptions and mourn-fully shaking his head.

"Are you looking for somebody in particular?"

"That I am. And may the flowers I'll lay on her grave not show their ugly faces above the ground till after me dying day!"

It would have killed Cassidy if he'd known what O'Rourke was up to, but somebody had to do it. For how could Mary Flatley turn out to be alive if nobody had made sure she wasn't dead?

They stopped at the first house. Cassidy smartened himself up and went around to the side, while the two brass buttons on the back of his old green coat kept a sharp watch on O'Rourke in case he decamped.

Not that O'Rourke would really have left him, even though he'd sworn that, one of these fine days, Cassidy would come back and there in the street waiting for him would be no cart and no O'Rourke.

Cassidy knocked, and a maid, armed with a coal shovel, opened the door.

"No hawkers!" said she, pointing to a notice Cassidy might have seen for himself if he'd had eyes in his head.

"And quite right, too! But on me honor, I've never dealt in hawks in me life, the terrible, sharp-eyed things! Have ye a hole in yer roof or a chair that needs mendin', me darlin' with the cherry lips and blackberry eyes?"

Cassidy had kissed the Blarney stone, all right, but by the squashed-in look of his nose, it must have been more of a collision than a kiss. There was none of your cheap good looks about Cassidy.

"Be off with you, you no-good Irish loafer!" said the maid, brandishing the coal shovel and preparing to shut the door, preferably with some portion of Cassidy in it. How was she to know that Cassidy was an angel now?

"Are ye acquainted," asked Cassidy hopefully, "with a lass by the name o' Mary Flatley? She's black hair and green eyes and a look on her that would bring Dublin Castle tumblin' down. Mary Flatley—though she might be wed to another, and I pray to God that she ain't, for she's been gone a year and a day, so she'll be just after eighteen!"

But the door had slammed long before he'd finished, so it was to the hardhearted wood he called out, "If ye should happen to see her, just say that Cassidy's come!"

He went back to the cart, and O'Rourke, who undertook all expressions of a gloomy nature, sighed. Nobody could have expected Cassidy to have done it for himself.

They applied at the next house, but with no more success, and so on all the way down the street. At last they came to a well-appointed residence with a pair of anchors propped up on either side of the front door, which seemed to declare that the owner would go no more a-sailing and had dropped those articles for good and all in a neat green harbor with a gravel path leading up to the front door.

Cassidy cleaned his nails on his teeth and went around to

the side. He knocked, and a female, all sails set, came to the door on a gust of freshly ironed linen. Cassidy took a step back. He felt she could have blown him clean out of the water.

"D'ye need yer roof mendin', ma'am?"

"I'll ask the master."

She shut the door and went away. Cassidy tried the door, but it was only from force of habit. The female came back.

"The master says there's two tiles off at the back. He'll give you five shillings to make it all shipshape and Bristol-fashion. But no thieving, mind! The master's a magistrate, so watch out!"

"Me thieve from you, ma'am?" said Cassidy, who could no more keep from courtesy than a cat from cream. "Why, 'tis me own heart ye'll be thievin' from me! But tell me, are ye acquainted with—"

The door was shut before he could so much as say "Mary."

He went back to the cart and told O'Rourke.

"A magistrate's house? No good will come of it, Cassidy."

"But it's the one, Mr. O'Rourke! It's the house!"

"How d'ye know that?"

"I feel it in me bones!"

"I'm warnin' ye, Cassidy."

"And I'm tellin' ye, O'Rourke. She's here!"

They took a pair of ladders off the cart and carried them around to the back, where a moldy old ginger cat fled at their approach and took refuge in an apple tree.

O'Rourke lashed the ladders together, and, when raised, they reached about two feet below the eaves. Cassidy began to mount. O'Rourke had no head for heights and consequently was always full of admiration for Cassidy's daring.

At every window Cassidy paused for a glimpse of the girl who'd have brought Dublin Castle tumbling down, while, below, O'Rourke prayed she'd not turn out to be high up, as the sudden sight of her would surely have done the same for Cassidy.

As Cassidy climbed, he leaned from side to side to take in a window almost out of reach. Sometimes he clung to the ladder with only one hand, so that, in his long green coat, he looked like a tottery caterpillar waving at the edge of a leaf.

From time to time he'd nod and raise a courteous finger to his head in recognition of having been caught looking in by somebody looking out.

In a lower parlor he saw the master of the house, a fine-looking old gentleman with seafaring eyes. Himself was sitting in a high-backed chair, and his poor gouty foot, all in a winding-sheet of bandaging and looking like the Raising of Lazarus, was sitting in another.

Cassidy saluted him, and the old gentleman scowled and made several upward jerking movements with his stick. Cassidy continued and at intervals saw and was seen by the tremendous female who'd answered the door and who seemed to be floating upward inside the house, like a wandering balloon.

He saw the lady of the house, a fine figure of a woman, who came to her window and asked him what the devil he was doing. Cassidy said he'd been on his way to mend the roof when suddenly he thought he'd gone too high and seen an angel, which was her ladyship's self.

The last window under the roof was all over stars, not on account of its altitude but because there was hardly an inch of it that wasn't cracked.

Cassidy looked in. He saw, seated at a table, not so much a broth of a boy but more of a stew, as he was on the thick and lumpish side. He was deeply engaged in trying to insert a small ship into a large bottle.

There was a card lying on the table, and Cassidy, by twisting his head almost off at the neck, was able to read it. Covered all over with hearts and arrows, it said: "FOR MARY."

Cassidy nearly fell with the shock of it. He recovered himself and tapped on the window, and a piece of glass fell out.

The boy looked up and, in his sudden fright, thrust the ship against the neck of the bottle with such force that the ship was instantly destroyed.

Cassidy said through the narrow triangle of air, "If that's for Mary Flatley, I'll trouble ye not to lay eyes on her again and tell her that Cassidy's come!"

The boy stared at the star-crossed face at the window and then at the shipwreck in his hands.

"It was for Mary Harris. And you've broke my window and I'll get the blame."

"So it's another Mary altogether!" cried Cassidy, unable to believe that there were two of them. "Heaven be praised, as we've both had a near escape!"

They stared at each other: the one mournful, though his Mary lived but two streets away, and the other beaming all over his face, though his Mary might have been anywhere from Brighton all the way around to Newcastle. Thus the two lovers met in midair.

"And is her hair as black as a raven's wing?" inquired Cassidy professionally, resting his elbow on the sill and cupping his chin in his palm, so that O'Rourke, down below, felt like shaking him off the ladder to remind him that he ought to be going up it.

"It's a sort of brown," said the boy. "I think."

"And are her eyes full of a green fire so bright that all the world goes dark when she sinks her lashes and puts it out?"

"No," said the boy. "They're a sort of brown, too. With speckles."

"That's a shame!" cried Cassidy. "But maybe she'll be able to see well enough without 'em one day!"

"Speckles," said the boy defensively. "Not spectacles."

A ship's bell clanged somewhere in the house. Four times.

"It's for me," said the boy, and went.

Cassidy examined the room. There were ships' posters all over the walls, advising able-bodied seamen, desirous of sailing to foreign ports, to present themselves aboard at ungodly hours of the morning.

Cassidy saw that all the vessels' names had been scored out and "Mary Harris" written in their place. It seemed that from China to the Cape there was no way to go but under the flag of the lass with the speckled eyes.

"Ah, but he's got it bad!" sighed Cassidy with all the satisfaction of finding a fellow sufferer.

He longed to compare symptoms and exchange pangs, for love is a sickness like any other, save nobody wants to be cured. A great tremble went through him, but this was because O'Rourke had shaken the ladder.

Cassidy went up and peered over the edge of the roof. Sure enough, two slates were gone, and you could see that, at the first breath of a wind strong enough to lift a feather, another dozen would be gone. The batten was halfway to being rotten, and all things considered, a new roof would be cheaper in the long run and twenty pounds well spent.

He came down and told O'Rourke, adding that there was a window broken that might bring in another shilling.

They knocked on the door and put it to the housekeeper, who went away and put it to the master, who put it that Cassidy and O'Rourke were a pair of loafing Irish rogues and five shillings was all they were going to get.

They went out to the cart, and Cassidy said, "It was another Mary, O'Rourke! Would ye believe it?"

O'Rourke nodded and sighed. They returned to the back of the house with rope and tackle and a basket of slates. Cassidy climbed the ladder again and looked in at the window under the roof.

The boy was back and with a friend. The friend was smallish and pale and gave off a strong sense of ink and intelligence. They stared at Cassidy in a state of suspended conversation.

Cassidy raised a finger in salute, and his heart went out to the first boy on whose face was frozen a look of boundless hope and boundless despair.

It was a lover's look if ever Cassidy had seen one, and he'd have given his right arm to have been of any help.

Then he and the ladder shuddered together, and O'Rourke shouted up, "Will ye get a move on, Cassidy, or ye'll be as old as Mary Flatley's grandfather by the time ye get down!"

Chapter Two

THE LARGER boy—and the room's principal inhabitant—was Bostock. He was thirteen and a half and stood, in a manner of speaking, on the threshold of manhood. In fact, he'd knocked on the door but as yet had received no definite answer.

His visitor was Harris, who, with a look of piercing inquiry, stood right behind him. Bostock wanted to *do*; Harris wanted to *know*.

They were friends and had been through thick and thin together, for which nature seemed to have formed them, Harris being thin and Bostock very thick.

At the present moment, however, their friendship was in the balance, as the Mary Bostock loved was Harris's sister.

Now Harris had several sisters, but unfortunately it seemed that Bostock had picked the most valuable and had nothing comparable to offer in return.

Harris had put it to him fairly, hence Bostock's boundless despair. Then Harris had made an offer, hence Bostock's boundless hope. Then he'd thought about it, hence the confusion of feeling that was reflected in his face.

They waited for Cassidy to vanish upward, then they resumed their conversation.

"Bosty, old friend," said Harris sincerely, "let me put it to you this way."

Bostock sighed, so Harris pointed out that Bostock, being the only known child of Captain Bostock, retired, was, in law, the heir to all his property.

Bostock agreed.

Harris went on. He didn't mean to suggest that Captain Bostock was in any immediate danger of "going out with the tide," as that sailorly man would have expressed it, but only that he was unlikely to be in full possession of his health and strength for some time to come.

Bostock looked doubtful, but Harris, being the son of Dr. Harris, who was looking after Captain Bostock's gout, and therefore in a position to know what he was talking about, assured Bostock that the captain would be unable to rise from his sick-chair and enjoy his property on the upper floors in the foreseeable future.

Bostock nodded. So far he was with Harris.

Therefore, said Harris, the property had passed, as it were, into the regency of Bostock, as it wasn't to be supposed his ma wanted it. It was in Bostock's gift, which any court in the land would uphold, and Captain Bostock himself, being a Justice of the Peace, would find it hard to deny. Not that Harris advised consulting him, but it was something to bear in mind.

Harris smiled and rested his case.

The property that particularly interested him and had given rise to these ingenious arguments was Captain Bostock's brass telescope. It was kept in a small room at the top of the house, known as the Crow's Nest, and was well beyond Captain Bostock's present range of activity.

Harris's reasons for wanting it were about as lofty as you could get. The heavens themselves. Pigott's comet, which was rushing across the sky at the rate of about an inch a night, foretelling the deaths of kings, the fall of governments, and other national benefits, was predicted to appear at its brightest on Saturday night, April 6. This was in three days' time.

Although the comet could hardly be seen at all and at best would appear as something between a bright pinprick and a flaming pimple, there was to be an outing to the top of Devil's Dyke to view the grandeur of the occasion.

There was to be chicken, veal pies, cheese, wine, and lemonade for the children. Also, if the weather proved kind, there was to be music and dancing. Pigott's comet, which, by the way, was a highly undistinguished object, would have been enchanted if it had known.

Everybody was looking forward to the occasion, and great plans were afoot for going with this or that companion and falling under the comet's romantic spell. In fact, you might have thought it was a kind of speedy Cupid, visiting Brighton for the Easter holidays and showering arrows down on the town.

But not on Harris. While every Jack thought of his Jill, Harris thought of Captain Bostock's brass telescope.

He'd always wanted it, but until Captain Bostock had been laid low with gout and Bostock had been laid low with love, he'd seen no way of getting it.

Now, however, with the happy onset of the two diseases— the one in Bostock's heart and the other in Captain Bostock's toe—he saw his way clear to realizing his ambition. In exchange for what was almost Bostock's telescope he felt himself able to offer the affections of his sister Mary.

He promised faithfully to advise and assist Bostock to the utmost of his ability and to leave no stone unturned in bringing Mary to heel. He gave him his solemn word that Mary would be his companion for the night of the comet.

Bostock beamed, and Harris shook him by the hand.

"There, Bosty, old friend! I can't say fairer than that! Now just get the telescope."

Bostock's beam faded and was replaced by a look of creeping doubt. He couldn't help feeling that something might go wrong. He didn't know why he should feel like that, with Harris looking so confident; it was just that there was a vague shadow at the back of his mind that worried him. As there wasn't much at the front of it, anything at the back was worrying.

Harris watched him closely. "You do want her, Bosty?"

"Oh, yes, yes!"

"Then get the telescope, old friend."

Bostock fidgeted. He longed to find some way out of his dilemma without appearing to question Harris's wisdom.

He respected Harris. He admired Harris beyond anybody else in the world. But did not Harris think his case was really hopeless? Mary was such a scornful, slender, acrobatic girl, and she never gave him a second glance unless it was to express twice the disdain she'd shown in her first.

How could Harris, brilliant as he was, have dominion over so wild and free a heart? Surely it was asking too much.

It wasn't.

"I know her, Bosty, old friend," said Harris. "She's my sister, flesh of my flesh and bone of my bone. I know her through and through, like a pane of glass." He smiled dreamily. "We were in the same womb, Bosty," he murmured reminiscently, and Bostock received an indistinct picture of Harris, in a warm dark place, scientifically observing Mary growing more complicated, month by month.

"But—but what if my pa gets better and goes up to the Crow's Nest?" pleaded Bostock, finding another avenue of escape.

"My pa says he'll be lucky to be on his feet by Christmas," said Harris, closing it. "And he's dosing him, so he ought to know."

"But—but after that?"

"Then I'll lend it to you back again," said Harris. "Until it's yours for good."

Bostock thanked him, and then the awful solemnity hinted at by "yours for good" saddened him.

"I think I'll be sorry, you know, when he goes. Out with the tide, I mean."

"It's got to happen to all of them," said Harris, carefully excluding himself. "Someday."

There was a pause in which they both stared at Cassidy's stoutly gaitered feet, shifting on the rung of the ladder. Then Harris, judging that he'd allowed enough time for Bostock to recover from his pa's future death, murmured, "The telescope, old friend."

Bostock said unhappily, "But how are we going to get it out without being seen, Harris?"

Harris pointed to Cassidy's feet.

"But what if my pa sees it going down past his window?"

"I'll go and ask after his toe. That'll take his mind off the window."

"But he said he never wanted to set eyes on you again for as long as he lived, Harris. And my ma says that aggravation only makes him worse."

"Makes him worse?" said Harris with a smile. "Then he won't be up till *after* Christmas, will he! The telescope, old friend!"

"You think of everything, Harris," said Bostock with unwilling admiration.

He left the room and in a little while came back with Harris's heart's desire. It was a sleek and beautiful object, of the brightest brass, that opened and shut like a flexible sunbeam. It had a neat leather cap at either end, like a pair of stoppers for keeping the more stirring sights within.

Somewhere inside its long dark heart, between glass and glass, there must have been a thousand dreaming ships, some becalmed, with sails as limp as Monday shirts, some leaning dangerously into the wind, and some in a kind of nightmare, dashing themselves angrily against rocks, as if to rid themselves of the tiny, itching figures that would not let go and be drowned.

Harris, raptly gazing at it, saw, in addition to Pigott's comet, stars of unimaginable brightness and planets hitherto unknown that would shortly bear a name. He saw Harris Minor, orbiting the sun, and Harris Major, constellated around with a host of lesser lights, among which would be a Moon of Bostock, for friendship's sake.

Cassidy, looping his green length down to pick another slate out of the basket, was also captivated by the splendid instrument. He saw himself sitting on a shoulder of the Downs, raking out all the streets until he saw Mary Flatley, maybe as she shook a sheet out of an upstairs window. And he'd call out, "Cassidy's come!"

Up she'd look, with her bright green eyes, and smile, for sure to God, she'd be near enough to touch, though she was a hundred miles away!

Even Bostock was stirred. He saw himself with Mary Harris,

right on the top of Devil's Dyke. He saw Saturday night as if it were here and now, for was it not the business of a telescope to bring what was far away near at hand?

He gave the telescope to Harris and received in exchange the absolute assurance of Mary's heart.

Harris opened the window and asked Cassidy if he would be good enough to take the article to a house, two streets away.

Cassidy, descending to a convenient height, took the instrument, removed the stoppers, and placed it to his eye. A sweeping blur of blue and green communicated itself to him, and then O'Rourke's face, with all its bristles and lugubrious aggravation, came up at him like a cannonball.

Deeply impressed by the nearness of his partner, he gave the instrument back and said it was a wonderful terrible thing, and it would cost a silver sixpence to take it, if Bostock was sure it was his own property, else why wasn't he taking it down by the stairs with his own two hands and out the front door like a Christian?

Harris said that any court in the land would uphold Bostock's rights over the property, so that whether it went out by the window or down by the stairs was of no consequence whatever, and threepence was his last offer.

Cassidy said to Bostock that his friend had the brain of a Jesuit, the way it went around corners in a straight line, and that fivepence was his last offer as he had overheads to think of, in the way of O'Rourke and the pony, and that threepence would have meant a penny each, which was insulting to man and beast.

Harris retired to the back of the room and conferred with Bostock.

"Fourpence," he said, coming back.

"Fourpence ha'penny," said Cassidy. "And have ye got it?"

Bostock produced the money—which was all he had—and Cassidy reached.

"On delivery," said Harris. "I'll be waiting."

"He'll end up as Pope," said Cassidy admiringly. "If the Protestants don't get to him first!"

Harris handed over the telescope.

"And which house is it to be?"

"Two streets down that way. You can't miss it. There's a brass plate outside. Dr. Harris."

"Harris, did he say?"

Bostock nodded.

"Not the Harris that belongs with that same Mary with the speckled eyes?"

Bostock nodded again.

"Then why didn't ye tell me in the first place?" cried Cassidy. "I'd have taken the article for nothing and been proud to! But now it's too late. I can't go back on me word. Oh, 'tis the very devil to be an honest man!"

He laid the telescope in the basket.

"May it bring us all our hearts' desires! A Mary for you, and a Mary for me, and health, wealth, and happiness for yer friend!"

Harris vanished, and Bostock watched the basket descend. Suddenly he had the terrible feeling of one who has not only burned his boats but neglected to get off them first. He wanted to call the telescope back, but it was too late. The basket was down, and in a moment Cassidy and his father's property had vanished from sight.

Chapter Three

CASSIDY had a terrible fight with the telescope. It kept slithering out from under his arm and standing bolt upright before him, like a brass serpent with a glass eye.

"Cass-ss-idy! Cass-ss-idy! Ye'd get a couple of pounds if ye slipped me to a pawnshop and nobody would be any the wiser!"

"Be silent, ye filthy beast!" cried Cassidy, grasping it around the neck as if he'd strangle it. "I'm an honest man!"

"Cass-ss-idy! Cass-ss-idy! Maybe even two pounds ten?"

"Hold yer tongue, ye brassy snake! Another word and I'll wrap ye 'round a railing and then ye'll not be worth a farthin' of anybody's money!"

So Cassidy fought with the devil all the way, but love had turned him into an angel, so he conquered in the end.

He found Dr. Harris's house without difficulty. He knew it for a doctor's right away, for beside the tradesman's door was a long stone trough on four carved paws, looking exactly like a coffin standing in its stockinged feet.

Not that Dr. Harris was a bad physician or would have advertised so plainly even if he had been. He had bought the trough when an old mansion at the top of the street had been pulled down to make way for a row of smart new villas. It was going to have flowers in it, but in the meantime it was used by butchers' boys, bakers' boys, and fishmongers' boys, who hid in it and frightened the wits out of the Harrises' maid by pretending to be dead.

As Cassidy approached, a hand rose out of the tomb and beckoned. It was Harris's. He lay in the tomb like a crusader, among earwigs, beetles, and leaves.

He was very much relieved to see Cassidy as the thought had crossed his mind, too, that the telescope would have been worth more than fourpence ha'penny, had Cassidy so desired. Harris had, in fact, been wondering, if the worse came to the worst and the telescope vanished from human sight, would he still be liable for the affections of Mary, or could he return Bostock's money and call it a day?

But Cassidy had turned up, so he handed over Bostock's money, and Cassidy handed over Captain Bostock's telescope. Bostock himself was not present, as Harris had told him to smarten himself up, as women, like moths, were attracted to clothes.

Harris had discovered this, both from personal observation and from a learned article on Courtship that he had consulted on Bostock's behalf. It was "The Courtship of Animals," but Harris did not see that it made any difference, and there was now lodged in his enormous brain a quantity of interesting information which he hoped to put into effect.

"Are ye acquainted with a lass—" began Cassidy, wondering if fate might at last reward him for his honesty and produce Mary Flatley then and there.

There came the sound of the front door opening. Instantly Harris and the telescope sank into obscurity, so Cassidy, raising a finger in salute, strolled back to the street.

He saw that a girl had come out of the Harris front door. She was dressed in pink-and-white spotted muslin and wore an Easter bonnet fit to charm the birds.

It was (or Cassidy was a Dutchman!) the Mary with the speckled eyes! At once he thought of the anguished lover at the window, and he felt an overwhelming desire to be of help. Perhaps, he thought, someone might do the same for him one day.

"And—and is it Miss Harris I'm addressin'?" he asked, hastening to catch up with her, for she went like a wind through a rose garden, all rustles and scent.

He asked to make sure, for God knew what mischief would follow if he got the wrong girl! Cassidy was nobody's fool!

She turned. It was her, all right. She had speckled eyes and her brother's little face, only she'd so improved on it that it was chalk and cheese and you'd not have known if she hadn't come out of the same house and answered to the same name.

"Yes? I'm Miss Harris. What do you want?"

"'Tis not what I want, me darlin'," he said. "Though were me heart me own ye should have it directly. I speak for another."

She looked at him in astonishment, then frowned angrily and tried to pass. But Cassidy, hopping backwards in front of her, kept pace and talked so eloquently on another's behalf that even a maid shaking a duster out of an upstairs window of one of the smart new villas could see his white teeth gleaming and his eyes gawping, right through the back of his head.

"I speak for him who's eatin' out his heart for the love of ye," panted Cassidy. "Oh, pity him, me darlin', for he's as fine a young man as ye're likely to meet with this side o' the grave!"

Miss Harris, still frowning so that Cassidy despaired of softening her heart, stepped this way and that, so that she and he seemed engaged in a sprightly springtime dance, she in dainty muslin and Cassidy in hopeless green.

Although she would like to have heard rather more about it, she wasn't going to lower herself in front of all the neighbors by bandying words with a flat-nosed Irish loafer with his syrupy words and treacly smile.

And yet... and yet he'd said somebody loved her. It was a good thing to have heard on a Wednesday morning, no matter from whom.

"Take pity on him!" Cassidy pleaded again, and Miss Harris, in spite of herself, racked her brains to discover on whom it was that she should take pity.

Although she wouldn't have admitted it for worlds, nobody sprang readily to mind.

She did not think of Bostock. She never thought of Bostock. And why should she? She was Miss Dorothy Harris, and she would have died of shame if she'd known that she'd been mistaken for her younger sister Mary.

At last she evaded Cassidy and stalked away, her mind an absolute ferment of young men who, just possibly, might have been madly in love with her.

Cassidy kissed his hand after her back and went off to find O'Rourke, feeling that he'd given love a helping hand.

"In Dublin's fair city, where girls are so pretty," he sang blithely.

"I first set me eyes on sweet Molly Malone!"

The maid at the upstairs window stopped shaking out her duster, and there was a look on her face that would have brought a good deal more than Dublin Castle tumbling down. It was Mary Flatley!

"So it's yerself, Michael Cassidy!" she sobbed. "Down there

in the street and smarmin' up to another bit of skirt in front of me very eyes! I'll give ye Molly Malone! Oh, Cassidy, Cassidy! Ye're a philanderin' villain with no heart but an onion, that ye peel and peel and find nothin' but tears! I'll give me heart and hand to the fishmonger's son!" she wept wildly. "For he's as true as ye are false! Though he's an Englishman and as quiet as a mouse and will never talk of raven's wings, nor sing, nor dance, he'll not make me cry, neither. I'll have him today if he asks. And ye've only yer wickedly wheedlin' self to blame!"

She shook her fist after the cheerfully singing Cassidy and then after the back of Dorothy Harris. She dried her eyes on the curtain and slammed down the window so that the glass cracked from side to side.

Chapter Four

DOROTHY Harris walked on toward the heart of the town. She was to meet her friend, Maggie Hemp, in Collier's Chocolate and Coffee Shop and talk about what they would wear for Saturday night on Devil's Dyke. As they were both, for the time being, without lovers, they meant to go together and stroll, laughingly, arm in arm, and watch the goings-on with disinterested amusement, come what may.

She walked quite briskly to begin with, and then fell into a gentle saunter, in which her head drooped, in musing contemplation of the cobbles. Then she looked up and hastened; then she slowed down again.

These changes in her pace reflected changes in her thoughts. That Irishman. What had he meant? She didn't really know what to make of it. Had he been making fun of her? Why should he do such a thing?

Common sense told her she ought to dismiss the whole thing from her mind. If she *did* have an unknown admirer, then surely she'd have known about it by now. And anyway, he wouldn't have left it to an Irish loafer to pass the good news on.

On the other hand, there *were* people who were so agonizingly shy that they ate their hearts out in private and went to their graves without ever opening their hearts to the girls they loved. You read about them—in books.

Yet if a person *was* so agonizingly shy, would he have confided his most sacred feelings to a perfect stranger? It wasn't very likely.

On the other hand (Miss Harris's mind was very full of hands that morning, and they all had a finger in the pie), *someone* had told the Irishman, for how else did he know her name and where to find her? That was a fact, and there was no getting around it, no matter how hard you tried.

So she walked, and so she mused, while the sun struck through her straw bonnet and dappled her face with flying gold—as if to add to her confusion.

"Could it be...him?" she wondered, giving way to the Dorothy part of her nature, and fixing on a distant youth who lived in one of the new villas and had once smiled at her absentmindedly. "Could it really be him?"

"No!" answered the Harris portion, which was rather more scientific and not given to flights of fancy. "It couldn't possibly be! He hardly knows you're alive!"

She walked on.

"But what if it's...him?" thought Dorothy, loitering again.

"Oh, I hope *not*!" declared the Harris half, shaking the jointly owned head. "I couldn't bear it! What would you say to him? Oh, no! Not him!"

She clutched her bonnet strings and hurried on in mock alarm, as if this last, undesirable one were already at her heels.

She slowed down.

"I don't suppose there's any chance that—that it could be...him?"

The Harris part didn't think so and, what was more, had some sharp words to say on the subject of foolish ambition and making herself a laughingstock. So she hastened on... until she found someone else in her Fortunatus's purse of dreams.

A young man driving a gig turned to look at her, either because she was behaving oddly or because there's always something heartwarming about the sight of a girl of fifteen and three-quarters smiling to herself and wearing the spring sunshine as if it had just been made for her.

Not that Dorothy Harris was what you would have called pretty. She wasn't likely to strike anyone all of a heap—unless she walked into him. She was small, like all the Harrises, but she certainly had an odd fascination, especially when she wasn't thinking about it.

She stared after the young man and instantly enrolled him as a suspect.

"Don't be ridiculous!" snapped the Harris in her. "You don't know him from Adam!"

"Oh, don't be such a wet blanket!" said Dorothy. "What ever would have happened to Eve if she'd listened to you!"

Collier's Chocolate and Coffee Shop was in Bartholomews, which was the oldest, noisiest, stoniest, fishiest part of the town. Most of the houses looked as if they'd been shrugged down North Street in a heap and were only just picking themselves up.

On Wednesdays, Thursdays, and Fridays, Mr. Collier served coffee or chocolate in delicate gold-edged cups for threepence, with a marzipan fancy for no extra charge.

Everybody went, and there was always a scramble for the best seats, which were in the new bow window that Mr. Collier, who liked to move with the times, had installed.

Maggie Hemp was there already. She beckoned imperiously to Dorothy, indicating through the window that she'd been guarding an empty chair with her life.

Eagerly Dorothy squeezed into Collier's; the doorway was still the old one and as narrow as sin. She joined her friend.

"Maggie!" she panted, sitting down with a flurry of muslin, and full to bursting with her news.

"You're late," said Miss Hemp coldly. She signaled to Mr. Collier, who was perambulating with his tray.

"Oh, Maggie!"

"I'll have one of those, Mr. Collier," said Miss Hemp, pointing thoughtfully to a marzipan crocus.

Dorothy bit her lip and picked a daffodil. She'd have picked Mr. Collier's thumb if it had been nearest, she was so impatient to talk.

"Maggie! You'll never guess what—"

"Mr. Collier!" called Miss Hemp, ignoring her.

"Yes, miss?"

"Could we have the sugar, please?"

"It's on the table, miss."

"Oh! Oh, I see."

"Maggie! You'll never guess what—"

"Dolly! Are you sitting on my glove?"

"No, I'm *not*! *Please*, Maggie, let me tell you what happened just now!"

"All right, Dolly," said Maggie Hemp, feeling that she'd punished her friend sufficiently for having been late. "Now you can tell me, dear."

So Dorothy, her spirits a little dashed, but reviving quickly, told Maggie about her meeting with the strange Irishman. She told it very amusingly and admitted that it was all probably nonsense and didn't mean anything at all. But wasn't it a strange thing to have happened?

She said it was nonsense not because she believed that it was but because she didn't want to make Maggie, who was rather touchy, jealous. She was rather hoping that they could both laugh and joke about who could possibly be in love with her. It seemed a pleasant subject.

However, as she rambled on, Maggie Hemp couldn't help noticing that Dolly kept staring around the room and even looking over her, Maggie's, shoulder to see who was passing by outside. Not even the burly fishermen who stumped into Saunders' Marine Stores and Fishing Tackle next door and came out in enormous new yellow boots were safe from her promiscuously roving eye.

Miss Hemp began to feel a little neglected. She felt that Dolly wasn't really with her. Also, she couldn't help feeling that, if the Irishman's words turned out to be only half true, then Dolly Harris would drop her like a hot potato, and that would be the end of Saturday night.

"He must have been off his head, Dolly!" said Miss Hemp briskly. "Or drunk, most likely. You know what those Irishmen are!"

"I *did* say it was probably all nonsense," said Dorothy. She was embarrassed to find that her wandering gaze had attracted a small boy, who, tired of gazing at unattainable shrimping nets and bouquets of mackerel knives next door, had come to make goldfish faces at her through the glass.

She blushed and concentrated again on her friend.

"But just for the sake of *supposing*, Maggie, who do you think it could be?"

"I really can't imagine, Dolly."

"But what if it's—"

"Oh, for goodness' sake, don't be so silly!" said Miss Hemp, losing patience. "I thought we were going to talk about Saturday night! We're still going, I suppose? You haven't changed your mind, Dolly?"

"Oh, no, Maggie! I wouldn't do a thing like that!"

"I can always find somebody else," said Miss Hemp warningly.

She was a year older than Dolly and a good deal prettier. She was particularly irritated as she'd felt she was doing Dolly Harris a favor by going with her. She had no intention of playing second fiddle to little Dolly's daydreams.

In fact, the more she thought about it the angrier she became. She believed Dolly had made the whole thing up. There never had been an Irishman . . . still less an unknown admirer. She began to bang her finger rhythmically against the edge of the table.

"I don't know why you're so cross, Maggie."

"I'm not in the least cross, Dolly. Why should I be cross with *you*, of all people?"

Dolly bit her lip. She wished she'd never told Maggie about her adventure. Somehow Maggie made it all seem so stupid. She shouldn't have told anybody. She should have kept it to herself. Nobody really understood the way she felt about things, except, possibly, that Mysterious Person, who also kept things to himself. *Who could he be?*

She picked up her cake and stared somewhat gloomily out the window, observing a young woman, in a green shawl and with a basket over her arm, going in to Saunders'.

"You haven't answered me, Dolly."

"I don't see what there is to talk about, Maggie."

"I asked you why you thought I should be cross with you."

"I don't know, Maggie. I really don't know . . . unless it's because you're jealous of what that Irishman told me."

"Jealous?" cried Miss Hemp, setting down her cup with a loud clatter. "*Jealous?* Me, jealous of *you*, Dolly Harris? Really, it's quite the funniest thing I've ever heard!"

She paused to express her merriment by a very ill-natured laugh indeed, and then went on to demolish her friend's pretensions by reminding her that she was hardly of a stature or appearance to drive men wild, and that, if it hadn't been for her—Miss Hemp's—generosity in the way of cast-off admirers, she wouldn't have got closer to a young man than to that stupid Pigott's comet!

Dorothy listened incredulously. She stood up. Her eyes were filled with tears.

"I hate you, Maggie Hemp! I really hate you!"

She left the table, and Miss Hemp, as a Parthian shot, offered, "And, what's more, Dolly Harris, I think you made the whole thing up. Unknown admirers, indeed! Pigs might fly, Dolly Harris, before I'll believe that!"

Blindly Dorothy left the shop and stumbled down the two steps outside. Her heart was in such a turmoil that she scarcely knew whether her adventure had taken place or not. She could only feel, as her one-time friend had pointed out, that she was plain, undersized, and unloved.

"Watch where ye're goin', miss!" cried the girl in the green shawl, coming out of Saunders' and knocking into her. "Oh! So it's yerself," she said, looking into Dorothy's face with angry recognition. "Well, ye can have him for all the good it'll do ye! Marry him today for all I care! And may he break his heart for the love of ye, which would serve him right!"

Dorothy tottered. She gaped. Her thoughts whirled around and around. It had happened again! She'd been told that somebody loved her! It hadn't been a dream, after all!

She looked back to Collier's. Maggie Hemp was standing in the doorway. She must have heard! Dorothy tossed her head.

So she'd made it all up, had she? Well! *Somebody* loved her. Somebody *loved* her. Somebody loved *her*, she thought, shifting the emphasis, like a figure in a quadrille, all the way down the line.

She marched away with her head in the air, every bit as high as Pigott's comet, while Mary Flatley stared after her, with eyes as green as unripe apples.

Then a fisherman's lad, in red-knitted cap and huge yellow boots, came out of Saunders' and led her away.

They had gone before Maggie Hemp had recovered herself sufficiently to demand the name of Dolly Harris's secret admirer.

Chapter Five

Miss HEMP remained standing in the doorway of Collier's, her breast heaving, her eyes flashing, her nostrils dilating, and her delicate, white-gloved fingers clenching and unclenching, like stricken blossoms. In addition to these little manifestations of her feelings, her left foot had begun to tap the ground with increasing force. There was no telling what it would all have come to if someone had not asked her to step aside as she was obstructing the entrance to the shop.

She scowled and walked away. She had heard enough—quite enough!—to realize that her friend had cruelly deceived her. Her friend—and Miss Hemp's lips curled scornfully over the word—had lied to her, had been deceitful and sly.

"Unknown admirer, indeed!" she muttered. "Oh, *very* unknown, when even a twopenny ha'penny servant girl knows all about him! *That's* a real mystery, that is! *That's* a *real* surprise! Ha—ha! 'I wonder who it can *be*, Maggie?'" she went on, imitating her friend's voice with bitter exaggeration. "'I really can't *imagine*! Who can have fallen in love with little *me*? Isn't it *strange*, Maggie? Isn't it *wonderful*, Maggie? Isn't it *mysterious*,

Maggie? Do you think it could all be on account of the *comet*, Maggie?'"

So Miss Hemp continued, jerking out her feelings, like teeth. Her anger fed on itself and drove tears into her eyes, so that she continually had to brush them aside.

She felt lonely and ill-used. Even though she was neat and pretty enough for young men to turn and look after her, nobody really liked her very much. She was just too honest. She never told lies herself, and if she thought anybody was being sly, she just came right out with it and said so. That was her nature and you could take it or leave it. Most people left it.

"You're a mean, sly beast, Dolly Harris!" she declared as she stalked along East Street.

"But *who could he be?*" she wondered, and she slowed down.

She shook her head and walked on quickly. Then she stopped; then she went on; then she stopped again, much as Dorothy had done, as a wide variety of young men presented themselves to her tortured mind.

"Could it be...him? Very likely! He's as sly as Dolly! Or... him? She's welcome to *that* one! But what if it was...him? Oh, the vile deceitful wretch! How could he? Oh, I hate and despise you all!"

She didn't know whether to be more hurt or angry that Dolly should have kept such a secret from her. Then she realized all of a sudden that Dolly had done it on purpose to trap her into speaking her mind!

Of course, that was it! Dolly must have known all along that Maggie would never have swallowed that cock-and-bull story about the Irishman! That's why she'd made it up! She'd done it on purpose to *force* poor, unsuspecting Maggie Hemp into a quarrel so she could get rid of her and go off to Devil's Dyke with her sly lover on her own!

"Oh, you nasty little calculating bitch!" cried Maggie

Hemp, her fury rising to great heights as she marched across North Street and was nearly knocked down by a cart. "Why couldn't you have come out with it instead of all that lying? Why couldn't you have said openly, 'Maggie dear, do you mind very much if we don't go and watch the comet together? You see, there's somebody else.' Why couldn't you have told the truth, you viper, you? I would have understood. I would have said: 'Of course, Dolly. I don't mind a bit.' But no! Not you, Dolly Harris! You're just like the rest of them, lying and cheating and being sly...like—like weasels and stoats and—and other things!"

As Miss Hemp's father was a butcher, it was only natural for her to associate the worst failings in character with animals you couldn't eat.

Poor Maggie Hemp! She never came across a deer or a nice tender lamb; she was always finding herself to be the one honest soul in a nasty sly world. And the worst of it was that when she found people out, they always turned on her in the cruelest way.

"Maggie Hemp!" someone once said to her after she'd told that person that she knew perfectly well what was going on. "You must have a mind like a corkscrew to think in the roundabout, twisted way you do!"

By the time she got home, her eyes were quite swollen from weeping, and the burning question of who was Dolly Harris's secret lover was still unanswered.

It so tormented her that she went straight up to her room and quite forgot her music lesson until her mother came to call her. She was a quarter of an hour late, and her teacher, Mr. Philip Top-Morlion, had become very agitated.

Ordinarily he was a mild young man who taught the flute and fiddle and helped out at dances. But lately his father, Monsieur Maurice Top-Morlion—a Frenchman who had married an English lady—had been laid up with a stomach disorder on account of shellfish, so all the work was loaded onto Philip.

In addition to his own instruments, he now had to teach the cello and the pianoforte to young ladies all over the town. If one pupil was thoughtless enough to be a quarter of an hour late, Philip, with his father's cello strapped to his back, had to run like a hare to his next lesson, as his mother, who taught drawing, singing, and dancing, always wanted the pony and cart.

Consequently he was rather abrupt with Miss Hemp. When he rose to go and she pointed out that she'd had only fifty minutes instead of the hour her pa paid for, he reminded her that she was the one who'd been late, and it wasn't fair to expect Miss Harris to suffer on her account.

"Miss Harris? Miss Dolly Harris?"

"Yes," said Philip with every appearance of innocence. "My father's ill so I'm giving her her lesson today."

"How very convenient," said Miss Hemp, as everything suddenly became as clear as crystal to her. "How *very* convenient for you, Mr. Top-Morlion!"

"Not really, Miss Hemp. It's quite a long way from here, you know."

"*Quite* a long way," repeated Miss Hemp. "And a very *twisting, roundabout* way, if I might say so."

"I don't understand you, Miss Hemp. It's quite a straight road once you're past North Street."

"You might call it a straight road, and *she* might call it a straight road," said Miss Hemp, grasping her flute like a truncheon. "But other people might think differently, Mr. Top-Morlion."

"I—I really don't know what you're talking about, Miss Hemp! Please, I must go now. I can't keep Miss Harris waiting any longer."

"Oh, no! That would never do! Don't keep Miss Harris wait-ing!"

"Please practice that last piece before next week."

"Oh, yes. Before Saturday, especially. We wouldn't want any-thing to go wrong before Saturday, would we! We must look after poor, silly Miss Hemp until Saturday, mustn't we! We must keep her busy!" said Miss Hemp, choking back her sobs in a series of moist explosions.

"Go on, Mr. Top-Morlion! Don't keep Miss Harris waiting! Go to her! Run—run, you—you tomcat, you!"

Chapter Six

PHILIP Top-Morlion, always in a hurry, trotted away from the Hemps' with his flute in his pocket, his fiddle under his arm, and his father's cello bumping against his back, where it was fastened by a complicated harness of straps. In addition, he carried an old leather case, so enormously bloated with songs, sonatas, duets, concertos, and the several beginnings of a grand symphony of his own composing that it was in constant danger of exploding and strewing his path with an autumn of tunes.

He was all music. He lived it, he breathed it, and even had dreams of eating it: whole platefuls of crochets the size of mutton chops. The very frown of perplexity that at present furrowed his brow declared itself in five parallel lines, like a stave.

"What the devil was she talking about?" he muttered.

He didn't know Miss Harris from Eve, and all that was happening on the Saturday night was that he and his family had been engaged to play music for dancing on Devil's Dyke if the weather proved kind. So far as he was concerned, Miss Harris and Miss Hemp could go wherever Pigott's comet was going. And the sooner the better.

He disliked all the young ladies to whom he was forced to give lessons, and he disliked their parents even more. He disliked them for the way they patronized music as if it were a mere pastime, and he disliked them for the way they patronized him.

True, when he entered a house and divested himself of his instrumental shell—his flute, his fiddle, his father's cello, and his music case—there stood revealed a somewhat threadbare youth, as thin and melancholy as a penny whistle. But there was a soul within him that soared in regions sublime. It ought to have been respected, instead of being received with, "It's only that Mr. Top-Morlion, dear. Now don't tease the poor young man!"

Crash—crash—crash! went horrid discords inside his breast, and huge fortissimos of anger thundered unheard as his maddeningly meek voice inquired, "And have you practiced your last piece, miss?"

Of all his pupils he disliked Miss Hemp the most heartily. He had been teaching her to play the flute for about half a year, and it was only by the greatest effort that he'd refrained from filling her spirit with music by way of thrusting that melodious instrument down her throat as far as it would go.

He detested her so much that he couldn't help thinking that Miss Harris, whatever she was like, must have had some good points, if only because she'd annoyed Miss Hemp.

With this in mind, he reached the Harris residence at about a quarter to four.

"Miss Harris?" he inquired as the maidservant answered his knock.

"Which one?" said she with a look of stupid cunning. "We 'ave four. There's Miss Adelaide, what's one. There's Miss

Caroline, what's eight. There's Miss Mary, what's rising four-teen, and there's Miss Dorothy, what'll be sixteen in July. Take your pick."

Somewhat taken aback by the quantity of Miss Harrises available, he frowned, and then supposed it was Miss Doro-thy. The maid nodded as if he'd made a wise choice. She went off to announce him while he unharnessed himself and stood in the hall, awaiting the appearance of Miss Hemp's enemy. He couldn't help looking forward to it with interest.

The Harrises were in the dining parlor, sitting uncomfortably around the table. Both the Harrises and the table were in a state of glazed decoration; pudding pies, jam tarts, marzipan fancies, and a large purple wine jelly vied in splendor with the gleaming Harris ladies. They were all awaiting the arrival of Dr. Harris, who was bringing two distinguished colleagues back to tea.

Harris himself had passed the news on, and if anyone doubted him, they might ask Morgan, the Harrises' nurse, who had been present when Dr. Harris had mentioned it.

Unluckily Morgan was out for the day, so Harris's word stood alone and unsupported. Ordinarily it was not an edifice calculated to inspire much confidence, but Mrs. Harris, who creaked awkwardly behind a doctor's ransom of silver and best china, could not, for the life of her, see any reason for her son's having told so stupid a lie. Even for him it would have been quite pointless.

"Are you sure your father said he was coming back at half past three?"

Harris was sure.

She stared hard at her son. He must have been telling the truth.

Harris stared unflinchingly back. He had not been telling the truth. It was not Dr. Harris and two distinguished colleagues who were coming to tea. It was Bostock.

Bostock was the important visitor for whom the silver had been polished, the best china set forth, the town ransacked for delicacies, the great wine jelly produced, the Harris ladies squeezed into uncomfortable finery, and three extra places laid. True, Harris might have said one distinguished colleague, but in his experience they usually came in pairs.

The whole splendid occasion was the product of Harris's remarkable brain. Being deeply committed to the disposal of Mary (who, by the way, he would have exchanged for a pair of spectacles, let alone a valuable brass telescope), Harris had devised the present scheme so that Mary would be unable to retire when Bostock arrived.

Usually, when Bosty called, she went off like a rocket, with a hiss and a giggle and a loud slamming of doors. In such circumstances, all the knowledge Harris had acquired from the learned article on Courtship would have been in vain. Both parties had to be present in order for anything to work. So Harris had arranged it, and now he awaited the appearance of Bostock with the utmost confidence in the learned article from which the scheme had derived.

The door opened.

"Young gentleman for Miss Harris," said the maid.

All the Harris faces, in various stages of age and appetite, turned and lit up, like a row of painted lanterns.

Young gentleman for Miss Harris? Which Miss Harris? But the maid, a bad bargain who cost little and gave less, had gone.

Harris stood up. He had divined that "young gentleman" referred to a Bostock who had smartened himself up beyond recognition. If he didn't get to the door first, somebody else would go and tell Bosty to clear off, as important visitors were expected, and so ruin everything.

"I'll go," he said.

Dorothy Harris also stood up. Her mind, still disturbed by the events of the morning, toyed madly with unknown admirers. Young gentleman for Miss Harris? It was *him*! It must be! He was out there in the hall! Oh, my God!

"Since when are *you* Miss Harris?" she demanded of her brother, her voice shaking.

"I thought she said Master Harris," lied Harris, making for the door at high speed.

"Come back!" commanded his sister, traveling with equal velocity around the other side of the table.

At all costs she had to stop that little beast from poking his nose in and ruining everything. Thus both parties, actuated by the same fear, moved rapidly toward the same point.

Dorothy, having started off with a small advantage in distance, arrived first. Then fortune favored Harris. The delay occasioned by Dorothy's having to open the door enabled him to grasp at the vanishing skirts of his sister's gown.

"It might be for me!" he suggested, to which Dorothy responded by jerking forward with all her might and striking out at her brother with her clenched fist.

Harris, in order to avoid the blow, relinquished his hold. Consequently Dorothy, on a final, violent jerk, flew through the door like an arrow.

"Ah!" she cried, traveling at a tremendous speed toward a dimly perceived figure ahead.

It was *him*! It *was* him!

Her aim was true. She struck home into the startled bosom of Philip Top-Morlion.

Never was there a happier meeting, never a luckier shot. Though she did not know it, Dorothy Harris, with her disheveled hair, her flashing eyes, and her small, oddly attractive face, was looking her very best. Had she strived for hours before her mirror, she could never have achieved quite the same breathless, enchanting abandon, and she made as deep an impression on the young man's heart as she did on his stomach and chest.

"Miss Harris?" he inquired, picking himself up and assisting the girl to her feet. "Miss Dorothy Harris?"

"Yes, yes! I'm Dorothy Harris!" she said eagerly. "We—we were just going to have tea," she added, as if by way of explanation. The young man couldn't help wondering if it was the custom of the house for Harrises to come out of the parlor like grapeshot, before tea.

One did come. Slowly. It was Harris. He frowned.

"Oh," he said, and went back again.

"My brother," muttered Dorothy reluctantly. What a vulgar little boy he was! What must the young man think!

She raised her eyes and couldn't help observing, with a slight pang, that her unknown admirer was rather pale, rather thin, and rather shabby.

To be brutally honest, she would have preferred something a little more eye-catching and calculated to inspire Maggie Hemp with envy. But beggars—and she was a beggar in lovers—can't be choosers, so, with a tiny sigh, she noted with approval that he had that full, strong mouth and those dreamy, sideways-looking eyes that come from playing the flute and reading the music at the same time.

"I called," said he, gesturing toward the cello, "to give you your lesson, Miss Harris."

Instantly fear clutched at her heart. Was it possible he wasn't her unknown admirer, after all?

"But—but I always have Monsieur Top-Morlion!"

"He's my father. I'm Philip."

"But why—"

"Your father's gone to see him," said Philip.

What did he mean? What *could* he mean? Only one thing. Her father had gone to call on his father to make sure that Philip's intentions were honorable!

What else was she to think after all that had happened to her that day, and with the young man himself standing there and looking at her in a way no young man had ever looked at her before?

The thought even crossed her mind that the two distinguished colleagues her father had said he was bringing back to tea would turn out to be Monsieur Top-Morlion and his son! It was just like her pa to keep things secret and want to surprise her. Dear Pa! Maggie Hemp would go quite *green*!

It never entered her head at all that Monsieur Top-Morlion had made himself sick from overeating and that Dr. Harris had gone to see him as a physician, not a father.

"I think it's shellfish," said Philip.

"Oh, no! A father has to be careful, Mr. Top-Morlion!" said Dorothy, supposing him to have said "selfish," as shellfish didn't make sense.

"I warned him," said Philip.

"You shouldn't have done that!" cried Dorothy, imagining high words between father and son, such as one reads about in books. "Really you shouldn't!"

"Why not?"

She didn't answer. She felt she'd taken a wrong turning somewhere. They smiled at each other in a puzzled sort of way. They shook their heads. It didn't matter. Though they might have been talking *at* cross-purposes, there was nothing cross in them at all.

"Will you have your lesson now, Miss Harris?"

"Who is it, Dorothy?" came Mrs. Harris's voice from the parlor.

"It's for me, Mama."

"You haven't answered my question, Dorothy."

"It's Philip Top-Morlion, Mama."

"Who?"

"Philip. Monsieur Top-Morlion's son. He's come to give me my lesson."

"Oh, dear! Can't he come back after tea?"

Philip grew pale. Crash—crash—crash! went the discords in his breast. He prepared to go, never to return.

"No, Mama. He couldn't."

Philip decided to stay.

"Oh, well, I suppose you'd better ask him to sit down to tea with us."

"Will you, Mr. Top-Morlion?"

"Thank you, Miss Harris. I'd like that very much."

"I'd like my lesson more."

"More than tea?"

She smiled. Music, not jam tarts and jelly, was the proper food for love.

They went into the parlor, where another place was laid, and they joined the remaining Harrises to await the arrival of Dr. Harris and two distinguished colleagues, who should have come at half past three.

Suddenly there was a loud and shuddering knock upon the front door. The maid jumped, put on her shoes, smoothed her apron, and went to see who was there.

Chapter Seven

It WAS Captain Bostock's best coat with its huge cuffs à la marinière, Captain Bostock's best waistcoat that had anchors embroidered over the pockets, and Captain Bostock's gold-braided hat that had been presented to him by his ship's company on his retirement from the sea.

Inside them all stood Bostock, stiff as a post.

He was, as Captain Bostock himself would have expressed it, all shipshape and Bristol-fashion—that is, if the fashion in Bristol was to wear one's hat an inch below one's eyes, and one's sleeves an inch below one's fingers, so that one looked as if one had lost one's arms and one's sight in the service of one's country.

He doffed his hat, revealing a head that shone like a cannonball and smelled powerfully of violets.

"Oh," said the maid. "It's you. Sorry, but they're expectin' quality. You'd best shove off."

Bostock, who, in the brief journey from his own house to Harris's, had rescued Mary from crocodiles, pirates, and sinking ships with consummate ease, tottered on the step. He didn't know what to do. Harris had told him to come at half past three, and he'd come. He was a little late, but then the rescuing on the way had taken longer than he'd realized. Harris hadn't told him that anybody else was coming. He felt frightened, and dwindled a little more inside the splendor of his apparel.

"But—but—" he croaked.

There was a frog in his throat. Most likely it was the frog that would a-wooing go.

"All right," said the maid, taking pity on him. "I'll go and tell Master Harris that you're here."

Not thinking it necessary to tell Bostock to wait in the hall, she didn't, so he followed her with doglike fidelity and was actually inside the parlor when Mrs. Harris said irritably:

"For goodness' sake, tell him to go away!"

Bostock panicked, not because of what Mrs. Harris had said—which she always said, anyway—but because of the huge number of people assembled in the parlor waiting for him.

There were hundreds of them! They were all shining like anything, in curls, ribbons, bangles, and necklaces, and they were all staring at him!

He was terrified. Everything was looking at him. The very jam tarts on the table seemed to be regarding him with a united, bloodshot glare, as if to say, "It's Bostock! Ha-ha-ha! Did you ever see such a sight!"

At once a morbid conviction was borne upon him that there was something peculiar about his appearance. Perhaps he'd forgotten to put on his breeches? Surreptitiously, and under cover of his father's hat, he felt for them.

"Why, Bosty, old friend!" said Harris, waving to him.

Good old Harris! Thank God for Harris!

"What an agreeable surprise!" said Harris. "Lucky you called, ha-ha! We were just going to have tea!"

What on earth did Harris mean? Bostock's misery increased. Had he made a mistake and come on the wrong day? Otherwise, why was he a surprise? He stared at Harris, appalled. Harris nodded reassuringly, Dear old Harris!

"I'm sorry I'm late," Bostock said.

"Late?" said Harris, looking at him oddly. "Why should you think you're late, Bosty, when we weren't expecting you at all? I can't imagine why you should say such a thing! Ha-ha!"

What a strange laugh!

"But you said half past three," said Bostock, making a desperate attempt to refresh his friend's memory. "For tea. Don't you remember, Harris? It was only this morning."

Now why had Harris gone so white? And why was his ma looking at him like that and reaching for the teapot as if she meant to throw it?

"If," said Harris, watching the teapot carefully, "I mentioned half past three, Bosty, it was with reference to my pa coming back with two distinguished colleagues. I think," he went on, chopping off his words as if they'd been Bostock's fingers, "that—you—have—got—hold—of—the—wrong—end—of—the—stick. Ha—ha!"

That laugh again.

Mrs. Harris put down the teapot and said evenly, "But I expect your father will get hold of the *right* end of the stick when he comes home."

What did she mean? What had Harris meant? Bostock felt he was in deep waters. He had the strangest sensation that, somehow, he'd betrayed his friend. He felt more frightened than ever.

"I'll come back later, Harris," he said hoarsely.

"Sit down!" said Harris shrilly, and then, mastering himself, added, "Now you're here, old friend."

Hurriedly he pointed to one of the empty chairs, as the terrified Bostock showed every sign of sitting down right where he was.

Harris blamed himself. He ought to have warned Bostock to keep his mouth shut. It was just that Harris, like God, preferred to move in mysterious ways. He'd wanted to amaze Bostock with what he, Harris, could accomplish when he really set his mind to it.

He watched as Bostock crossed the room with the general air of one who expects at any moment to fall down in a fit.

"Here, Bosty. Next to me."

Bostock sat, and Harris, dismissing any future unpleasantness from his mind, waited for the learned article on Courtship to take effect.

Courtship in nature, it had explained, was to be observed in the performance, by the male of the species, of those interesting actions that were ingeniously arranged to arouse in the female a willingness to accept him as a mate. Among such actions perhaps the most striking was the display of bright plumage and the discharge of perfume or scent.

Well, it was done. There was Bosty, got up like a dog's dinner and whiffing like one o'clock. And there was Mary, sitting opposite and at point-blank range. Harris didn't see how Bostock could fail to strike.

"Pooh!" said Mary, waving her hand in front of her nose, as a powerful discharge of perfume from Bostock's hair oil reached her. "What a stink!"

Harris, satisfied that Bostock had struck, punched him violently in the ribs to indicate that he should take advantage of the impression he'd made by engaging Mary in animated conversation. Otherwise, whatever it was he'd aroused would subside again.

Bostock opened his mouth, but nothing came out. Harris

kicked him under the table. Bostock moaned. Harris trod on his foot, and Bostock smiled feebly. It was hopeless.

If only Harris had brought a raging lion into the parlor, Bostock would have snatched Mary from its jaws. If only Harris had set fire to the house, Bostock would have saved Mary from the flames. But animated conversation was utterly beyond him.

He was just too modest. In his heart of hearts he couldn't believe that he was worthy of anyone's interest, or that he was anything other than dull, clumsy, and unattractive to behold. And, to be honest, nothing had ever happened to him to make him change his mind.

He sat, paralyzed by the presence of his beloved, who was almost within touching distance, in her best white dress with green ribbons in her hair. From time to time, when nobody was looking, she put out her tongue at him with the rapidity of an angry serpent. Apart from this, she took no notice of him at all.

Harris began to get angry. He'd gone to considerable trouble to put Mary in the way of Bostock, and, what was more, his family had gone to considerable trouble, too. Now it was all being thrown away. A glance at his mother confirmed that she felt the same … perhaps even more strongly than he did himself. Fortunately, however, the music teacher had stayed to tea so Harris was safe, as his ma never blew up in company.

Harris stuck a fork into Bostock to draw his attention to the music teacher, who was setting an example Bostock might well have followed, in the way of animated conversation.

Philip Top-Morlion hadn't stopped talking once, and Dorothy, who was sitting next to him, was hanging on to his every word.

More than ever she was convinced he was her unknown

admirer, and she wished with all her heart he'd stop talking about music for long enough to ask her to go with him to Devil's Dyke on Saturday night.

In vain she plied him with jam tarts and pudding pies and asked him slyly if he cared about comets or stars. He only smiled his sideways smile and went on about Bach, Handel, and Bononcini until she could have screamed.

Everybody was eating now, as it was plain Dr. Harris wasn't coming, and all the good things dwindled away. Presently nothing remained of the feast but a plate of tarts next to Bostock—who hadn't opened his mouth either to let anything out or to put anything in—and the great wine jelly in its silver dish.

It was an exceptionally fine and costly jelly, full of claret and brandy and all manner of outrageous things. It had been prepared for the outing to Devil's Dyke and would have done Mrs. Harris great credit if only it had been spared.

But it was going to be spared. Mrs. Harris had made up her mind. She would have taken it off the table at once if Monsieur Top-Morlion's son hadn't been present; as it was, she sat and watched the jelly with an attention beside which the stare of a hawk was but a casual glance.

At the smallest motion in its direction, she frowned menacingly and shook her head. It was not going to be touched.

All right! she thought: he (she could not bring herself to mention her son's name) had turned the household upside down. He had caused her to drag herself and her daughters into their uncomfortable best gowns. In addition, he was responsible for her having spent a fortune on cakes and then had had the impudence to invite his idiot friend who was sitting there, stinking the house out with his horrible hair oil.

But that was enough. There had to be a limit. And that limit was the wine jelly. IT WAS NOT GOING TO BE TOUCHED.

◆

Bostock was feeling a little easier. He was sorry that he'd let Harris down, but there it was: you might bring a Bostock to the tea table, but you couldn't make him talk; any more than a horse. It was a pity there hadn't been a lion or a fire. Then Harris would have been proud of him!

He gazed achingly at Mary. She wasn't looking at him. Maybe she was thinking about him?

She wasn't. She was thinking about the last plate of jam tarts. She reached toward them.

I'll help her! thought Bostock gallantly. Harris will be pleased!

He also reached toward the dish. Mary, not wanting to be forestalled, hissed warningly. With bewildering rapidity she snatched the tarts away, so that Bostock, taken by surprise, continued after the dish for a short distance. Then he uttered a faint cry and withdrew his arm to its former position. After which he made no further movement and seemed to have stopped breathing.

He was dying. His sleeve was full of blood. He did not know what had happened. He felt no pain and wondered if his heart had burst.

He wanted to die quietly, sitting at the table next to Harris, and with Mary looking on. His dearest friends. He did not want any fuss. He wondered if he ought to apologize to Mrs. Harris. She was certainly looking very angry. Why was she looking so angry? What was she staring at?

Oh! The jelly. Now that was strange. There was the dish, but where was the jelly? It had been there a moment ago. What had become of it?

Bostock thought, which is to say, he knitted his brows and

hoped the rest would follow. It did. He was not dying. His sleeve was not full of blood; it was full of jelly. He had scooped it up in his father's enormous cuff à la marinière.

One problem solved, another presented itself. Why wasn't he dying? He wanted to die. If possible, yesterday. He could see no other satisfactory conclusion to the afternoon.

He sat in abject misery, a prey to thoughts of self-destruction, and attempting, by a series of fitful jerks, to persuade the huge, clammy jelly to slide out of his father's cuff and into his father's hat.

At the other end of the table Mrs. Harris stared at him with incredulous loathing, while beside her, as if nothing had happened, Philip Top-Morlion still talked of Bach, Handel, and Bononcini, and Dorothy tried to put in a good word for the stars.

Then Dr. Harris himself came in, and Dorothy couldn't help being mildly disappointed that Philip's father wasn't by his side.

The doctor, seeing Philip, greeted him affably.

"I've just seen your father," he said.

Dorothy's heart began to dance. She could hardly wait for the next words. Would they be, "He has given you his blessing, my boy," as she'd so often read in books? Involuntarily she reached for Philip's hand under the table and squeezed it. Philip looked surprised but squeezed back.

"It was the shellfish all right," said Dr. Harris.

Dorothy let go of Philip's hand.

"I've given him some medicine," went on the doctor pitilessly. "But I'm afraid you'll be troubled with his pupils for a day or two longer yet."

Dorothy stood up. Her face was crimson with shame and embarrassment.

"Your lesson," said Philip. "Will you have it now?"

"I've had it!" sobbed Dorothy. "I've learned my lesson once and for all!"

She fled from the room and rushed upstairs, wishing with all her heart that she was dead, while Bostock and Harris, taking advantage of the confused situation, vanished like ghosts.

Chapter Eight

HARRIS comforted Bostock. He walked the streets with him, trudged along the beach with him, and went back home with him, where he stayed until Bostock was almost asleep.

Having departed at high speed from the tea table, Harris was in no hurry to return, being anxious to give Time, the Great Healer, every opportunity of acting on his behalf.

Also he was really worried about Bostock, who looked so miserable that Harris feared he'd give up all hopes of Mary and want the telescope back.

"Bosty, old friend," he said gently, as Bostock sat on his bed and mournfully contemplated the ruin of his father's best coat and hat, "trust me."

Bostock looked up. "It's no good, Harris. She doesn't like me."

Harris smiled. "How little you understand these things, Bosty."

"I know when somebody can't stand me!" said Bostock with a flicker of irritation.

Harris dismissed this and explained that the ingenious

process of Courtship pursued its course regardless of personal feelings. He, Harris, had studied the matter and knew what he was talking about.

Bostock had really done rather well. Having displayed himself in bright plumage and discharged scent, he had made a definite impression on Mary.

Bostock agreed but felt it hadn't been a very good one. Harris laughed triumphantly. That was exactly as it should have been!

Did Bostock not know that the female always responded to the beginning of Courtship with a display of hostility? Had Bostock not seen the peahen dart out her beak like a dagger, the bitch bare her teeth, the vixen snarl, the mare kick, and even the docile cow heave and moo?

So it had been with Mary. It was the female's way of displaying her independence before subduing herself to the male of her choice. Which, in this case, was Bostock.

If Mary had smiled at him, then he, Harris, would have been doubtful. If she had held his hand, then Harris would have feared that all was lost. But to have her respond with the venomous dislike they had both witnessed filled Harris with confidence.

"Tell me this, Bosty," said Harris, pressing home point after point as if he were pinning down a butterfly. "Was she worse than usual?"

"I think so, Harris. Yes. Now you come to mention it, I think she was."

"Then that proves it, old friend! Don't you see, Bosty? The ritual of Courtship has begun! There's no stopping it now, Bosty, no stopping it at all!"

They shook hands and Harris went home. Bostock was happy again, and so was Harris. He was glad to have restored the admiration of his friend.

Curiously enough, this admiration was as important to Harris as the telescope itself. Although the telescope might have revealed the wonders of the heavens, Bostock revealed the wonders of Harris. Without Bostock, Harris dwelt in darkness, a dead star, a lonely, unconsidered thing.

The house was quiet. Time, the Great Healer, had acted on Harris's behalf, and everyone was asleep. He climbed in through the scullery window and went upstairs.

He heard, in passing, his sister Dorothy sobbing in her sleep. Time had healed nothing for her, and over and over again she relived in her dreams her humiliating mistake about the music teacher's son.

"Oh, no—no—no!" she moaned.

Harris frowned. There was always a female crying somewhere in the house.

He mounted the last flight of stairs and entered his room, which, like himself, was somewhat removed from the rest of the world.

It was a remote, squeezed-under-the-roof Pythagoras of a room, containing one right angle and a great many wrong ones. Wherever you looked, it was impossible not to propose a theorem, and equally impossible to solve it. Even in the darkness there was a sense of immense problems and immense solutions.

Harris sat on his bed and considered the whole question of Courtship. In addition to the display of bright plumage and the discharge of scent, the learned article had described the clashing of beaks and pursuit, music, both vocal and instrumental, and the performing of dances or other antics. There was the presentation of prey or of inedible but otherwise stimulating objects, and, as a footnote, there was noted the curious behavior of the snipe, which plummeted down at a great speed while uttering hoarse cries.

Harris shivered, not at the thought of Bostock plummeting, but because there was a draft. It was blowing through a hole in the window that had been brought about by Harris's having accidentally poked the end of Captain Bostock's telescope through the glass.

The instrument itself lay on the windowsill, gleaming faintly, as if with a mysterious light of its own. Harris gazed at it thoughtfully.

Might not the telescope, which brought the heavens nearer, bring other things nearer, too? Might it not reveal the secrets of human courtship?

He went to the window and opened it, and looked out into the night. It was dark, very dark. Somewhere aloft, under a blanket of cloud, Pigott's comet pursued its frantic course; otherwise there were dark houses, dark trees, and a long dark shoulder of the downs, making a landscape of ink. To the north, on top of Dyke Hill, rose St. Nicholas's Church. Both were as black as sin.

Harris set the telescope to his eye. Instantly chimneys, roofs, and the tops of trees swept past in a dark hurry, as if anxious not to be seen.

He thought he saw an owl, with something in its beak, winging its way back to its nest, but he could not be sure. He studied windows, doorways, and the quiet corners of streets. Nothing. Human beings, it seemed, were more secret than the night itself.

Then suddenly a light flickered. It was no more than a tiny yellow pinprick, but in the wide darkness it was an explosion of interest, like a gold tooth in a pirate's beard.

He lost it, then he found it again. It was by the church. It was moving so that every now and then it vanished behind bushes, emitting no more than a fragile sprinkling of yellow, like the pricking of buds.

He put down the telescope rather quickly, as if the distant object of his scrutiny might have turned and seen Harris's eye, suspended in the night.

It was a courting couple all right, performing their mysterious antics in St. Nicholas's churchyard, far from prying eyes.

Harris left his room in great excitement, intending to observe, as closely as he could, an actual human courtship, so that he might put his knowledge at the service of his friend.

He hastened down the stairs, left the house, and sped through the night. He was desperately anxious not to be too late and miss the whole thing.

Not until he was three quarters of the way up Dyke Hill and approaching the churchyard itself did the possibility of his having been mistaken occur to him.

Trees whispered, tombstones loomed, and monuments glared. Harris faltered. He listened in vain for the murmur of lovers' voices and the music of amorous sighs. Regretfully he abandoned the idea of a courting couple and considered instead the possibility of grave robbers, body snatchers, murderers, and other likely inhabitants of a churchyard by night.

He could still see the light, moving about in a thoroughly spectral fashion, and he could hear the slow, heavy thump of mysterious feet.

Harris felt a strong desire to be back in his room, with his head under the blankets, and asleep.

The light drew near, and a long black shadow fell across a grave. Harris, mentally bequeathing his possessions to Bostock and his murdered body to science, moaned and went horribly white.

"Holy Mother of God!" shrieked O'Rourke, coming out from behind a bush and beholding the apparition of Harris. "'Tis a murdered boy!"

Indeed, it was a ghastly, spectral Harris, whose corpse-like pallor would have deceived any body snatcher into taking him into stock at once.

They both stood, trembling violently and glaring at each other and inspiring as much terror as they felt.

O'Rourke crossed himself and required Harris, in the name of St. Patrick, to vanish and return to those mysterious regions whence he'd come.

Harris would willingly have obliged, but was unable to do so. Paralyzed with dread, he remained motionless in O'Rourke's lantern light.

Then O'Rourke perceived that the terrible, white-faced thing was the friend of the magistrate's son, and Harris perceived that the huge gaunt figure with the lantern was one of the Irish roofers he'd seen at Bostock's house.

"Wh-what are you doing here?" inquired Harris in a tone of voice that suggested that, if O'Rourke didn't choose to say, then he, Harris, would not press the point.

But O'Rourke was so relieved to discover that Harris was flesh and blood—although, by the look of him, there wasn't all that much blood about—that he was only too thankful to talk.

"I was lookin' for somebody," he said, casting his light around the graves. "And I pray to God that I won't be lucky enough to find her."

"Somebody dead?"

"Now would I be lookin' for a livin' lass with her name on a stone and her pretty self under it?"

"Then she is dead!"

"Never say such a thing! If Cassidy heard ye, he'd go right out of his mind! Just say she's somewhere, that's all. And may

Cassidy be the first to find her, though he'll fall off his ladder and break his neck!"

O'Rourke beckoned. "Come over here and sit with me on this stone, young sir, and I'll tell ye a tale of love and courtin' that'll bring the tears to yer eyes, even though ye're as small as a wink in a blind man's cup!"

He held out his hand as if to assist the uncertain boy. "I'll tell ye of Cassidy and sweet Mary Flatley, that's been gone for a year and a day. But I tell a lie, for it's tomorrow already, so it'll be a year and two days. 'Twas in Dublin's fair city, and she in the fish business like Molly Malone before her, and Cassidy comin' up to mend the thatch of her father's roof...."

So they sat on the tombstone with the lantern between them, which turned the black midnight yews into a golden bower, while O'Rourke told sadly of Cassidy's courting and Cassidy's seeking and Cassidy's singing under every window, down every street in the land.

Then his face grew longer and even more lugubrious as he told of his own quiet searching down streets of a different kind, where the houses had no windows, and were dwellings for only one.

"But she's in one or the other, and that's for certain-sure, and whichever way it is, no good will come of it, for it'll break Cassidy's heart or break Cassidy's neck."

He put out his lantern, and the trees, the stones, the church, and they themselves sank back, like dreams, into the darkness of the night.

Harris went back to his home, and O'Rourke went back to the King's Head, a little public house in The Lanes, where he and Cassidy shared a room.

"She wasn't there, Cassidy!" he whispered, bending over his sleeping friend. "She wasn't there at all, so ye can still be an honest man!"

Chapter Nine

O'ROURKE shook the end of Cassidy's bed so that Cassidy came out of his dreams with a great start, or, rather, a great stop, which was what O'Rourke had put to them.

"'Tis tomorrow!" he shouted. "Ye loafin' great bundle of sleep!"

"Where am I?" inquired Cassidy in a grumbling kind of fright.

"In the King's Head!"

"And what monarch might that be with a thought like Michael Cassidy inside of him?"

"'Tis the public house, ye mad thing—" began O'Rourke, when he saw that Cassidy was deceiving him, so he went on to inform him that half the world was up and about its business and, most likely, taking the bread from their mouths.

"Another minute!" sighed Cassidy, brightening up his eyes with his knuckles. "Only another minute and she'd have been in me arms! Ye're a hard man, O'Rourke."

He began to array himself for the day's work, taking particular care with the scraping of his whiskers and the whitening of his teeth, which he polished, first with his tongue and then with a bit of old rag.

"Do I look all right, O'Rourke? D'ye think she'll have me?"

"Ye look fine, Cassidy! Handsome enough to lead a parade!"

"Today's the day, O'Rourke! Today's the day I'll find her! I feel it in me bones!"

O'Rourke nodded. He did not have the heart to remind Cassidy that he'd felt it in his bones every single morning since they'd landed in Liverpool, and it was a marvel that Cassidy could still stand upright, with bones inside of him that told such terrible lies.

They left the King's Head and went down into Bartholomews, where O'Rourke collected a pane of glass from a glazier's, and came back all sideways, like an Irishman in an Egyptian picture, carrying nothing at all.

They went to the stables and Cassidy said they ought to take the pony to the doctor's, as he looked sick as a dog.

"D'ye really think so, Cassidy? For it'll cost us money!"

"Just look at him, O'Rourke! Did ye ever see such a poor beast with so many spots behind his eyes?"

Gloomily, for O'Rourke was no joker and Cassidy always caught him out, he gave Cassidy the glass and the pair of them got up onto the cart.

Then O'Rourke jerked the reins, and Cassidy began to sing, pausing only to pay his high-flown compliments to every pretty girl they passed. Nor did he overlook the plain ones, for Cassidy found something to be charmed by everywhere.

"In Dublin's fair city, where girls are so pretty...Good mornin' to yer ladyship! And what might ye be doin' so far from Dublin with such cherries in yer cheeks?

"I first set me eyes on sweet Molly Malone!...Oh, but if I'd seen ye first, me darlin', I'd have had no eyes for that Molly Malone! Chalk and cheese! Chalk and cheese!"

So he went on, singing and saluting, and sometimes holding up the glass at a girl as if she were a picture, crying out for a frame, while O'Rourke boomed steadily, "Tiles and slates! Chairs to mend! Pots, kettles, and pans!"

At last they came to the row of smart new villas that sparkled in the sun. "There's the house!" cried O'Rourke, pointing to the end of the row. "'Tis a window upstairs in the front!"

He'd spied the cracked glass on the previous day and obtained the business of mending it from the lady of the house herself. They halted.

"And while ye're up there, Cassidy, ye might take a look at the roof and see if ye can wheedle a slate or two down, for she's not a lady to begrudge a shillin'," said O'Rourke.

"That wouldn't befit an honest man," said Cassidy, climbing down.

"For God's sake, Cassidy, it's business and there's nothin' personal in it at all!"

Cassidy beamed.

"She died of a faver, and no one could save her," he sang, carrying the ladder to the front of the house.

"Must ye sing, Cassidy? 'Tis a respectable house!"

"I must, O'Rourke. I must!" said Cassidy, and went on with, "And that was the end of sweet Molly Malone!" so that O'Rourke couldn't help feeling that it would have been a good thing all around.

"Her ghost wheels her barrow, through streets broad and narrow,

"Crying: Cockles and mussels, alive, alive-o!"

He laid the ladder against the wall.

"Alive, alive-o!"

"Go easy, Cassidy, or it's the dead ye'll be awakening with that great bellow!"

"And haven't they been sleepin' long enough, O'Rourke?"

demanded Cassidy, and went on trumpeting his song at the top of his voice.

He began to mount the ladder.

"Alive, alive-o!"

He's like a bird! thought O'Rourke with unwilling admiration, as the smart buttons on the back of Cassidy's green coat winked and twinkled down on him.

Cassidy went dancing up, alive and alive-o-ing all the way. He reached the cracked window and tapped on the glass.

"Alive, alive-o!"

The window flew up.

"Alive, alive—OOOOH!" shrieked Cassidy as Mary Flatley herself looked out.

Like a bird! thought O'Rourke, as down plummeted Cassidy with a hoarse cry.

"Dead!" howled O'Rourke. "Cassidy, are ye dead?"

"Not dead! Not dead!" screamed Mary Flatley, coming out of the window almost far enough to follow after. "Don't say ye're dead, Michael Cassidy! Never say that in me hearin'!"

"So it's yerself!" wailed O'Rourke, staring up at the cause of the disaster. "And didn't I always tell him ye'd break his heart or his neck?"

Cassidy lay among bushes, green as a giant leaf, with a face on him as white as any blossom—and him just singing, "Alive, alive-o!"

"Oh, Cassidy, Cassidy! Tell me ye're not dead!"

Never a word out of him, never a look. His eyes lay under lids as quiet as stones.

"Oh, Michael Cassidy, Michael Cassidy!" wept Mary Flatley, coming out of the front door and joining O'Rourke in his lamentations. "I'll not wed another if only ye'll tell me ye're not dead! For what should I be doin' in this old world without ye?"

The mistress of the house appeared, then neighbors came,

and presently there was a little crowd gazing down on the fallen Cassidy and wondering what to do.

Then somebody remembered that a doctor lived nearby, and ran off to fetch him, while Mary Flatley wept and picked leaves and twigs from out of Cassidy's curly black hair.

Dr. Harris came and everybody made way for him. He looked up at the window and down at the ground, for all the world as if he expected to find Cassidy somewhere between. Then Mary Flatley showed him where Cassidy was, and he looked at Cassidy and felt him and listened to him through his green coat and right down to his heart. Then he said that Cassidy was alive and that his neck was as good as yours or mine.

"'Tis a miracle!" said O'Rourke.

"'Tis Michael Cassidy!" said Mary Flatley. "And that's miracle enough for me!"

Then O'Rourke took one end of him and two of the villa people took the other, and between them they eased him off the bushes, and Mary Flatley picked up a silver sixpence that had fallen from his pocket and tucked it into his shirt.

They laid him on his ladder and carried him out to the cart, and the lady of the villa said she'd pay the doctor's fee as poor Cassidy had fallen in her service, in a manner of speaking. And Dr. Harris said no, not at all, she wasn't to think of it, as he'd only acted out of common humanity. And O'Rourke, who was all for saving money, agreed that there never was such a common piece of humanity as Michael Cassidy, God bless him!

"He'll need liniment," said Dr. Harris to O'Rourke. "Can you fetch it for him?"

But before O'Rourke could answer, the lady of the villa, anxious to be of service, said she'd send her very own maid.

"We're livin' in the King's Head," said O'Rourke. "The establishment in The Lanes."

"I'll be there before ye!" cried Mary Flatley, and flew back into the villa to put on her best dress and fill a basket, so that Cassidy, when he woke up, should have something good to look at, as well as good to eat.

They put him in the back of the cart where he lay like a fallen knight collected for burial. Sorrowful O'Rourke briefly turned his countenance—to make sure Cassidy hadn't tumbled off—and the cart trundled away. It was a scene of ancient chivalry, bright as a tear and a thousand years old.

Chapter Ten

HARRIS saw it all. Leaning out of his window like an angel on a bracket, that had, for reasons of short-sightedness, been equipped with a telescope, he had watched Cassidy go climbing up his ladder, singing at every rung.

He had seen the girl come swiftly to her window, her face all wild with longing as she heard her lover's song. And then, just as O'Rourke had predicted in the churchyard, down had plummeted Cassidy with a hoarse cry, remarkably like the snipe.

Harris had witnessed the courting of Cassidy and Mary Flatley, and he could hardly believe his luck.

He had seen everything he needed to know, hanging in a miraculous bubble of light, suspended before his eye.

Fascinated, he observed the girl fly out of the house and rush to Cassidy's side, kneeling and weeping all over him, as if to water him back to life.

Quietly he put the telescope by. The problem was solved. What had moved one Mary could hardly fail to move another.

Courtship, love, and the very springs of passion were, to Harris, now an open book.

He left his room and went downstairs, passing on his way his sister Dorothy, to whom, unhappily, courtship was a book that had been slammed shut. She sniveled, dabbed her swollen eyes, and stared at her brother as if, somehow, he were the author of all her misfortunes.

He departed from the house and went around to the side. He looked into the stone coffin, but Bostock wasn't there, so he went down to the beach.

On the other side of the road Philip Top-Morlion was hanging about, trying to summon up courage to call on Miss Harris and propose another time for her lesson. He was still bewildered by her tempestuous departure from the tea table, particularly after she'd held his hand. He saw Harris and waved.

Harris ignored him. He had a great deal on his mind. Bostock was sitting on a breakwater, hurling stones with tremendous force into the sea, as if to provoke it. But it lay, flat as Sunday, scarcely bothering to lap at the pebbles before drawing itself back with a noise like soup.

The friends shook hands, and Harris perched himself on the breakwater by Bostock's side. Philip Top-Morlion, who'd tottered after, watched from a distance and wondered if he should ask Harris if he thought his sister would like her lesson now.

The two boys appeared to be deep in conversation, and of a very private kind. They kept looking up at the wheeling, shrieking seagulls as if fearing they were eavesdropping on the secrets that each was confiding to the other.

Philip smiled indulgently. What secrets could they have at their age, when their hearts were still sleeping and they knew nothing of the pangs of wounded pride?

He eased his various musical burdens and waited for a suitable moment to approach the two boys. Although he felt that the presence of a grown-up person like himself would probably be flattering, he was sensitive enough not to want to interrupt.

Her brother appeared to be doing most of the talking. He was waving his arms about earnestly, and every now and then he laid a hand on his friend's shoulder with an affectionate, reassuring air.

Presently Bostock stopped throwing stones and began to nod, as if he'd been talked into something. Then, to Philip's surprise, Harris started to sing. It was uncanny, as if there were a bird somewhere inside him that had cut its foot on something sharp.

Philip, the musician, winced, but Philip, the music teacher, felt that the suitable moment had arrived.

He crossed the road and stumbled bulkily over the pebbles of the beach.

"You should take lessons," he said, as if Harris's singing, though pleasing in an artless way, would have benefited tremendously from paid tuition.

Harris looked mildly affronted.

"I think you have talent," lied Philip, not wanting to make an enemy of Miss Harris's brother.

Harris nodded, and Bostock did not look surprised.

"I was wondering," said Philip, "if your sister Dorothy would like her cello lesson this morning."

"It's Thursday," said Harris. "She goes to Collier's. Free cakes."

"Ah, well," said Philip casually, "perhaps another time. Collier's, did you say? I might even see her there."

Harris looked at him carefully. "You won't get in, you know," he said.

Philip Top-Morlion stepped back as if he'd been struck. His eyes filled with tears.

"Thank you," he said shakenly. "Thank you very much!"

He'd never been so insulted in all his life! To be told by a child—a sordid, vulgar, hateful boy!—that he wasn't good enough to be admitted to that cheap little coffee shop in Bartholomews! And after he'd told the boy he had talent!

Philip Top-Morlion raged hopelessly against the injustice of it. Why hadn't he struck the boy? Why hadn't he punched him in the face? Why was he always so sickeningly meek when everywhere you saw stupid arrogance honored? When every loud-mouthed fool was hailed as a genius because he said he was!

Why did he never tell the parents of his simpering pupils what he *really* thought of them? Why did he always say, "Thank you," when he meant, "Damn you!"?

He longed with all his heart to be able to explode with outrage and spread a peacock's tail of anger across the sky. He longed to strut, to give grand concerts and be greeted with reverence and wild applause.

Above all, he longed to see Miss Harris again. She, at least, understood him, and she loved music.

He went down to Bartholomews. He couldn't help himself. It was almost as if he *wanted* to be humiliated. People like Philip Top-Morlion—sensitive, artistic souls—seem to have a passion for exposing themselves to anguish. It's as if only by suffering can they create the masterpieces that give the heedless world its joy.

So Philip Top-Morlion tried to fix his mind on a poignant passage in his grand symphony as he walked past Collier's with knitted brows.

She was there! She was sitting in the window, talking to Miss Hemp. He retraced his steps. Miss Hemp saw him first. She would! She nodded slightly and compressed her lips, as if to say, "You won't get in here, you know."

He smiled, as if to say, "Thank you. Thank you very much."

She said something to Miss Harris. He walked on slowly. He looked back. Miss Harris was staring at him. She was smiling and beckoning!

"Good morning, Mr. Top-Morlion," she was mouthing through the glass.

He walked back.

"Good morning, Miss Harris."

"What did you say?"

"I said good morning."

"I can't hear you! Why don't you come inside?"

"I—I—"

"Please!"

"All right. Just for a minute!"

"What?"

"I said—oh, never mind!"

He vanished, and Dorothy looked expectantly toward the edge of the curtain that screened the bow window from the door.

After her terrible night of tears she'd decided to try to make things up with Maggie Hemp before it was too late to go with her to Devil's Dyke. She hated herself for doing it, but there was so little time left and nothing else in view. Now, however, things had changed.

"I don't know why you asked him in!" said Miss Hemp with the beginnings of irritation.

"I wanted to ask him about my lesson, Maggie. That's all, really."

She continued to look toward the curtain.

"I wonder what's happened to him?"

"I expect he's changed his mind. You know what men are!"

"He said he was coming...just for a minute."

"I thought you said you couldn't hear a word!"

"I'll just go and see where he is!"

"Really, Dolly! You're man mad!"

"I'm not!" said Dolly, fidgeting out of her chair. "Really I'm not! I won't be a minute, Maggie!"

She left the table and whisked around the curtain.

Ah! He *had* come in! Or mostly in. He was standing in the doorway and looking rather flushed.

"Won't you join us, Mr. Top-Morlion?"

He shook his head.

"Why not?"

"I can't."

He tried to smile but felt more like crying. He was the victim of a peculiarly unfortunate circumstance. His father's cello had become wedged in the narrow doorway, and he was strapped to it as firmly as to a stake. The boy Harris had been right. He couldn't get in to Collier's, and, what was worse, he couldn't get out, either.

"Let me help you," said Dorothy, trying not to laugh.

"It ought to be the other way around," said Philip wretchedly. "I mean, isn't it the knight who's supposed to free the lady?"

Back at the table, Miss Hemp began to breathe heavily and to tap her foot. What were they doing? She took Dolly's cake and ate it. What were they talking about? She stared toward the curtain and could just see the edge of Dolly's dress.

If it was only Dolly's lesson, why were they being so secretive about it? She leaned over as far as she could and strained her ears.

Collier's was very noisy. Everybody was clattering cups and talking at once. Nevertheless, over and above it all, Maggie Hemp heard quite distinctly the sound of laughter. His and hers. What were they laughing at?

Her face grew red and her eyes filled up with tears. They were laughing at *her*!

It was as plain as anything. *That's* why they hadn't come back to the table! They wanted to have a good laugh together over silly, honest Maggie Hemp! Oh, they were beastly and sly, like—like monkeys or—or goats! She should never, never have made it up with Dolly Harris! She would never speak to her again!

She stood up and stalked around the curtain toward the door. Yes! She was right! There they were—the pair of them —laughing like cats! It was horrible—worse than she'd supposed. Dolly actually had her hand on that odious Mr. Top-Morlion's shoulder as if she'd just been whispering in his ear!

"Oh, *Maggie*!" cried Dolly, killing herself with laughter.

"Oh, *Dolly*!" said Maggie, as if she would gladly have helped. "Get out of my way!"

Before Dorothy could move, Maggie Hemp's anger boiled over and she gave Philip Top-Morlion a sharp push.

At once there was a grating sound, as of a cello being freed from a doorway, and Philip Top-Morlion, with a hoarse cry, flew backwards down the two steps.

Dorothy, still holding on to the straps she'd been trying to unfasten, accompanied him, and, with a painful clashing of noses, they completed their journey in the street outside. As on their previous meeting they lay in each other's arms, mightily surprised.

"Are—are you hurt, Miss Harris?" asked Philip, feeling dazed, his eyes watering.

"Oh, no, no! Are *you* hurt, Mr. Top-Morlion?"

"No, no! Not at all..."

"But why don't you ask me?" sobbed Maggie Hemp, standing in the doorway and trembling with rage. "Why don't you ask Maggie Hemp if she's been hurt? Why don't you, you—you hyenas, you!"

Chapter Eleven

MAGGIE Hemp rushed away from Bartholomews, half blinded with tears. They were all laughing at her! People were even staring out of Collier's big window and laughing! She could never go there again! Her whole life was ruined!

Dolly Harris, lying on the dirty ground and showing a good deal more of her stumpy legs than she needed to, was laughing till she cried, and so was that snaky Top-Morlion, all tumbled up beside her!

Oh, tears are cheap, aren't they! But not the boiling, scalding ones that ran down Maggie's cheeks as she ran and ran with her hands to her ears.

All the world was laughing at her, and she couldn't bear the sound of it. It was a horrible world! You only had to look around a curtain, and what did you find? Grins and slyness going on behind your back! Everybody despised you if you were honest.

It was indeed a cruel world for people like Maggie Hemp, who couldn't keep a lover for more than a week because she just couldn't help telling him things for his own good.

Poor, pretty Maggie Hemp whom nobody understood! Surely there was somebody, somewhere, who would see, wide blue eye to wide blue eye, with her.

She stumbled along with her eyes awash and her nose growing as red as a berry. She'd been so happy to have made things up with Dolly Harris, and talked about what they should wear for the night of the comet on Devil's Dyke! Now it was over forever!

The comet! She hated it. She wished that stupid Pigott had never invented it. If she did go to watch it, it would have to be with her dull-as-ditchwater ma and pa, who'd talk about beef and pork and sausages all the time. Never! She'd sit at home and sew rather than that!

She sniffed and sobbed her way through the narrow, twisting Lanes, with hateful images of jeers and sneers and whispers cut off short thronging her brain. She never really noticed, as she passed, that many was the head that turned, and many the sympathetic smile, for the pretty, brokenhearted girl.

"Sure to God they're not tears, me darlin'?" came a voice in her ear, together with a strong smell of spirits in the air. "'Tis the mornin' dew on yer cheeks—for ye're as pretty as a primrose, and I don't tell a lie!"

It was Cassidy, who'd been loafing outside the King's Head. He was bandaged as if he'd been embalmed, for O'Rourke had told him that Mary Flatley herself was coming down with some liniment, and he wanted to show her he needed it. Though he might have done with a roll or two less of the bandage and not come to any harm, it was, as he said to O'Rourke, but a couple of yards of white lie.

"Oh, please go away!" sobbed Maggie Hemp, mightily embarrassed by the Irishman, who stank of brandy. "Or I'll call for help!"

But there was no getting rid of Cassidy as easily as that. The very sight of a female in tears was more intoxicating to him than all the brandy that ever came out of France...there not being a drop of good Irish whiskey to be had in the King's Head for love or money.

And talking of love, who was it who had made her so unhappy? Say but the word and Cassidy would give his right arm! Or was it that she'd lost a lover by drowning, maybe? It was a fate very common among them who lived by the sea!

If that was it, then she should dry her eyes and consider that more good men came out of the sea than ever went into it, and they were like pebbles on the shore.

"So give over weepin', me darlin'," said Cassidy. He held out his green arms and took Maggie Hemp's surprised hand into his own two bandaged ones, holding it as if it had been a rare and delicate butterfly.

So that was how he was standing, like a whited sepulcher, holding a pretty girl's hand and calling her "darlin'," when Mary Flatley, in her best dress and shawl, with a bottle of liniment, a basket of apples, and her last drop of good whiskey, came running down to give him her heart.

She stopped as if she'd been shot, and her eyes blazed up so that Cassidy felt the heat of them, though he was six yards off and trying to look the other way.

"Ye dirty scoundrel!" she cried. "Smarmin' up to another bit of muslin skirt! Me mother was right, Michael Cassidy! Ye've not even the decency to be dead!"

Away she went like whirlwind, and Cassidy, whose bandages were like shackles, was left far behind.

She flew through The Lanes, losing apples from her basket as fast as tears. She was off for the fishmonger's son! She'd marry him now—this very minute! He'd only to say the word. Though he was quiet and a bit on the dull side, at least he was honest and true!

She rushed across Bartholomews toward Saunders', and there, standing next door and smiling to herself, as if all were well with the world, was the doctor's speckle-eyed daughter, the one with the poky little face!

"'Tis no use yer smilin'!" sobbed Mary Flatley. "For he'll break yer heart as soon as spit! He's found another, so ye've lost him even before ye had him, the dirty, philanderin' rogue!"

Then she vanished inside Saunders' and was lost among huge hanging nets and clusters of green glass floats.

Chapter Twelve

LOST HIM? thought Dorothy Harris. The girl's out of her mind! She stared into Saunders' and was confronted by the slow grins of several huge fishermen who loomed out of the marine gloom like monsters of the deep.

She retreated and shook her head. If the girl had really meant Philip Top-Morlion, then she'd never made a bigger mistake in her life.

She smiled. Although she was mildly shocked that Philip should have been mixed up with the Irish girl, there was no doubt it gave him a touch of mystery that wasn't at all displeasing.

Anyway, he was coming to give her her lesson at nine o'clock that very evening. He'd have come earlier, but the bridge of his father's cello had been broken when they'd fallen down the steps, and he had to get it repaired.

He'd asked if nine o'clock was too late. No, she'd said, but wasn't it inconvenient for him? Surely he had more exciting things to do with his evenings than to give young ladies lessons on the cello?

"More exciting things than music?" he'd asked seriously.

"I love music," she'd said. "Better than anything."

"So do I," said he.

"Till nine o'clock, then?"

"On the very stroke, Miss Harris."

Well! If that was losing him, then give her more such losses! She would bear them with equanimity. If only she could keep him off Bach, Handel, and Bononcini, she was absolutely certain he'd ask her to go with him to Devil's Dyke on Saturday night.

She went home and set about making herself hauntingly beautiful. This necessitated dressing and undressing some twenty times and waiting for suitable moments to enter her mother's room and borrow articles of jewelry and French scent.

By five o'clock she was ready and faced the prospect of sitting in her room, like a vase, for four hours.

Twelve of them passed, and it was half-past five. She put her ear to her clock. It was still going.

"Dorothy?"

"Yes, Mama?"

"What are you doing?"

"Nothing, Mama."

"You're very quiet."

"Yes, Mama."

"Dorothy?"

"Yes, Mama?"

"Have you been using my scent?"

"No, Mama."

"Then why can I smell it all over the house?"

"I can't smell anything, Mama."

At seven o'clock she was summoned for dinner. She couldn't eat. At half past seven she remembered her cello and began to look for it. At eight o'clock she was still looking. At a quarter past eight she saw her brother leaving the house.

She called down to him from her window. "Have you seen my cello?"

Harris looked up. "Cello?" he said wonderingly.

"Yes. My cello. Have you seen it?"

"When?"

"Now!"

Harris looked around carefully.

"No."

She stared after him thoughtfully, then went back to searching for her vanished instrument. Harris went down to the beach.

Bostock was by the breakwater. He was wearing a blue cape with silver frogs, and an expensive wig that lay on his head like an old salad.

They had been presented to Captain Bostock by Mrs. Bostock on the occasion of his elevation to the Bench, as she wanted him to look like a gentleman.

The friends shook hands.

"Harris?" said Bostock.

"Yes, Bosty?"

"Do you really think that—"

"I don't think," said Harris, silencing his friend with a smile. "I *know*. It's science, Bosty, and science means to *know*, not to think."

Bostock nodded.

"Harris?"

"Yes, Bosty?"

"Don't you think we ought to be going?"

"In a little while, old friend. In just a little while."

They sat in silence, dreaming their dreams. From time to time Bostock stole a glance at Harris and marveled that a head that was really quite small could contain a brain so large.

Little by little the sky darkened. The stars winked and the friends left the beach with a noise like pearls.

They walked, still in silence, to Harris's house. Lights shone from all the upper windows. Harris pointed.

"That's hers!"

Bostock blushed and stared.

Harris pulled him away and around to the other side of the house.

"What is it, Harris?"

Harris raised his finger to his lips and, with infinite caution, removed his sister's cello from the stone coffin in which he had concealed it.

The learned article on Courtship had stated music, vocal or instrumental, so Harris, anxious to take no chances and to leave no stone unturned, had decided on both.

"Oh, Harris! You think of everything!"

Harris nodded. He did.

"I'll kill him!" gasped Dorothy, aloft.

The time for her lesson drawing near, she had been watching from her window when she'd seen her hateful brother stealthily lifting her lost cello from its hiding place.

"I'll kill him! *And* that idiot friend of his!"

She rushed from her window and returned with a bowl of dirty water. Then, hearing the unmistakable grumble of a cello below, flung out the water with an enraged screech.

"Take that, you filthy little beast!"

◆

She missed them. Harris and Bostock, capering deftly, arrived back under Mary's window, panting and unscathed. They did not even suspect the narrowness of their escape.

They looked up. Mary's window was open to the spring night. Harris twanged the cello and, marvel of marvels, Mary appeared! Harris felt quite awed by his own success. It was happening exactly as he'd seen it happen that morning, through the telescope. The girl had been drawn to her window by an instinct she could not deny. What had moved one Mary was quite definitely moving another.

She looked down. She saw Bostock and Harris. She made a noise like a rocket and vanished from view.

"In Dublin's fair city," croaked Bostock, while Harris twanged loudly by his side.

"Where girls are so pretty..."

Mary came back.

"I first set my eyes on sweet Molly Malone!"

Mary beckoned. Bostock approached, and Mary emptied the contents of a chamber pot over Captain Bostock's cloak and wig.

It was five minutes after nine o'clock and the last echoes of Bostock's cry of anguish had died away. Dorothy Harris waited by her window, listening for the sound of her admirer's step.

At ten o'clock she began to cry. At eleven o'clock she was still crying. At twelve o'clock she blew out her candle, got undressed, and went to bed.

The Irish girl had been right all the time. He *had* found someone else. Philip Top-Morlion had not come.

She cried herself to sleep, sobbing, over and over again, "Why, why didn't you come?"

In point of fact he had come. And on the very stroke of nine. He'd glimpsed her at her window and had had the happy idea of announcing his presence, not by a commonplace knock on the door, but with a melodious flourish from his grand symphony, on his father's cello. What could have been more romantic than that?

He had been rewarded with a stream of filthy water and a loud screech of abuse. He had fled, soaked to the skin. He had never been so insulted in all his life!

Chapter Thirteen

NEXT MORNING Philip Top-Morlion rose from his bed, shuffled across his room, and, blinking in the sunlight, put his hand out of the window. Sure enough, there was his coat and shirt, where they'd been hanging out to dry, like a suicide.

He shuddered. It was all true. It had actually happened to him. It hadn't been a horrible dream. She really had thrown water all over him.

Why—why? What had he done to offend her? He was used to being ignored, he was used to being slighted, but he was not used to being soaked to the skin and called a filthy little beast!

It was the end. He hated the world. He wanted to die on her doorstep with, if possible, an explanatory note attached: "This is your doing. I hope you are satisfied."

And he might die, too. Sensitive people like him caught chills very easily. You were always reading about them, coughing their lungs up in a garret and being found by their landlady, dead and with a flower of blood coming out of their mouths.

Already he was beginning to feel feverish. He dressed and ate a hurried breakfast. He ought to see a doctor. It was foolish to neglect himself.

Unfortunately, the nearest physician was Dr. Harris—her father. Well, it couldn't be helped. His health came first. If it meant swallowing his pride before he swallowed any medicine, then he'd do it. Posterity would never have forgiven him if he'd sacrificed himself so young.

He put on his cello, took up his flute, fiddle, and music case, and walked unsteadily to her street and stood outside her house. He wondered if, by any chance, she could see him. He crossed to the other side of the street to give her a better chance. He coughed three or four times and looked exceptionally frail.

He couldn't see her, and he felt very angry indeed. He crossed back again. Perhaps she'd be in the hall when he asked the maid if he could see the doctor. He'd ignore her. Or, better, he'd give one deep, accusing look that would strike her to the heart. That is, if she had a heart.

He knocked on the door. The maid answered.

"I'll go and tell Miss Harris you're here," she said, and went before he could even open his mouth to say that she was the last person he wanted to see.

He was about to go away when there was Miss Harris, coming down the stairs, two at a time, in a blossomy gown and looking like a storm in an orchard. She looked flushed and eager. He wondered if she'd dare to beg his pardon?

Dorothy Harris, who had been watching Philip Top-Morlion from behind her curtain, wondered if he had come to beg her pardon.

She couldn't understand why else he should have been loitering on the other side of the street like a criminal and clearing his throat. Perhaps he really had come to explain that something extraordinary had happened last night that had prevented his keeping the appointment?

And would she forgive him, after all she'd suffered? Of course she would! Only—only she'd be dignified about it. She wouldn't just throw herself at his head. She'd had quite enough of that! She'd be a little cool and distant to begin with. She'd show him that she had her pride.

"Well?" she asked breathlessly. "What is it that you want, Mr. Top-Morlion?"

Can't she see how ill I look? thought Philip. Can't she see that I need a doctor?

"I—I would like to see your father, Miss Harris."

"My father? Why?"

"I think you can guess, Miss Harris," he said quietly.

He wants to *marry* me! thought Dorothy with a rush of amazement. He wants to ask Pa for my hand! Oh, no! He can't—he mustn't! It—it's ridiculous! Oh, I like him well enough...but I hardly know him! Besides, I'm much too young to think about getting married! Perhaps he doesn't know I'll only be sixteen in July. I know I look older, but—but—Oh, dear! This is awful!

"I—I think you ought to wait a little while, Mr. Top-Morlion," she said with a nervous smile.

"How long?" asked Philip.

"About a—a year?"

My God! thought Philip incredulously. A year to see the doctor? And in my state of health? She really hasn't got a heart at all!

"Thank you!" he said bitterly. "Thank you very much. But, under the circumstances, I think I'd better find someone else."

He tottered away, coughing consumptively.

Dorothy stared after him, unable to believe her ears. So! Just like that! "*I think I'd better find someone else.*"

It was horrible! Women were nothing to a man like that! The Irish girl had been right all along! He really would break your heart as soon as spit!

She ran back up to her room and slammed the door with a violence that shook the house. She sat on her bed, breathing tempestuously and not knowing whether to scream or cry.

What evil fate was forever crossing her path so that, whenever she offered her heart, it was thrown back in her face? What had she done to deserve it?

She began to sob. Perhaps in a year or two she'd have taken such things in her stride, even as, a year or two before, she wouldn't have been walking that way at all. But now she was in the middle of it. Every shadow was a pit and the very morning sunshine was a gilded iron cage.

Presently she grew a little calmer. A man like that wasn't worth crying over. She sniffed and, remembering that it was only Friday, wondered if there was any chance at all of making things up with Maggie Hemp before Saturday night. She felt dreadful about it, but what else could she do?

She stood up and looked in her glass. Maggie would be bound to notice she'd been crying. Oh, well, maybe it was for the best! Maggie might feel sorry for her and be kind.

She changed her April dress for one that had a touch of March about it and suggested blossoms blasted in the bud, and left the house. She walked quickly until she came to the row of smart new villas at the top of the street.

"And have ye taken pity on him, me darlin'?" inquired Cassidy, stepping out from where he'd been loafing at the side door of the house where Mary Flatley worked. "For ye'll never forgive yerself if he dies of a broken heart!"

She stared at him with hatred. She'd like to have known just when and where Philip Top-Morlion was going to die as she would like to have watched.

The side door opened and someone came out. Dorothy hurried away, as she didn't want to be caught in conversation with the shabby Irishman. Anyway, people didn't die of broken hearts! *Her* heart was broken and she'd never felt better in her life!

She reached Collier's and there was Maggie Hemp sitting in the window just like old times! Dear Maggie! She went in.

"You look terrible, Dolly," said Maggie with affectionate satisfaction. "Like something the cat's brought in."

Dorothy sat down.

"Oh, Maggie!" Then, "I—I was wondering if you think I ought to wear my blue velvet cape for Saturday night?" asked Dorothy.

Miss Hemp compressed her lips. She knew perfectly well that something had gone wrong with Dolly's plans and she was trying to make things up as if nothing had happened.

But she wasn't going to let her. She wanted Dolly to be honest with her. If they were going to be friends again, then there were going to be no secrets or slyness.

"You've been crying," she said.

"Are—are you going to wear your lovely new silver dress, Maggie?"

"Your eyes are all red and puffy, Dolly, like giblets."

"I—thought of wearing my grey one...if you think it would look all right, Maggie?"

"I do believe you're *still* crying, Dolly!"

"I'm not!"

"Yes, you are! All over your cake. Look!"

"Oh, Maggie!"

"Tell me about it, Dolly. Tell me everything. After all, we *are* friends!"

She had moved closer, to comfort her unhappy friend and

to screen her from curious eyes, when she became aware that she was being watched through the window.

Of all people, it was the drunken Irishman who'd accosted her yesterday in The Lanes. She remembered he'd called her "darlin' " and held her hand. She shook a warning finger. He responded by raising his own in salute.

Dorothy looked up, and Cassidy saluted again.

"Do you know him, dear?"

"No! No!" said Dorothy quickly. "I don't know him from Adam! Do you know him?"

"Of course not, dear."

"I wonder why he waved?"

"Oh, you know what men are, dear!"

Dorothy nodded. She knew. They were beasts, they were brutes, and they would break your heart as soon as spit!

Maggie smiled tenderly. She was glad they were of one mind. They were friends again. She held Dorothy's hand and together they sat, in Collier's window, two frail females alone in a forest of monkeys, weasels, vipers and—and MEN. But nothing would come between them any more. Nothing would separate them again.

She gestured angrily through the glass, and Cassidy went away.

Chapter Fourteen

CASSIDY, having applied at the villa, had been told that it was Mary Flatley's day off and that she wouldn't be back till late.

"And where might she be spendin' it, ma'am?"

"With Andrews, of course. The fishmonger's son."

"No!" said Cassidy, white as a ghost.

"Yes!" said the housekeeper. "And a lucky girl she is!"

"Don't tell me they're courtin', ma'am?"

"I'll tell you what I like, young man!"

"And him an Englishman?"

"Every decent, hard-working inch! He's Mr. Saunders' sister's boy. Mr. Saunders, with the shop in Bartholomews."

"The villain!" Cassidy had cried. "The dirty philanderin' villain!" And away he'd gone to Bartholomews, hoping to plead with Mary Flatley before it was too late.

He saluted the two young ladies in Collier's window and then went inside Saunders' Marine Stores and Fishing Tackle, where he blundered about among rods, lines, hooks, choppers, yellow boots, and terrible festooning nets, like a frantic green fish with a bandaged head.

At length, finding no one about, he stopped and scratched his head.

"In Dublin's fair city," he began to sing, in a small voice as if he'd swallowed a tiny Irishman, "where girls are so pretty..."

He peered into the ill-lit depths of the shop, hoping that his song would draw the girl out. Instead, it drew the proprietor, a hard, knobbly man with a nose like a shrimp.

"Yes?"

"I was wonderin', sir, if ye're acquainted with a lass by the name o' Mary Flatley? She's black hair and—"

"I am."

"And have ye seen her this mornin', sir?"

"I have."

"And where might she be, sir?"

"Out with my sister's boy."

"And where might they be walkin', sir...if it's not too much trouble to ask?"

"They ain't walking. Wears out boots. They're in the boat."

"At sea?"

"Well, they ain't rowing down North Street!"

Cassidy hurried from the shop and went down to the beach. He stared wildly over the water, but the sun, spilling all over it, turned it to a sea of fire and blinded him.

The only vessel he could see was in his mind's eye, and it was a grand painted barge with a tasseled canopy, under which sat Mary Flatley and Andrews, side by side.

Cassidy groaned as he thought of Andrews, with his crafty silver tongue, offering Mary Flatley the kingdom of the sea, with cockles big enough to ride in, and mackerels, proud as bishops, to draw her along.

"But what of me Michael Cassidy, who's followed me so far and loved me so long?" said she with a wistful smile.

"Forget that no-good Irish loafer! What can he do for you that an Englishman can't do ten times better?"

"Ye dirty lyin' rogue!" wailed Cassidy, stamping and stumbling along the beach and not looking where he was going, for it didn't matter any more.

"Will you wed me, Mary Flatley?" asked Andrews, smooth as silk. "And become a decent Englishwoman?"

"That I will!" said she with a sigh. "If ye happen to have such a thing as a ring?"

"A ring?" said he with a laugh, and straightway produced an article with a pearl the size of an egg, maybe.

"Don't take it! I'll give ye a diamond as big as an apple!" cried Cassidy, though he'd no more than a shilling and the life he stood up in.

He stumbled on till he came to a breakwater half sunk in the sea, so that its last posts poked up out of the water like a row of executed heads.

He climbed over it, still looking out to sea, and came down on the other side and trod on something soft.

It was a coat and a pair of breeches, huddled in a heap. Beside them lay a pair of battered boots and stockings, wrinkled like empty worms.

"You're standing on somebody's property," came a cold voice from the shadow of the breakwater.

Cassidy started and then saw it was the pale and brainy boy to whom he'd taken the telescope. He was sitting against the breakwater, shrouded in darkness, with the instrument firmly to his eye.

Cassidy begged his pardon for any inconvenience and hoisted himself back onto the breakwater and continued to scour the sea.

At last he saw the boat. It was not so far out as he'd been

looking, nor so grand as he'd feared. It lay no more than sixty yards away, to the west of a line of nets with green glass floats winking and sparkling like emeralds of the deep.

It was a rowboat with shipped oars that stuck up like ears, and the sea kept shrugging it in and out of a pool of sunshine so that it came and went like a dream.

At one end sat Mary Flatley, as small as a thimble, and at the other sat Andrews, as big as a house. Cassidy shuddered at the size of him. A man like that could have given a girl a hundred pound and not even missed it!

Even as Cassidy watched, the big fellow fumbled in his pocket and then held out his hand. Was he giving her a ring?

"What's he doin' out there?" groaned Cassidy.

"None of your business," said Harris from the shadows below.

"Maybe not," said Cassidy sadly. "But what's he givin' her? Can ye tell me that, young sir?"

"Yes," said Harris, not taking his eye from the telescope. "It's what you might call an inedible but otherwise stimulating object. It's part of the ritual of Courtship, you know."

"And is she takin' it?" asked Cassidy, his worst fears confirmed.

"It'll knock her flat," said Harris confidently.

"Oh, Mary, Mary! How could ye?"

"Instinct," said Harris. "She can't help herself."

"Will ye lend me a squint through the glass, young sir, so's I can see for meself?"

"No," said Harris.

"I'll give ye a shillin', young sir."

"No."

"Ye're a hard case!" said Cassidy bitterly. "An Englishman through and through."

He began to make his way to the end of the breakwater so he could see for himself what was going on in the boat, while the hard case remained in possession of the telescope below.

Now Harris was not a hard case. In fact he considered himself to be quite warmhearted. He'd not parted with the telescope because of Bostock. He did not want Bostock's present activities to be witnessed by eyes other than his own.

Bostock, as Harris had inferred, was engaged in procuring the inedible but otherwise stimulating object mentioned in the learned article on Courtship, the presentation of which was destined to knock Mary flat. Mary Harris, not Mary Flatley—for what the devil did she have to do with it anyway?

Music, both vocal and instrumental, having met with a conspicuous lack of success, Bostock had naturally been depressed. In fact, he'd turned quite nasty, and Harris had had quite a struggle with him.

Patiently Harris had pointed out that failures, however disagreeable, were really a good thing. It stood to reason. The more you failed, the less chance there was of failing next time. You were reducing the chance of error by using it up. That was science. Did Bostock not know that nothing great had ever been achieved without many mistakes on the way? How many baths did Bostock think Archimedes had to take before the water overflowed?

Bostock had pointed out that there'd been an overflow from Mary's window the first time, and that was enough for him. But Harris, explaining the easy success in courtship of foolish creatures like herons, magpies, and oyster catchers, at last persuaded Bostock that the presentation of prey or of inedible but otherwise stimulating objects was worth a try.

The particular objects to which Harris had directed Bostock's attention were the green glass floats used by fishermen to hold up their nets. Mary already had three of them, hanging over her bed like a pawnshop, and Harris assured Bostock that another pair would send her wild with delight.

Bostock said he didn't have any money, as he'd given Harris his last fourpence ha'penny. Harris said not to worry, as Bostock could nick them from the nets floating out at sea.

It was quite all right, Harris explained, because as long as they were floating, they were flotsam, and, as such, belonged to the Crown. But, as it wasn't to be supposed that the king wanted them, he, Bostock, had the law on his side—which any court in the land would uphold.

All that was needed was a strong swimmer and a sharp knife, to cut the floats free from the nets.

Bostock was the swimmer, and the knife was a handsome, ivory-handled article that had been presented to Captain Bostock by the Brighton Exploring Society on the occasion of his election to the presidency, and was engraved with his name. It had been the sharpest knife Bostock had been able to find.

So now Harris waited confidently in the shadow for the triumphant return of his friend, while not very far away Cassidy squatted forlornly on the last stump of the breakwater like a green frog with brass buttons that had missed its chance of being kissed into a prince.

He stared at the rowboat as hard as he could. What was going on out there? What was he saying to her, and she to him? What had he given her? Had he really parted with a ring? What was a ring to a big Englishman like that?

The Englishman had not parted with a ring. In fact he hadn't parted with anything more than a lump of stale bread he'd given to Mary Flatley to feed the seagulls with.

Andrews was a huge, good-natured youth, the color of a kipper, and as straight and true as a plank of wood, but he was a bit on the stingy side.

Mary Flatley was his second girl, the first having given up after he'd spent no more than a shilling on her in eighteen months, and then when it was raining.

He was, you might have said, a careful youth who was saving up for something, but he never said what, as he was a bit close with words, too.

"Are ye savin' up for a house, maybe?" said Mary Flatley, scattering all the crumbs at once. "Or a fine new boat of yer own to bring home fish for yer wife and little ones when ye have 'em?"

Andrews, of the silver tongue, looked down at his knees and smiled at them affably.

"A penny for yer thoughts, Mr. Andrews!" said Mary Flatley.

He looked up with interest.

"Eh?"

Mary Flatley sighed and reflected that, if it hadn't been for that smarmy, faithless Cassidy, she'd not have been sitting here now, as flat as a drink of water. She hated him; she loved him. He was her worst friend and her best enemy.

"I was thinkin'," said Andrews, as if still pursuing the offered penny, "that we might row over to the nets and look at the fish. That's what I was thinking."

"If ye're sure they'll not charge us for it?" said Mary Flatley.

"No," said Andrews. "It's all the same to them."

"Then let's take a look," said Mary Flatley. "For it's all the same to me, too."

He spat on his hands, and, grasping the oars, began to row vigorously toward the nets. Mary Flatley, sitting in the stern, watched the blades rising and falling like choppers. She gazed over them to the beach. Sitting on the end of the dwindling breakwater was a lump of green that looked a bit like Cassidy.

She waved. The lump waved back. She stood up and waved again. The boat rocked and Andrews clouted the water with a steadying blade.

At once there was a scream and a terrible bubbling howl! Something wild and streaming, with a knife between its teeth, came up on the end of the oar. It was Bostock.

"*Harris!*" shrieked Bostock, who, having been struck on the head, was seeing a great many stars, suns, moons, and comets without the aid of any telescope whatsoever. "HARRIS!"

Captain Bostock's ivory-handled knife fell out of Bostock's mouth and vanished into the sea, where it sank and, doubtless, became jetsam and the property of the Crown.

Bostock shrieked again. Mary Flatley screamed and Andrews struggled to dislodge the monster from his oar. Knowing nothing of Bostock, his hopes, his dreams, his abiding love for Mary Harris, nor the learned article on Courtship that was responsible for his appearance, the occupants of the little boat could only regard him with terror and revulsion and fight to escape his grasp.

Bostock, still dazed from the blow, fought back and overturned the boat.

Now Cassidy entered the lists. He stripped off his coat, plunged into the sea, and sank like a stone. He couldn't swim a stroke, but he'd seen his girl in danger of drowning, and he meant to save her even if it killed the pair of them.

He came up roaring water and waving his arms; then he went down again to the bottom of the sea. His past life flashed before his eyes and he didn't regret a minute of it, though he wished it had been longer and a bit more drawn out.

He came up five times in all, for you can't drown an

Irishman in three; then Andrews got hold of him by the hair and dragged him up onto the beach.

He'd seen Cassidy in difficulties, and, leaving Mary Flatley safely holding on to the boat, he'd swum to his rival's aid. He was truly a good-natured youth, as kind and brave as any knight, so long as there wasn't any expense.

Back went Andrews for the boat, and, with himself and Mary Flatley astride the keel, paddled away for shore.

"He's dead!" cried Mary Flatley, rushing to the sodden Cassidy, from whom water was running like whiskey on St. Patrick's night.

Andrews picked him up and held him upside down till the rest of the water came out. Then he laid him down, and Cassidy opened his eyes.

"He's alive!" cried Mary Flatley. "Mr. Andrews, ye've saved Michael Cassidy's life!"

Andrews stared down at his feet, affably.

"Oh, Cassidy!" cried Mary Flatley, kneeling down beside him and wringing the sea out of his hair. "Did ye hear that? Mr. Andrews has saved yer life! So what can I do, me darlin', but wed him today, if he asks? For I've nothin' else to give him for his trouble but me hand and me heart!"

"Oh, Mary, Mary!" groaned Cassidy. "I'd never have needed savin' at all if it hadn't been for the love I bear yerself! I'd nothin' else to give ye but me life!"

"But ye're still alive, Michael Cassidy, so what's the use of that?"

Chapter Fifteen

THE BEACH was empty. The unlucky boating party and the passers-by who'd stopped to watch had all departed. Nothing remained but a large wet patch on the stones, compounded of seawater and tears. The scene was finished. It was time for the others to take their bow.

Bostock and Harris emerged from the shadow of the breakwater. Bostock, due to the action of the sea, was looking peculiarly clean, like a scraped potato. Harris was supporting him, as he was still weak from his exertions and unable to speak.

They went first to Harris's house. Harris concealed the telescope in the stone coffin while Bostock looked on with chattering teeth.

Then they went to Bostock's. Harris observed that the Irishmen's cart was once more outside, but there was no sign of the owners.

They went into the house through the side door and Harris helped Bostock upstairs.

There was a long, lugubrious face at the window. It was

O'Rourke. He had replaced the broken pane and was engaged in cleaning his own finger and nose marks from the new glass.

He took no notice of the two boys. Unlike his partner, he did not feel talkative when he was high up. He was terrified of heights.

Bostock began to take down the ships' posters with Mary Harris's name on them.

"What are you doing that for, Bosty?"

"It's finished, Harris. It's all over."

He rolled up the posters, tied them with a piece of string, and laid them on his bed. Idly Harris picked up a roll and, applying it to his eye, observed Bostock.

"It's still only Friday, Bosty. There's still time—"

"It's no good! Everything's ruined now!"

"Oh, Bosty, how little you understand!" said Harris. "We've only just started! We've only just scratched the surface of things! That's why they look such a mess! Nothing's ruined, old friend!"

He explained that there was still a great deal more in the learned article on Courtship that they hadn't tried. It would be madness to give up now. For instance, there was—

Bostock lost his temper. When he'd said everything was ruined, he hadn't been talking about the learned article. He had been referring to his pa's best coat, his best hat, his best wig and cape, and, most recently of all, the knife that had been presented to him by the Brighton Exploring Society and had been engraved with his name. His pa had been very proud of that knife and used it to peel apples when company came. Gone!

In view of all this, didn't Harris think that he, Bostock, had sacrificed enough?

Harris, somewhat taken aback by Bostock's outburst, remarked that Mark Antony had sacrificed a whole empire for Cleopatra, so wasn't Bostock being a little close-fisted about Mary? And anyway, Captain Bostock was a sick man and not in any state to discover his losses before Christmas.

He turned the rolled-up posters toward the window and peered past O'Rourke into the distance, as if to demonstrate how far away Christmas was.

But Bostock, who always looked forward to Christmas as a time of warmth and presents and kindness from his parents, was enraged by the thought of having even that snatched from his grasp. He glared at Harris, and, being reminded by the roll of posters of yet another item in the catalogue of his father's missing property, said, "And I want the telescope back!"

Harris stiffened. He removed the roll from his eye and stared at it as if it were the ghost of the fine brass instrument that was so close to his heart. He stood up.

"I'm going now, Bosty."

"The telescope, Harris!"

"Good-bye, Bosty."

"Harris!"

But Harris had gone, and without shaking hands. Bostock stared at the closed door, at first with anger, then with bewilderment and dismay.

At first he wanted to run after Harris and tell him he hadn't meant what he'd said, but he was still too deeply hurt by Harris's abrupt departure. He wondered if he ought to wait for Harris to come back and then tell him it was all right.

"Oh, Harris!" he whispered. "Even if I never get Mary, you can keep the telescope!"

The door opened. It wasn't Harris. It was the housekeeper. She looked around the room and frowned at Bostock.

"You're for it!" she said.

Bostock smiled feebly. She always said that.

"Where have you put it?"

"Put what?"

She shook a polishing rag menacingly. "You know what I mean."

Bostock knew. She meant the brass telescope.

Ordinarily it was not an article that interested the good lady, but, having seen the recent commotion at sea from an upstairs window, she'd gone to polish the master's telescope and look through it, in case anybody she knew was drowning.

It hadn't been there, so her thoughts had gone to Bostock.

"If it's not back today, I'll tell the master," she said. "And then you'll be for it!"

Her tone of voice suggested that, if Bostock did not comply with her demand, he could count himself lucky that the house wasn't equipped with a yardarm, as he'd undoubtedly be hanged from it.

"But—but I haven't got it!" he moaned. "Whatever it is! Word of honor!"

He didn't know what to do. He thought with anguish of what would happen if he asked Harris for the telescope again, and he thought with equal anguish of what would happen if he didn't. There seemed no way out.

The housekeeper, unmoved, repeated her threat, and then, raising her eyes, saw O'Rourke's absorbed face at the window.

The thought crossed her mind that, in spite of appearances and everything she knew about him, Master Bostock might be innocent, and those no-good Irish loafers might be to blame.

She glared at O'Rourke and remembered his partner, who, she suspected, was as crooked as his nose. So she said, as loudly as she could, "I'll give you till tonight to put it back.

Either that or I'll go straight to your father, Captain Bostock, J.P.!"

She had the satisfaction of seeing Bostock on the point of collapse, and O'Rourke in a similar state as he vanished below the sill.

Chapter Sixteen

YE DIRTY thief, Cassidy!" shouted O'Rourke, coming violently into their little room in the King's Head, where Cassidy was sitting before the empty grate, wrapped in a blanket, with his wet shirt hanging out the window and his dripping breeches depending from the mantelpiece, for he was a modest man.

"Say that again, O'Rourke," cried Cassidy, rising like the ghost of Julius Caesar—the blanket being full of holes, "and I'll knock ye down!"

"Then I'll not make a murderer of ye as well," said O'Rourke. "So I'll keep me opinions to meself till ye're hanged for 'em!"

But he couldn't. He was too angry and frightened. He began pulling out Cassidy's belongings, going through his pockets and looking under the bed, raging and railing at Cassidy all the time.

"What are ye lookin' for?" demanded Cassidy, being pushed from wall to bed and back again as he got in the way of the search.

What was O'Rourke looking for? Well might Cassidy ask!

He was looking for whatever it was that Cassidy had thieved out of the magistrate's house.

O'Rourke, having heard the housekeeper's threat, jumped at once to the conclusion that Cassidy had been guilty of backsliding. It was as plain as the nose on Cassidy's face. He'd lost Mary Flatley, so he cared nothing for anybody any more. The loss of the love that had turned him into an angel had put him right back among the devils again.

O'Rourke was almost in tears. Hadn't he watched over Cassidy like a father and humored him every yard of the way? And now Cassidy repaid him by stealing out of the house of the very gentleman who could have them both hanged!

In vain Cassidy protested that he was as innocent as a newborn babe. O'Rourke was too mad to listen; he'd been frightened to death by the housekeeper and the gallows glare in her eyes.

Then Cassidy, who'd been racking his brains for the cause of it all, remembered the brass telescope. O'Rourke collapsed on the bed.

"Then ye *did* steal it?"

"Never! I gave it straight into the hand of the doctor's son. I swear it, O'Rourke!"

"Did he give ye money for it?"

"Fourpence ha'penny for me trouble."

"Then it's trouble indeed, Cassidy! Ye're worse than a thief. Ye're a receiver of stolen property, and as such ye're liable to the full strength of the law!"

"Never!"

O'Rourke looked at him pityingly, then went to his carpet-bag and took out a battered book. It was a volume entitled *The English Lawyer*. O'Rourke had stolen it from a bookshop in Liverpool, for how could he keep Cassidy from breaking the laws of the land unless he'd a list of them to know what was what?

He found the page, and Cassidy, following O'Rourke's huge finger, saw for himself that his friend was quite right. It was all written down, and it proved him to be as guilty as the thief.

He'd get fourteen years' transportation if he was lucky. Otherwise he'd be hanged. And poor O'Rourke, being party to the criminal, would get the same.

O'Rourke began packing up. They'd have to leave the town at once. Cassidy lay on the bed with the blanket over his head and swore that he'd sooner be hanged than leave Mary Flatley to marry the Englishman. So long as she wasn't a wife, there was still hope, even if it was only to be Cassidy's widow.

O'Rourke dropped Cassidy's bag with a thump.

"Then it's good-bye to ye, Michael Cassidy. I'll not be hanged for another man's girl."

Up came Cassidy's head. "Then ye'll leave me?"

"What good would we be to each other, hangin' on the end of a rope?"

"Could we not get the article put back, O'Rourke?"

"D'ye mean steal it out of the doctor's house?"

"I'm still an honest man, O'Rourke."

"Thank God—else ye'd be hanged twice over!"

"I was thinkin' of goin' to the boy himself. Give me a chance, O'Rourke! He's only a boy. He's flesh and blood. He's not a boy of stone that would see a man hanged for a bit of brass!"

O'Rourke came back from the door.

"He's flesh and blood, Cassidy," he said, remembering the night in the churchyard. "I'll grant ye that."

"And will ye grant me the chance to try him?"

O'Rourke fumbled in his pocket. He produced a grubby scrap of paper, which was the firm's worksheet. He consulted it.

"Ye're in luck, Cassidy. There's a window needs mendin' in the doctor's house. It's the window of the boy's own room."

Cassidy leaped from his bed as if it were on fire. He dragged on his breeches and shirt. O'Rourke stood back.

"I'm not saying ye'll fail, Cassidy," he said. "But if ye should and the boy denies ye, will ye promise to come with me out of the town tonight?"

Cassidy promised. How could the boy deny him? Had it been an old man, now, stern and calloused with years and well past the age of loving, it would have been another matter. But a boy, still young and tender enough to cry over a lost kitten, maybe? Ah, there was nothing to it!

They went out together, and even O'Rourke felt that it would have been an unusual boy indeed who could have remained cold and unmoved in the face of Cassidy's love and Cassidy's desperate plight.

The ladder was off the cart and up against the wall almost before the pony had stopped, and Cassidy was halfway up when O'Rourke shouted out, "Ye've forgot the glass!"

But Cassidy went on like a green shoot rising, and, when he came to the broken window, he looked down and waved to O'Rourke. The boy was inside.

Cassidy began to talk through the hole in the glass, and when Cassidy talked, the world stood still. Ah, that Cassidy! He could have charmed the birds from the trees and every lass from her glass! Oh, Cassidy! Who could turn aside from the pleading look on your face? Who could deny you, with your golden tongue? What heart in all the world would not be melted by the aching love of Cassidy for Mary Flatley?

But he was a devil of a long time about it!

Cassidy came down like the weather.

"O'Rourke," he said, "ye'll not believe it, but he *is* a boy of stone. Somebody ought to tell his father, the doctor, and maybe he'll put him in a bottle."

"What did ye say to him, Cassidy?"

"I told him of Mary and me."

"And what did he say to that?"

"Nothin'. He just stared at me with them terrible eyes of his."

"And then what did ye say to him?"

"I told him we'd be a pair of dead men if the instrument wasn't put back in the magistrate's house within the hour."

"And what did he say to that?"

"Nothin'. So I asked him if he'd have us on his conscience just for a bit of brass?"

"And what did he say to that?"

"Nothin'."

"And what did ye say to him then?"

"Why, I told him he was made of stone and that if ever I was to meet with him on a dark night, I'd punch him into the middle of next week or further. Let's go, O'Rourke, before I damn meself forever by goin' back and committin' murder on a child!"

They put the ladder on the cart.

"A child!" repeated Cassidy, still unable to take it in. "Now had it been an old man, all crabbed and horny, I could have understood it better. A man like that wouldn't have cared any more for lovers and their sighs. But a child—"

"An old man would have been better, Cassidy," said O'Rourke, jerking the pony into life. "Though he'd have been past love, he'd have remembered it, for it's not somethin' ye're likely to forget. But a child, not yet come to it, can't remember where he's never been!"

"Ye're a charitable man, O'Rourke. Will ye be charitable enough to let me say good-bye to Mary Flatley?"

"That would be foolishness, Cassidy, not charity. It would be cruel to the pair of ye. Let her wed her Englishman in peace, while you and me go lookin' for work."

And he reminded Cassidy that they'd scarcely a shilling left to bless themselves with, being out of pocket to the tune of two pieces of window glass and a third that had been put in at the magistrate's house and not claimed for, on account of O'Rourke's having left in a fright.

They turned the corner at the top of the street. Cassidy gazed up at the villa where Mary Flatley worked and saw her best green dress hanging out of her window to dry.

"God bless you," he said, "and send you a good life."

He turned to stare back at the house they'd left, and muttered, "And may God forgive ye, if He's a mind to, by keepin' ye out of me way!"

The cart rolled on and took the road to Patcham, and Harris put down the telescope with a deep sigh of relief.

Chapter Seventeen

HARRIS breathed heavily. He was not made of stone. He rejected the Irishman's accusation indignantly. He was human. He was composed of flesh and blood, disposed in vessels and layers about his bones in accordance with the strictest principles of Anatomy. And he was proud of it.

Harris had a liver, a spleen, a sweetbread, and lights, just like anybody else. He also had a heart that drove his blood from place to place and nourished his brain.

It was Harris's brain that was unusual. It was very powerful and helped him to see things more clearly than most people.

He saw, for instance, that the Irishman was a very dangerous and unpleasant fellow and it was a good thing that he'd gone. He saw that he'd been talking through his hat, and that if anybody was going to be hanged for Captain Bostock's telescope it would probably be Bosty, which was unlikely in the extreme.

He wondered if Bostock had put the Irishman up to it in order to exert pressure on Harris. If so, it would have been blackmail and very wrong. Harris wouldn't countenance anything like that. He was surprised at Bosty.

In short, he was not going to give the telescope back. What would become of Pigott's comet if he did?

Suddenly Pigott's comet became very important and Harris felt that, if he didn't observe it at the proper time, somehow it would be disappointed—as if it were a visitor who'd come a long way to see Harris and found him to be out.

It was quite impossible to give the telescope back. He looked through it again—not at the sky, but at the villa at the top of the street where the green dress was hanging out of the top window. It jumped toward him, almost close enough to touch.

He thought, inexplicably, of Cassidy going up his ladder, and the look on Mary Flatley's face as she'd come in answer to the song. He thought of the night in the churchyard, and O'Rourke's gentle words, and he felt a curious aching sensation in the lower part of his chest.

He shut up the telescope with a snap. It was out of the question to give it back.

He really couldn't. It would be as good—or, rather, as bad—as admitting failure to Bosty. He'd never failed before, and he wasn't going to be pushed into it now, not for a hundred Irishmen and their girls!

He gazed down at the shortened brass cylinder in his hands.

"Keep me!" it seemed to say. "I bring things nearer, almost close enough to touch!"

Harris extended it.

"Almos-ss-st!" hissed the polished joints.

He shut it, and the aching sensation in his chest seemed to spread upward till he felt it in his very teeth. With shaking hands he put the leather caps back on the two glass eyes and blinded them. He left his room, taking the telescope with him. He was very angry.

He went out of the house, slammed the door, and set off down the street. He met Bostock at the corner.

"Harris!" said Bostock with a desperately frightened look. "Have you got the telescope?"

Silently Harris gave it to him. As the instrument left his hands, he had the queerest feeling that he was still looking through it, only through the wrong end. Everything was unutterably remote.

"Oh, Harris! You're a brick!"

"No," said Harris bitterly. "Stone."

He walked away, trembling with a sense of outrage and injustice. He had intended to surprise Bostock with his magnanimity. He'd thought of bursting in upon him when Bosty had given up hope. He'd pictured it all very clearly and had been actually looking forward to it. But now, to have been met on the way, as if Bostock had expected it all the time, was intolerable!

He returned to his house in a state of profound agitation. He'd been treated monstrously. He'd worked hard for Bosty, and now, just when the fruits of victory were within his grasp, they'd been cruelly snatched away.

But Bosty wasn't going to have it both ways! He, Harris, would see to that! It had always been the telescope or Mary. Well, he'd gotten the telescope back, so that was the end of Mary. Once and for all Bostock would see that it was madness to cross Harris. Harris could undo just as well as he could do. Nothing was beyond him.

He went straight to Mary's room. She was sitting on her bed, frizzling up the hair of that little cow Caroline.

"Go away!" said Caroline. "This is a ladies' room. No boys allowed!"

Harris ignored her and addressed himself to Mary. "Bosty's found somebody else," he said. "Another girl. So he won't be going with you tomorrow night. It's all over."

He made a gesture of wiping his hands of the whole affair and withdrew before he could be questioned further.

That had fixed Bosty! A period had been put to his romantic aspirations, a very full stop indeed. Harris nodded grimly. What he, Harris, put asunder, no man on earth could join together again.

He went to his sister Dorothy's room. She was trimming a hat and, for once, wasn't crying.

"Don't you ever knock?" she said.

Harris, feeling no answer was called for, gazed around the room for a subject for conversation. He felt like it.

"I see you found your cello," he said.

Dorothy's face darkened, and her eyes filled up with their familiar burden. "Get out!" she said.

Although music might have soothed the savage breast, any reminder of the musician served only to inflame it. And almost everything reminded her.

Harris went away and drifted into the nursery, where Morgan was cleaning up his last sister, Adelaide. She began to cry.

"Why do you always come in like a ghost?" said Morgan. "Go away!"

Harris departed and vanished from the house with the mysteriousness that characterized all his movements. He walked down to the beach, reflecting that his whole life seemed to consist of unseen comings and goings. He wondered, if he vanished altogether from the face of the earth, if anybody would notice that he'd gone.

He sat down on the stones and noted, with melancholy interest, that they were a good deal harder than he was. There was no doubt that the Irishman's hurtful accusation still rankled.

Ordinarily, insults did not affect Harris, but the Irishman had offered to supplement his with injury. He had meant it, and Harris had been impressed.

So had he only yielded to the threat of being punched into the middle of next week? Had he just been frightened? He looked around, half hoping to see the Irishman, as the middle of next week, however he reached it, offered more attractions than here and now.

It was half past six. He wondered how long he'd need to stay out before somebody came to look for him and tell him that supper was ready.

No one came. The sky grew dark and the huge sea frittered itself in a fringe of silver and sighed over the expense. The stars came out and winked at Harris, as if to mock him with their remoteness.

He frowned and tried to make out which of the tiny pricks of light was Pigott's comet. He stared from one to another, trying to detect a scrap of movement, till his eyes watered with the effort. But the stars played blindman's buff with him, so he got up and went home.

He had lost everything, even the comet. It was as if the telescope, in its death agony, had turned and struck down even its most devoted admirer. Harris had lost Bostock, too.

"Bosty!" sighed Harris, expiring in sleep. "Dear old friend!"

Chapter Eighteen

THE DAY that Harris had schemed for, that Bostock had yearned for, that Dorothy had sobbed for, and that Maggie Hemp had had such agonizing suspicions about dawned in heedless splendor.

It was rather like a guest who, not having been told that the party's off, arrives in foolish magnificence, at a house in tears.

First Dorothy awoke, from a dream of dancing on the top of Devil's Dyke with Philip Top-Morlion—to the unspeakable envy of Maggie Hemp—and wished herself back asleep again.

Next, Maggie Hemp awoke, from a dream of a world without slyness, in which she danced on the top of Devil's Dyke with a youth of spotless honesty—to the unspeakable envy of Dolly Harris—and she wished herself asleep again.

Bostock awoke from dancing on top of Devil's Dyke with Mary Harris, and he wished himself back asleep again. And Cassidy, in a small room at the Black Lion in Patcham, awoke from a dream of dancing all the way back to Dublin with Mary Flatley on his arm, and he wished himself asleep again.

Even Harris, who'd had the most horrible nightmare of

299

being shut up inside the telescope with the Irishman, Captain Bostock, Pigott's comet, and various invisible slimy things— all of which had hostile intentions toward him—awoke and wished he hadn't. Anything was better than the emptiness of the coming day.

He tried to think, to scheme, to devise some means of renewing his hopes and saving his friendship without loss of face, but it was in vain. His thoughts rose, only to fall back exhausted, like a bird with a broken wing. He had the feeling that he was fluttering against a huge black wall, as if he had reached the end of the universe.

He went to the window and looked out, hoping that Bostock would be there. He wasn't. Harris put on his crumpled clothes, which gave him the odd appearance of having been discarded, and went downstairs.

His sister Dorothy passed him on the first landing. She was on her way to her mother's room to borrow scent and whatever else she could find that would suit her rather more than a lady of Mrs. Harris's advanced years.

She vanished quietly and Mary Harris darted across the landing on an identical errand to Dorothy's room. At such times every woman's most urgent needs turn out to be in the possession of another.

Harris went down to the kitchen where his mother was supervising the filling of hampers and baskets for the evening's outing.

His mood darkened at the festive sight. He breakfasted frugally on a veal pie and wondered about going out. Then he remembered the Irishman, and his blood ran cold. The fellow was probably lying in wait for him with a pistol or a cudgel.

Although Harris had returned the telescope, Cassidy couldn't have known and would probably hit him without waiting for an explanation. Harris, in addition to his other misfortunes, was virtually a prisoner in his own home.

He went back upstairs, noting, without interest, that Caroline was crying. He looked out of his window. No Bostock.

He heard the front door open and bang shut. A moment later he saw Mary, in a white dress with green ribbons, scamper up the street, like a stick of celery.

He looked toward the villa on the corner. The green dress was gone. He could just make out vague movements in the window. He missed the telescope more than ever.

Mary came back, flushed and windy. She saw her brother looking down and put out her tongue. Still no sign of Bostock.

The morning continued with idle comings and goings, but Harris stayed where he was, his mood fluctuating between anger, bitterness, sadness, and despair.

Soon after midday he went down to the kitchen and removed another pie. Caroline was still crying.

At about two o'clock he saw Andrews, the fishmonger's son, call at the villa and wait at the side door till Mary Flatley appeared. She was wearing the green dress and was carrying a basket. Andrews put a small bag into it. It was his contribution to the feast. They walked off in the general direction of Devil's Dyke.

Harris tried to make a phantom of his mind and send it into Bostock's house to tap him on the shoulder and bid him come.

"Bosty! Bosty, old friend!"

No Bostock. Instead, he saw the Top-Morlion family, all in their pony cart, proceeding along the road at the top of the street.

Mrs. Top-Morlion, who was excessively tall and thin, held

the reins. She sat bolt upright and, with her long neck and small round head, looked uncannily like a treble clef, driving. Monsieur Top-Morlion, who had recovered from his illness, cuddled his cello, and Philip, in addition to his fiddle, flute, and music case, was clutching a bouquet of music stands. They too were moving in the general direction of Devil's Dyke.

At half past three Maggie Hemp arrived, in a state of black and silver satin and tearful indignation. She wondered if there would be room for her in Dr. Harris's carriage?

She was not going with her ma and pa even if it meant walking all the way. Her pa was taking a whole hamper of cooked mutton chops and was going to sell them, like a common tradesman.

Maggie had never been so ashamed in all her life. It was just as if Dr. Harris were to take pills and things. As it was, all the town seemed comet mad. Even Mr. Collier was selling marzipan comets at threepence each, and that little shop next to Saunders' was selling special smoked spectacles for viewing the comet in comfort, while the greengrocer's and the fishmonger's were all selling rides on their carts, at two shillings there and back.

It turned out that there was room in the Harrises' carriage as Mary and Caroline had quarreled and Caroline wasn't going. Maggie Hemp subsided and told Dorothy it was a pity she wasn't wearing her gray dress as the blue one she'd put on rather clashed with Maggie's hat, but there was still time to change, and didn't Dolly think she'd overdone the scent?

At five o'clock the Harris family, with the exception of Adelaide, Caroline, and Harris himself, piled into the little carriage, along with baskets, hampers, and warm blankets.

Mournfully Harris watched them. He thought of running downstairs and confessing to Mary that Bosty had not found somebody else. He felt, in some strange way, that he'd interfered with Providence, and that, if he undid what he'd done, then Providence would relent and set everything to rights.

But this was all nonsense, and Harris, the scientist, knew it. Fate, Providence, and Hostages to Fortune were all in the realm of magic. Harris was above such things, and with a shrug and a frown he conquered his impulse to confess.

The carriage departed, leaving Harris behind, with a victory as joyful as ashes. Caroline was still crying.

Chapter Nineteen

HARRIS thought about the Irishman. He reasoned that Cassidy, being of Celtic blood and of a violent temper, was unlikely to be possessed of much patience. Therefore, if the fellow had really been lying in wait for him, he'd have shown his hand by now.

He looked up and down the street. No hand. Cautiously he left the house and proceeded to the corner. His reasoning proved correct. Cassidy was nowhere to be seen.

Happily Harris bolted around to Bostock's and knocked loudly on the door. How much better it was, he thought, to show such generosity to Bostock by making the first move, instead of remaining at home in a somber resentment that nobody could see.

Bostock would be so overcome by the loftiness of Harris's spirit that he could hardly refuse him admission to the Crow's Nest and the use of his pa's telescope to behold the glory of Pigott's comet. Everything was for the best, after all!

The housekeeper came. Harris smiled.

"No need to ring the bell," he said. "I'll go straight up."

"Oh, no, you won't."

"Why not?"

"Because he's gone out."

"OUT?"

"Out."

"Where?"

"Up to Devil's Dyke. Didn't you know?"

Harris made a stupendous effort to control himself.

"Oh, yes—yes. Of course. I—I forgot," he said.

In no circumstances could he expose the fact that Bostock had actually done something without his, Harris's, knowledge, and that he hadn't arranged.

"I—I expect he's waiting for me," said Harris, and tottered away with a despairing jauntiness. "He'll be wondering what's happened to me. Ha—ha!"

He went back to his house. He looked into the stone coffin, not for Bostock, but in the hope of finding some scrap of graveyard philosophy to sustain him...such as, we are all food for worms, and what does anything matter anyway? In a hundred years who would care whether Bostock had betrayed Harris or not?

Not much comforted, he went inside the house. Morgan, who had been feeding Adelaide, shouted to him not to bang the door. But, as he'd already banged it, her remark seemed unnecessary.

Everything was unnecessary. He began to mount the stairs. Caroline was still crying. He went toward her room with the general idea of being disagreeable. He had no pity for her. She was a female and Harris loathed and despised all females. They always caused trouble and never seemed to get the blame. He opened her door.

"Go away!" sobbed Caroline.

She was sitting on her bed, holding a doll, and with her eyes as red as poppies.

"Shut up!" said Harris sternly.

Caroline's face crumpled up, as if an invisible fist were squeezing it to get more tears from her eyes. She looked very small and insignificant. Harris felt vaguely touched and inquired as to the source of her grief.

More tears and a frantic rocking of her doll, who persisted in smiling glassily. Harris told her to pull herself together.

It turned out that Caroline's grief proceeded from an undying hatred for her sister Mary. Mary, it seemed, had inexplicably wished to disassociate herself from Caroline. She had threatened to punch Caroline in the stomach and scratch her eyes out if Caroline so much as came anywhere near her once they got to Devil's Dyke.

Harris nodded; he understood both points of view. For the first time in his life he found himself sympathizing with two of his sisters at the same time. He thought.

"I'll take you," he said. "We'll walk up to the Dyke together." It had occurred to him that, by producing Caroline on top of Devil's Dyke, he would be destroying Mary's happiness, probably destroying Caroline's, and he would be discomforting Bostock by catching him out. In short, he would be killing a large number of birds with one stone. Also, he wanted very much to go to Devil's Dyke, and he was feeling so lonely that even his small sister's company was better than none.

"What are you doing with Miss Caroline?" demanded Morgan, coming out of the nursery with Adelaide under her arm.

"He's taking me up to the party on Devil's Dyke," said Caroline, proudly clutching her brother's sleeve.

"Now don't you go and lose her!" said Morgan, her wild Welsh mind muddled with ancient memories of changelings and foundlings and lostlings on the downs. "And don't bang that door!"

Devil's Dyke was five miles off and uphill every weary step of the way. Long before they were halfway there, Harris yearned to realize Morgan's worst fears and lose his bitterly complaining sister for good. She was hungry, she was thirsty, her toe hurt, and there was a tickling in one of her ears—had an animal gotten in?

Harris poked his finger in, and Caroline shrieked. They went on. Caroline hated Harris, and Harris hated Caroline; nevertheless they clung together as it was beginning to get dark.

At about seven o'clock they passed the old inn before the top of the Dyke itself. Already fires had been lighted, for the downs were chilly when the sun went down, and it was still only April.

Smoke was rising from the high place where, long ago, the Devil had stood and scooped out the deep, precipitous Dyke that was meant to let the sea come rushing in and drown all the churches of the Weald. It was as if his footprints were still hot.

There was a red glow in the air and a throng moved against it, mysteriously black. Then a wind blew. The smoke flattened and a million golden sparks danced and raced, as if Pigott's comet, to signify its arrival, had shaken out its tail.

A pleasant smell of cooked food was wafted across the downs, together with the cheerful sounds of plates, bottles, faintly jingling harness, and the pigmy out-of-doors voices of the comet watchers, as they laughed and strolled and found best places for their feasts, around the dancing green.

"Look!" cried Caroline, dragging on Harris's sleeve. "There's Dolly with Maggie Hemp!"

Harris, much relieved, hastened to dispose of Caroline. He appeared like a specter in Dorothy's path. She halted.

"That's Ma's brooch you're wearing," said Caroline observantly. "I'll tell."

"For God's sake!" said Dorothy in a rage. "Go away!"

Nobody, she thought, can expose you to the contempt and ridicule of the whole world better than your own family!

Maggie looked at the brooch. "It is a little old for you, dear," she said.

Dorothy wondered why she ever went out with Maggie Hemp, who always managed to say something hurtful. She longed for the dancing to begin, even though she didn't have much hope of a partner.

"Look!" she said. "There's Mr. Top-Morlion and his family! I wonder when they'll start to play."

Maggie Hemp pulled Dorothy the other way. "Look!" she said. "There's Mr. Collier selling those comet cakes! Come along and I'll buy you one, Dolly!"

Away they went.

"Look!" shouted Caroline. "There's Mary! Over there! Look! She's with—"

But Harris was no longer by her side. He had seen not Mary but the murderous Irishman! At once the prospect of personal violence had flashed upon his inner eye, and with a faint cry of alarm he had vanished from human sight.

The abandoned Caroline began to howl and scream, but it was too late. Harris, when he vanished, vanished for good.

Cassidy also had been surprised. He kept gazing about him and seeing the familiar faces of Brighton folk, ringing the firelight like demons. He felt he was drowning all over again, and yesterday was flashing before his eyes.

He and O'Rourke, having been unable to pay their bill at the Black Lion, had been obliged to work off their debt by carrying part of the landlord's family and a stock of Patcham beer and pies "up yonder hill."

Not being geographers, they'd toiled up in all innocence from the Patcham side. Not Sir Francis Drake himself, leaving Plymouth and then coming back to it without having turned a corner, could have been more astonished than Cassidy and O'Rourke when they beheld what they thought they'd left behind.

There was Mary Flatley herself, walking arm in arm with her Englishman, who was as tall as a lamppost, only without the shine.

All Cassidy's hopes came back to him and then were dashed when he saw the size of his rival. He longed to distinguish himself, to do something valiant—to save a life, maybe... hers if it could happen without putting her in danger! But it was hopeless. What could he do beside Andrews, who had everything he lacked, and a rowboat besides?

"Look!" said O'Rourke. "There's that boy who'll see ye hanged, Cassidy!"

"Where?"

"Ah, he's gone now. Most likely he's gone for the magistrate. Ye'd best keep out of the way, Cassidy!"

"I'll kill him!" said Cassidy, retreating into obscurity with a tray of Patcham Ales (None Finer). "I might as well be hanged for a boy as for a brass telescope I never had!"

So Cassidy went looking for Harris, while Harris stayed where he was, trembling and perspiring under the Top-Morlions' cart.

He saw Cassidy's stoutly gaitered legs coming near. Urgently he searched for some means of defense. He found a brick wedged under one of the wheels. He pulled it free, meaning to sell his life dearly.

Cassidy, not finding Harris—and not really wanting to—put down his tray of Patcham Ales (None Finer) and rested against the cart, while nearby the Top-Morlions tuned their instruments for the beginning of the dance.

Monsieur Top-Morlion, observing out of the corner of his eye the tray of Patcham Ales, wondered if they were an additional tribute to the musicians—a kindly refreshment, such as was always offered in France? He put down his cello....

"My God!" said Mrs. Top-Morlion, poking her son in the back with the bow of her fiddle. "Look at your father! He's done it again!"

Monsieur Top-Morlion was swaying in his chair and clutching his sensitive stomach with every appearance of agony.

"He's a pig!" said Mrs. Top-Morlion furiously. "He's just drunk a whole bottle of beer after all that wine! He's nothing but a pig!"

Monsieur Top-Morlion fell off his chair and rolled on the ground, groaning piteously.

"I'd better fetch Dr. Harris," said Philip, no less furiously. "Maybe he can give him something right away."

He hurried away to where the Harris family were settled and explained the situation. Dr. Harris came at once.

"He should never have had that beer," he said after he had examined Monsieur Top-Morlion. "I warned him about straining his stomach."

"Can't you do something, Dr. Harris?" pleaded Mrs. Top-Morlion. "Just so he can play for this evening?"

The look on her face suggested that, after that, she didn't care.

Dr. Harris said there was nothing he could do, and Mrs. Top-Morlion said it was intolerable that everybody's pleasure should be ruined because of her husband's irresponsible greed.

Dr. Harris sympathized, and, wishing to be of service to his patient's family and the company in general, suggested that, if the music wasn't very difficult, his daughter Dorothy might take the cello part. She was, after all, Monsieur Top-Morlion's pupil and would most likely do him credit.

At once Philip's heart began to beat violently. He assured Dr. Harris that the cello part was simplicity itself. A child could manage it, let alone an accomplished young lady like Miss Harris.

"I'll go and find her," said Dr. Harris.

"She's over there!" said Philip rapidly.

Dr. Harris approached his daughter.

"Really, Pa!" said Dorothy, her heart beating violently. "The very idea! Besides, I haven't practiced for ages. I'd just be making a fool of myself!"

Maggie Hemp agreed. Dolly couldn't possibly do it!

"On the other hand," said Dorothy, dragging Maggie toward the Top-Morlions, "I don't want to be a spoilsport. And—and you can turn the pages for me, Maggie!"

She greeted Mrs. Top-Morlion politely and looked daggers at Philip. He needn't imagine she'd come to make things up.

"We really are obliged to you, Miss Harris," said Philip icily. "I think you'll find the music is quite straightforward."

She sat down, and Mrs. Top-Morlion passed her the cello. Philip leaned over to open the music.

"Miss Hemp will turn the pages for me," said Dorothy. "There's no need for you to stand so close, Mr. Top-Morlion."

She smiled triumphantly at Maggie, who smiled uncertainly back. She didn't trust Dolly an inch.

"Are you ready, Miss Harris?"

Dorothy nodded, and they began to play, almost together. A stir went through the firelit crowd, a hastening to and fro.

Then the music launched itself into "Nancy Dawson," which children know as "My Grandmother," and two by two the dancers came, shyly and awkwardly onto the green.

"Please try to keep in time!" muttered Philip, briefly lowering his flute.

"I *am* in time!"

"Then you're out of tune!"

"Please don't criticize. I'll stop if you go on like that!"

"You should practice more."

"How can I? Nobody bothers to teach me!"

"What do you mean by that? And don't keep stopping every time you talk!"

"I wasn't stopping. That was a rest. Oh, I see—it was a smudge. If you'd come to give me my lesson that night—"

"I *did* come!"

"Philip!" said Mrs. Top-Morlion. "For goodness' sake, don't keep stopping!"

"You didn't come! I waited till—"

"I did come. And you threw water over me! *And* you called me a filthy little beast!"

"I didn't! Oh, my God! Was it you?"

"Who the devil else would be playing the cello under your window?"

"Miss Harris! Philip! Please keep playing!"

"I thought it was my brother," said Dorothy savagely, and then: "Oh, Mr. Top-Morlion, what must you have thought of me?"

"A great deal, Miss Harris!"

"Will you ever forgive me?"

Would he? He thought about it. He would. Suddenly he felt

that his skin was too small to hold in the bursting happiness it contained. He felt an overwhelming desire to hop and skip and fly with Miss Harris in his arms.

Impulsively he turned to Miss Hemp, who was suddenly his most talented pupil of the flute.

"Here," he said, thrusting the instrument into her hands. "Would you mind, Miss Hemp? The music's quite easy, you know!"

Then, before Maggie Hemp could say more than "VIPER!", he released Dorothy from the cello and escorted her onto the green.

"Philip! Miss Harris!" wailed Mrs. Top-Morlion, as the dancers clumped and turned and bowed to the scraping of a single violin. "Come back!"

Too late. With the lady on his left, and his right hand holding her left, Philip led Dorothy in the dance.

Drive with the left foot; step forward on the right...all move around one place...

Dorothy floated and Dorothy flew, as she danced on the top of Devil's Dyke with Philip Top-Morlion, to the unspeakable envy of Maggie Hemp!

"Serpents! Weasels! Hyenas and goats!" sobbed Maggie Hemp as her worst suspicions came true. "I *hate* the world!"

She flung down the flute and went to sit on the back of the pony cart, to cry and cry and cry.

Unfortunately it was the very cart under which Harris was concealed, and from which he had removed the securing brick. Looking up, he was alarmed to see the cart begin to move under the tempestuous weight of Miss Hemp.

Fearing exposure, Harris began to crawl away, taking good care to choose the opposite direction from where he could still see Cassidy's feet.

In consequence of this, he was forced to brush lightly

against the pony's legs. At once the ignorant beast snorted, tossed its head, and jerked its tethering post out of the ground.

Maggie Hemp screamed, and the pony, frightened out of its wits, set off briskly in the direction of the wild, plunging Dyke itself.

Cassidy, picking himself up from where he'd fallen when the cart had left him, saw at once an opportunity of distinguishing himself and shining in Mary Flatley's eyes.

"I'll save ye! I'll save ye!" he roared and stared wildly around for Mary Flatley, just to make sure she could see him.

But for God's sake, she was nowhere to be found, and there was the poor girl screaming her head off and being rattled along to her terrible death, maybe hundreds of feet down below!

"I'll save ye! I'll save ye!" yelled Cassidy frantically, and shut his eyes in terror and waited for the faraway crash!

It wasn't that he was a coward; it was just that he was so frightened of going over the edge with the cart that he couldn't move a step.

He heard shouts, he heard cries, but, Heaven be praised, he heard no crash. He opened his eyes and saw that the cart had been stopped and the poor, weeping girl was standing upright on the ground. Who had saved her? ANDREWS!

The dirty scoundrel had poked his nose in again! He was a professional rescuer, and that's all there was to it! Poor Cassidy never stood a chance. A fellow like that would have beaten St. George himself to the dragon...the great big hulking lump of wood! Cassidy sat down and cried.

"Will ye not come and dance with me, Michael Cassidy?" said Mary Flatley's voice, while Mary Flatley's hand came down and stroked his hair.

He looked up, and she looked down, and there was a look

in her eyes that would have raised Dublin Castle up if ever it had tumbled down.

"But—but yer friend over there?"

"He's no friend of mine, Michael Cassidy," said Mary Flatley, offering him her hand. "D'ye think I've got the time of day for a fellow that's always goin' after rescuin' and leavin' me standin' on me own?"

Cassidy stood up.

"And d'ye think, Michael Cassidy, that I've not got eyes in me head to see that ye love me truly? For wasn't it yerself that risked yer life to save me from drownin' when ye couldn't swim a stroke? So I'll never forget that it was yerself that didn't risk yer neck for *another* girl, and not him!"

They walked onto the green to join the waiting dancers, and the lonely lady fiddler struck up again.

Hop on the left foot, step with the right; ladies turn under the gentlemen's arms. All move around one place...

"I don't know how to thank you," said Maggie Hemp, drying her eyes and cautiously examining her savior from beneath lowered lids. "Really I don't."

Andrews didn't know either, although he appeared to be giving the matter some thought. He felt vaguely distressed to see that he'd lost Mary Flatley and, with her, his contribution to the feast. He looked wistfully toward her as she and Cassidy danced together, like two green leaves.

"Would you—would you like to dance with me?" asked Maggie Hemp, feeling that such a sacrifice was the least she could make.

"I'm not much of a dancer, miss."

"I don't believe you!" said Maggie Hemp, taking hold of Andrews' huge hand. "I really don't!"

Onto the green they went and joined in the growing dance.

Andrews tripped and stumbled and trod on Maggie's foot. Just as he'd said, he wasn't much of a dancer, but at least he'd told the truth and not been sly. *That* was something. And compared with that weedy Top-Morlion, he was a real Apollo, even though he smelled of fish. She hoped Dolly Harris could see her and go green with envy over her catch!

For a little while Harris, his danger past and his person secure, watched the revolving dancers on the green.

Hop on the right foot, step with the left... partners give right hands and make a turn... all move around one place...

He turned away. Not for him the happiness of finding a partner, only the sadness of losing a friend. He looked up, hoping to catch a glimpse of the comet, which surely was as solitary as himself. But the air was too full of smoke and flying sparks.

The dance went on. Flushed faces bobbed; eyes winked like stars.

Gentlemen bow... and rise up on their toes...

Dark figures against the fire, weaving in and out... little shrieks as bright embers touched the hems of swinging skirts and then went out. All move around one place...

All but one. At the end of the line a single figure hopped and capered as if unaware that his partner had long since fled his company.

"Bosty!" shrieked Harris.

"Harris!" shouted Bostock.

Shining with delight and relief, he left the dance and rushed upon his friend. They shook hands.

"Harris!" said Bostock. "You're a genius!"

Harris blinked away a tear.

"You did it, Harris! Just as you always said. Mary danced with me... and I danced with Mary! Oh, Harris, Harris!"

Then, as Harris listened, Bostock told him that not only

was he the most brilliant but also the most magnanimous person that he, Bostock, knew. He was ashamed, he said, to think how wonderful and forgiving Harris had been. Even though he'd asked for the telescope back, Harris had still kept his word and given him Mary.

She'd come around to his house that morning and asked him to be her companion on Devil's Dyke. Bostock had been absolutely overwhelmed by Harris's generosity. But how had he done it? How had he accomplished such a miracle?

Harris smiled and frowned and thought. How had he done it? For the moment he was not quite sure.

In point of fact, he had done it by accident. But that didn't detract from his achievement. Most great discoveries are made by accident. After all, Archimedes had meant to wash, not to soak the bathroom.

Harris had wrought his masterpiece when he'd told Mary, in a fit of anger, that Bostock had found another girl. That was all. Mary, when she'd gotten over her incredulity, wondered who it was that Bostock had found. Who would go out with that idiot? Then she fell to wondering if, perhaps, there was more to Bostock than she'd supposed. Then she'd decided she'd better try Bostock for herself in case she'd been missing something. Also she'd be hitting another girl in the eye, which was a satisfaction in itself.

So she'd secured Bostock and threatened Caroline, as she wasn't going to have that little cow laughing her head off while she danced with her brother's awful friend.

Now she'd gone, having discovered that the only aspect of Bostock to which there was more than she'd supposed had been his feet. But she *had* danced with him.

"Oh, Harris!" said Bostock, quite overcome by the memory. "How *did* you do it?"

"It was really quite simple, Bosty," said Harris, emerging

from his ponderings like a sagacious retriever, with the answer in his mouth. "It was only a question of knowledge properly applied."

Quietly he explained to Bostock about the learned article and how the whole ingenious ritual of Courtship had been followed and at last fulfilled. First there'd been the display of bright plumage and the discharge of scent, then the performing of music and the presentation of prey, and finally, right on top of Devil's Dyke, had come the execution of the dance. That had done it.

It was just, said Harris shrewdly, that you had to go through the lot. There were no shortcuts. Omit one and the rest would never have followed. It was rather like a figure in a quadrille.

"To prove it," said Harris, "we could do it again if you like."

Bostock shook his head. He'd had his moment and he'd treasure it all his life. Perhaps in the future—a long way off—he'd think differently. But not now. To be honest, he was rather glad it was all over and he and Harris were friends.

They began to walk away from Devil's Dyke, leaving the dance behind. Once more a great warmth of affection glowed between them, and a great depth of friendship, no matter how ruffled the surface had lately been.

At last they came to Bostock's house, and Bostock asked Harris if he'd like to come in and watch Pigott's comet through his pa's telescope, up in the Crow's Nest.

Harris said he would, and together they climbed to the top of the house. There, while Harris scoured the heavens with an eager eye, Bostock thought of Mary and the cost of her in terms of his pa's property, ruined or lost. But he wasn't worried any more. Christmas was a long way off, and Harris would be sure to think of something. Harris was a genius, after all.

LEON GARFIELD (1921–1996) was born and raised in the seaside town of Brighton, England. His father owned a series of businesses, and the family's fortunes fluctuated wildly. Garfield enrolled in art school, left to work in an office, and in 1940 was drafted into the army, serving in the medical corps. After the war, he returned to London and worked as a biochemical technician. In 1948 he married Vivian Alcock, an artist who would later become a successful writer of children's books, and it was she who encouraged him to write his first novel, *Jack Holborn*, which was published in 1964. In all, Garfield would write some fifty books, including a continuation of Charles Dickens's *Mystery of Edwin Drood* and retellings of biblical and Shakespearian stories. Among his best-known books are *Devil-in-the-Fog* (1966, winner of *The Guardian* Children's Fiction Prize), *Smith* (1967, published in The New York Review Children's Collection), *The God Beneath the Sea* (1970, winner of the Carnegie Medal), and *John Diamond* (1980, winner of the Whitbread Award).